I0687531

Double Two

Steve Schach & Sharon Stein

Wandering in the Words Press

Copyright © 2016 Stephen R. Schach and Sharon M. Schach. All rights reserved. No part of this book may be reproduced, stored in a retrieval system or transmitted in any form or by any means without the prior written consent of the publishers, except by a reviewer who may quote brief passages in a review to be printed in a newspaper, magazine, blog or journal.

To request permission, visit www.wanderinginthewordspress.com.

All characters in this book are fictitious, and any resemblance to real persons, living or dead, is coincidental.

PUBLISHED BY WANDERING IN THE WORDS PRESS

ISBN-10: 0-9967878-7-9
ISBN-13: 978-0-9967878-7-1
First Edition

To Jackson and Mikaela

Also by Steve Schach

Old Bach Is Come
Highly Satisfactory
A Matter of Trust

Also by Steve Schach and Sharon Stein

Coopers Island
Bakerloo Line

PROLOGUE
Near Eaglesham, Renfrewshire, Scotland
Saturday, May 10, 1941

Standing in her apple orchard, Flora MacDougal heard the sound of a plane flying toward her. After a few seconds, she saw it approaching at a low altitude in the darkening sky. The sputtering of the propellers revealed that it was nearly out of fuel. Then she saw the Iron Cross painted on its side. She shook her fist and cursed in Gaelic, "Nazi *blaigeard* (bastard)."

Suddenly the aircraft started to climb. Then it leveled out, the canopy opened, and a white parachute blossomed in the purple sky. Now pilotless, the plane twisted downward in a death spiral before smashing into a pasture on Floors Farm.

The parachute descended slowly. Standing at the edge of the field he had just plowed, David McLean watched the pilot land clumsily on one leg, then fall into his chute as it collapsed. McLean grabbed his pitchfork and ran toward the German airman as fast as he could.

CHAPTER ONE

Duntress Castle, Renfrewshire, Scotland
Thursday, September 9, 1993

"Benedict, did you know that Rudolf Hess landed less than five miles from here?" Hamish asked.

Short and overweight, and with a puzzled expression on his chubby face, Benedict turned toward Hamish and asked, "Who's Rudolph Hess?"

"Are you serious?" Hamish asked, raising his eyebrows. "Do you really not know who he was?"

"My son is forty-six years old," Sebastian said. "He was born two years after the Second World War ended." Sebastian was half a head taller than Benedict and considerably thinner than his son.

"But you sent him to your old school," Hamish persisted. "Benedict, didn't you learn anything there?"

"Just Latin and Greek, I'm afraid," Benedict said ruefully. "And I've already forgotten most of it. Who was he?"

"Who was who?"

"Rudolf what's-his-name. The man who landed near here. And I didn't know that there's an airport anywhere in the vicinity of the castle."

"There isn't. We're about twenty miles south of Glasgow, in the middle of the countryside, and the nearest airport is in Glasgow."

"I'm confused," Benedict said. "I thought you said Rudolf landed less than five miles from here. Where did he land?"

"He landed near the edge of a field in Floors Farm near Eaglesham." Hamish was careful to pronounce the name of the village correctly. It sounded to Benedict something like *Ee-giz-ham*.

"So, who was he, and why did he land in a field?"

Hamish still could not decide whether Benedict was teasing him. While trying to make up his mind, he looked around the great hall of the ancient castle, the walls crammed with full-length paintings of previous Earls of Duntress and their Countesses. Many of the men wore the uniform of a senior officer in the Black Watch, the Royal Highland Regiment; some were resplendent in the formal kilted attire of the Chief of Clan Duntress.

Hamish, the eighteenth Earl of Duntress, looked older than his seventy-nine years. His elongated face was heavily lined, his brown watery eyes weak. The few remaining wisps of white hair revealed the many age spots on his head. Hamish had invited Sebastian and Benedict to spend two weeks with him at Duntress Castle. During the evenings they sat in the great hall, drank his superb whisky, and talked about the day's trout fishing. But that evening the conversation had turned to the past and was beginning to touch on events that Sebastian preferred not to revisit.

It all started when Sebastian innocently remarked that a painting hanging on the nearest wall reminded him of a Gainsborough portrait in the National Gallery in London. For some reason, that observation triggered a wartime memory stored deep in Hamish's brain, and he asked Sebastian if he remembered the lunchtime piano concerts that Dame Myra Hess gave in the art gallery during the Second World War. Reminiscing about concerts that were organized in the early 1940s to raise wartime public morale was fine. But then Hamish segued from Myra Hess to Rudolf Hess, a topic to be avoided, at least as far as Sebastian was concerned. Before Sebastian could stop his friend, Hamish had informed Benedict that Rudolf Hess had landed some five miles from where they were sitting. Sebastian looked meaningfully at Hamish, hoping that he would change the subject, but Hamish was staring at Benedict, still trying to decide whether to answer his question.

Hamish finally made up his mind. "Benedict," he said, "Rudolf Hess was the Deputy *Führer* of Nazi Germany. He was number three in the power hierarchy of the Third *Reich*, after Adolf Hitler and Hermann Göring. More than fifty years ago, in 1941, he flew solo to Scotland on an unauthorized peace mission—he wanted to negotiate a truce between Britain and Germany before Hitler opened a second front by invading the Soviet Union.

"Hess was under the mistaken impression that the Duke of Hamilton was a Nazi sympathizer, so Hess flew to Scotland to meet the duke and draw up the terms for an armistice. He couldn't locate his destination, Dungavel House, the duke's estate, which isn't too far from here. Nearly out of fuel, he parachuted to the ground, hurting his foot. An astonished plowman named David McLean arrested him at pitchfork-point and handed him over to the police.

"The authorities imprisoned Hess in the Tower of London. We returned him to Germany at the end of the war. He stood trial at Nuremberg where the court convicted him and sentenced him to life imprisonment. They transferred him to Spandau Prison in Berlin where he committed suicide in 1987, at the age of ninety-three."

As far as Sebastian was concerned, Hamish had let the genie out of the bottle. If Hamish wanted to raise the subject with Benedict then so be it, but now Hamish was obligated to tell Benedict what really happened. Consequently, Sebastian said quietly, "Hamish, we both know that what you've just said isn't the whole story."

Hamish looked shocked, but he said nothing.

"The documents were impounded for fifty years," Sebastian went on, "and the authorities duly released them in 1991. The contents of the papers are public knowledge."

Hamish glanced sideways at Benedict as if to say, *Not in front of your son.* Sebastian looked him firmly in the eye; his message to Hamish was, *You started this.*

Somewhat curtly, Hamish replied, "Just some of the papers have been released."

"Almost all of them," Sebastian answered. "And Hess has now been dead for six years."

"May I remind you that, in terms of the Official Secrets Act 1939, everything regarding the Hess affair is Most Secret?" Hamish said.

"It's all over now. We can talk openly about it."

Hamish abruptly changed tack. "Benedict," he asked, "just how much do you know about what your father and I did during the war?"

"Nothing. Father has either refused to answer or he changed the subject when I asked him."

"Hmm. And do you know why?"

"No. But I've come up with a theory."

"And that is?"

"I think he was involved with some secret operation that went terribly wrong."

"Not exactly," Hamish replied. "The work we did together certainly was secret, but most of it turned out quite successfully. But that's not why he won't say a word about what happened. Tell me, Benedict, did your father ever tell you why he chose your name?"

"I've never asked him."

Hamish turned to Sebastian. "Can I tell him?"

Now it was Sebastian's turn to think deeply for a long while. He back-played his role in the events of the first two years of the Second World War. Then he said, "Why not? It can't do any harm now."

"I agree. And your son needs to know what his father accomplished for his country."

Hamish turned back to Benedict. "Your father and I met as new recruits to MI5. You do know what MI5 is, don't you?"

"Of course. It's our intelligence service."

"It's much more than that. MI5 stands for 'Military Intelligence, Section 5.' Its official name is the Security Service, and it's responsible for domestic counter-intelligence and security; MI6 handles the foreign threats. Well, early in 1939, your father and I were invited to join MI5. After training, they assigned us to the Double-Cross System. Do you know what that was?"

"I've no idea, I'm afraid."

Hamish looked at Sebastian, shook his head sadly, and then turned back to Benedict.

"The *Abwehr*, the German military intelligence agency, sent numerous spies to Britain before the war and smuggled in dozens more after the war started in September 1939. Some of them handed themselves in to the authorities as soon as they arrived. Most of the others made elementary mistakes within hours of coming here, and the police arrested them even before they could send their first radio message to Berlin. We offered captured agents a choice: execution as spies, or becoming a double agent and transmitting to Nazi Germany radio messages that we composed. Almost all of them chose the second option, which didn't come as any sort of surprise to me; my experience was that most spies are craven cowards. Of course, the messages that we ordered them to transmit to their *Abwehr* handlers were filled with disinformation. And because the Nazis never realized that we'd turned their agents, they believed the contents of our messages."

"Are you serious?" Benedict asked. "Do you really mean to tell me that the Germans couldn't tell that the messages they received from Britain consisted of disinformation put together by MI5?"

"It wasn't quite as simple as that," Hamish replied. "Our messages consisted of a mix of factually correct information and deceptive material. Also, we occasionally sent genuine top-secret information, but we made sure that the Nazis received it a little too late to be able to make any use of it. And we made sure that all the messages we constructed formed a coherent whole, thereby strengthening the credibility of each separate transmission."

"And we had another trick up our sleeves," Sebastian added. "By that time we'd broken almost all the German codes, including the Enigma ciphers. As a result, we knew what the Germans were thinking, so we told them what we knew they wanted to hear. Nothing makes a spy more credible than sending a message that makes his handler exclaim, 'That's exactly what I've been saying for past three months.'"

"Anyhow," Hamish resumed, "one of the agents they sent to Britain early in 1939 was a beautiful young woman named Helga Ziegler. That was a brilliant move on the part of Admiral Canaris, the head of the *Abwehr*. Who would've thought that a gorgeous female would be a spy? Yes, during the

First World War, Mata Hari seduced allied generals and passed on the information she learned from them to her German spymasters. But Helga wasn't a *femme fatale*; they trained her as a regular secret agent and then sent her to Britain in the guise of a refugee; that was a ploy they often used with their male agents.

"The day after war broke out she went to Scotland Yard, informed the desk sergeant that she was a Nazi spy, and showed him the radio transceiver that the *Abwehr* had given her. The police arrested her immediately, of course. After a week of interrogation, we asked her whether she was willing to work as a double agent. She unhesitatingly declared that she was keen to cooperate. MI5 put her in a flat in Knightsbridge, under twenty-four-hour armed guard. All the double agents were comfortably housed in individual apartments to ensure their cooperation, but they knew that if they tried to escape their guards would shoot to kill—we couldn't take the risk of the secret of the Double-Cross System reaching the Germans.

"Your father and I were her handlers. Among our other duties, we were responsible for composing the encoded radio messages that Helga sent to Germany, tapping out the letters one-by-one with her Morse key. For security, we both operated under a *nom de guerre*, a false name; Helga knew me as Johnson, your father was Carlyle.

"She was killed early one morning in an air raid. That night, we went to my flat in London to drown our sorrows in the local product, the incomparable single-malt whisky they make a few miles south of here at Lochervan; you've been enjoying it all week. There was no way we could even consider getting drunk in a pub; we both knew far too many secrets. I'm sure you know from first-hand experience that alcohol tends to loosen your tongue.

"After we'd finished off a bottle of the eighteen-year old, the crowning glory of the whisky maker's art, your father blurted out that he'd been secretly in love with Helga. Of course, he'd never said a word to anyone, least of all to her." Sebastian cleared his throat loudly and looked meaningfully at Hamish. Hamish had the grace to blush before he continued. "And then I admitted to him that I, too, had fallen in love with Helga during the year or so that she'd been our double agent. But it wasn't just her stunning physical beauty, her long blonde hair, beautiful big blue eyes, perfect face, and a figure to match. Her mind had enchanted us, too. Helga had come to London in January 1939, a committed Nazi. But after months of intensively studying a vast number of books on a wide range of topics, she slowly began to realize that Hitler and his minions had been feeding her and the German people with lies. Helga started to change, slowly but steadily. In particular, she wouldn't accept anything without first evaluating it carefully. And by the outbreak of war she was utterly committed to democracy and our British way of life. If she hadn't been killed, there's no doubt that when peace came she'd have ended up as an academic at a top British university. Brains and beauty—what a remarkable combination!"

Hamish paused. His old eyes probed the room as if he was looking for Helga. Perhaps he was.

Then he continued. "I've always believed that true love comes to each of us at most once in a lifetime. That's probably why neither your father nor I ever married. You know, of course, that your birth parents, your father's twin brother and his wife, were killed when a drunken driver smashed into the back of their car while they were driving you to their parish church for your baptism. A passerby snatched you out of your mother's arms and pulled you to safety seconds before the fuel ignited.

"Your uncle immediately offered to adopt you. Your parents had kept secret the name they'd chosen for you; they'd wanted the rector to announce it for the first time at the baptismal font. Consequently, your adopted father now had to come up with a name. At the time, he informed his friends that everyone considered your survival to be nothing short of a miracle and therefore he'd decided to call you Benedict, which means 'blessed' in Latin. What he didn't tell anyone is that Helga is a Norse name meaning 'blessed' and that—"

"So, Father—or should I call you Carlyle—it seems that you named me after a beautiful Nazi spy. I'm not sure I really like that."

"Benedict," Sebastian replied, "You haven't been listening to Hamish. Helga turned herself in when the war started because she no longer believed in National Socialism. On the contrary, she worked for us willingly because she opposed Hitler and all he stood for."

"That makes me feel a little better," Benedict said. "But what has all this got to do with Rudolf Hess? Were you and, er, Johnson involved?"

Sebastian looked Hamish in the eye. "Can I tell him?"

"Hmm, I suppose so."

It was clear that Hamish disapproved strongly. But he said nothing more, so Sebastian started to explain. "Two years after Hess died in 1987, Hugh Thomas, an eminent British military surgeon who had treated Hess in Spandau Prison when Thomas was stationed in Berlin, wrote a book entitled *The Murder of Rudolf Hess*. He claimed that Hitler had the real Hess killed in 1941 and that the man who flew to Scotland and ended up in Spandau was a look-alike, a double. Thomas based his allegation on the fact that the man in Spandau had no scar on his chest, whereas Hess received a bullet wound there during the First World War. Then Thomas alleged that the double didn't commit suicide. Instead, British agents had murdered him to prevent his revealing certain wartime secrets. Historians and legal authorities widely debunked the theories that Thomas put forward in his book. Finally, a BBC journalist named Roy McHardy found a copy of Hess's original 1917 medical file in the Bavarian State Archives in Munich. The file contained the description of two bullet wounds, an entry wound and the corresponding exit wound, both of which left only tiny scars, and in a different location than Dr. Thomas had claimed. Finally, the very idea that, after the war, a double would sit quietly in Spandau

Prison for more than forty years and serve out a life sentence for crimes committed by the real Rudolf Hess is beyond belief."

Hamish did not react visibly to what his former MI5 colleague was saying. In particular, his face stayed quite expressionless. Sebastian decided to go on.

"Yes, it's true that both the Nazis and ourselves made extensive use of doubles during the war to protect our leaders against assassination attempts. We also used look-alikes to spread disinformation. For example, we sent an actor named Clifton James, a General Montgomery impersonator, to North Africa to fool Hitler into believing that the D-Day invasion would be launched from there to the South of France. James wrote a book about it that he entitled *I Was Monty's Double*; it became so popular that they made it into a film starring James as both himself and General Montgomery. On the other hand, Dr. Thomas's book received widespread ridicule, even though underlying his bizarre claims was the undeniable fact that both sides did make wide use of look-alikes." Sebastian paused again. He looked directly at Hamish and slowly raised an eyebrow.

Hamish nodded almost imperceptibly as if to say, *proceed.*

"Then, earlier this year, Greg Iles wrote a superb thriller, *Spandau Phoenix*. It was his first book. The novel is nearly seven hundred pages long, but I just couldn't put it down; the tension never flags from beginning to end. The core of Iles's plot is that both

Hess and a double were in the two-seater plane that Hess flew to Scotland. Hess safely parachuted out when the plane reached the coast of Scotland; the look-alike landed on the Eaglesham farm and ended up in prison in Spandau."

Sebastian paused for the third time and, to his great surprise, Hamish took up the story.

"Both Thomas and Iles got the story wrong. It wasn't a question of Hess and his double: There were *two* doubles."

CHAPTER TWO
MI5 Headquarters, London
Thursday, May 15, 1941

Punctual as always, Air Commodore Archibald Pankhurst walked briskly into the basement room for the daily team meeting at a quarter past nine. Soon after the outbreak of the Second World War, the War Department moved the prisoners out of Wormwood Scrubs Prison in order to use the building as a secure headquarters for MI5. The basement conference room in "The Scrubs" was where Pankhurst met every morning with the members of his team.

The five British military officers and two MI5 intelligence officers seated around the table immediately rose stiffly to attention. Pankhurst nodded to indicate that they should sit. His bushy white eyebrows were lowered to the level of his hooded eyes, a sign that he was not at all happy. Another indication was the scowl on his craggy face. Johnson flashed a warning glance to his colleague

Carlyle. The message was clear: *Be careful. Archie is in one of his moods.*

"Gentlemen, we have some critical problems to discuss today," the air commodore began. "In the last two days, there have been two serious threats to the Double-Cross System. Since the beginning of the war, MI8 has been using direction-finding equipment to locate secret radio transmitters used by enemy spies in Britain. The MI8 people have deployed fixed receivers and mobile units all over the country."

"How can they tell whether a transmission they pick up is from a German agent?" Squadron Leader Harkness asked.

"At the start of the war," Pankhurst said, "the government banned all amateur radio transmissions. In fact, Defence (General) Regulations 1939 made it illegal for anyone to even possess any form of transmitting equipment. We confiscated as many transmitter components as we could lay our hands on. But we left all the receivers, and that decision has turned out to have extremely useful consequences.

"The amateur radio operators are helping us by supplementing the MI8 effort. Many ham radio operators, as the amateurs like to call themselves, have been called up, of course. But in spite of that, we have more than one thousand five hundred Voluntary Interceptors, to use their official name, who actively listen for radio signals beamed to the enemy. We simply cannot take the risk of an *Abwehr* agent somewhere in Britain sending a radio message to Berlin that contradicts the disinformation that we provide for the double agents to transmit. We know that we've been successful in preventing illegal transmissions because more and more evidence is accumulating that the Germans believe our messages that the double agents send out when we order them to do so. Yes, there may be *Abwehr* agents still at large in Britain, but if there are, they're not transmitting any messages.

"Questions or comments?" Pankhurst asked.

No one said anything. Squadron Leader Harkness shook his head.

"Fine," the air commodore continued. "Now for the latest developments. Last night MI8 detected a short unauthorized radio transmission. It was in a book code, but we don't know what book they used and, as a result, we can't decipher the message. It came from Western Scotland, from somewhere outside Oban. That area is sparsely populated, and there are exceedingly few amateur radio operators in the region, so there are almost no Voluntary Interceptors in the West Coast area of Scotland. As you probably know, all that a direction finder can tell you is the bearing of the transmitter; you can't tell how far away it is. So, you draw a line on a map. The position of the transmitter will be somewhere along that line, but you won't know where. But if you have readings from two different direction finders, the transmitter will be located near to where the two lines on the map intersect. I say 'near' because these instruments aren't totally accurate. Of course, if you have three or more readings, then you substantially increase your chances of pinpointing the transmitter.

"In the case of the Oban transmission, the Royal Navy signal station near Ganavan was still out of action last night after the German bombing raid earlier this week, so all we have are reports from two mobile units located too far from Oban to obtain an accurate reading. Our scientists are looking into the data from the mobile units.

"Here's a map of the Oban district. The two red straight lines are the readings from the direction finders. This large black circle indicates the area where the illegal transmitter was likely to have been located."

"But sir," Lieutenant Reginald Wallstead of the Royal Engineers interrupted, "that's well over a thousand square miles. I've hiked many times in that part of Scotland. Much of it is woodland. And there are endless hills thickly covered with heather, bracken, and gorse. Trying to search that area would be a nightmare."

"Precisely, Wallstead. However, the radio boffins informed me that their best guess is that the illegal transmitter was located on top of one of the hills outside Oban. I don't have to remind any of you that I know absolutely nothing about science, but I think that they were trying to tell me that mountains can block radio transmissions. Or something like that.

"Take a look at the map. They suggested that the transmission probably came from here, here, or here. Or possibly there, to the northeast of Oban. All four of those hills—I've marked them with an X—are thickly forested, making it easier for the perpetrator to escape detection."

"But sir," Wallstead interrupted again, "if the transmitter was in a forest on top of a hill, that would mean that the device is portable."

"Spot on, Wallstead. But the experts assured me that the transmitter was connected to an electricity supply; they insisted that batteries couldn't have provided enough power for Berlin to be able to detect the transmission. The MI8 people have suggested that, in addition to inaccuracies caused by the distance between the mobile units and the transmitter, one or perhaps both the operators weren't quite as accurate in their measurements as they might have been, possibly as a consequence of the briefness of the message; they just didn't have time to get a precise fix. MI8's conclusion is that there's definitely an illicit transmitter somewhere in the West Coast region of Scotland, possibly in the vicinity of Oban, but they can't be more precise than that. In the meantime they've rushed additional mobile units into the area in case there are any more transmissions. The more ears the better, of course, so they've also alerted the handful of ham radio operators in the area and asked them to listen in as well.

"Any questions, comments, or suggestions so far?"

Not even the irrepressible Wallstead had anything to say, so Pankhurst continued.

"And as if that wasn't bad enough, there was another short illegal transmission two nights ago, probably in the same book code. This one also came from a sparsely populated area, one that has no fixed or mobile units at all and, like Western Scotland, comparatively few ham radio operators. Two of our fixed receivers picked up the second transmission, one sited in London, the other near Hastings—much too far away for any sort of accurate measurement, I'm afraid. The signal seemed to come from the middle of the Norfolk Broads, somewhere in that marshy network of rivers and lakes between Norwich and Great Yarmouth.

"Look at this other map. As you can see, the two towns are more than twenty miles apart, and the Broads extend at least that far from north to south, so we can hardly claim to have pinpointed the location. Furthermore, it's quite possible that the radio we're looking for is actually further inland, over here in the vast Fens region between Cambridge and King's Lynn. And before you can say anything, Wallstead, allow me to point out that again we have to deal with an area of more than a thousand square miles."

But Pankhurst's attempt to forestall Wallstead failed miserably.

"Sir," the lieutenant insisted, "not only is this second area larger than the other one, but it's flat as a pancake. There simply are no hills that might be likely sites for the transmission. We'd have to search every square inch."

"Not exactly, Wallstead," Pankhurst said. "We have one piece of good news. The transmitter again appears to have been plugged into an electrical supply, but there aren't too many dwellings in that area, just a few farmhouses. So that should help to reduce the search area. Of course, they've rushed mobile units to that part of Britain as well, and they've contacted the few ham radio operators in the vicinity.

"Ordinarily, I wouldn't have raised this matter here. After all, there's nothing to be done until we manage to decode the messages or if the listeners detect more illicit radio signals. And if there is another transmission, the MI8 people will handle it; that's their job, not ours. However, something happened five days ago that may well be tied to these two mysterious transmissions."

The air commodore waited for a few seconds to make sure that he still had their full attention. Then he continued. "What I have to say now was announced on Munich Radio the day before yesterday. However, no announcement has been made in this country yet, so for now keep what I'm about to tell you to yourselves. Last Saturday night, Deputy *Führer* Rudolf Hess flew to Scotland. He landed by parachute in a field some miles south of Glasgow. Now that I come to think of it, Johnson, Hess must have come down quite close to your father's place."

Johnson nodded in acknowledgment, making a mental note to ask his father about it once the Ministry of Information had released the details to the public.

Pankhurst continued. "We found the wreckage of a Messerschmitt Bf 110 modified for long-distance flight. It's a two-seater plane, but Hess claims that he flew alone. He stated that he wanted to open peace negotiations with the British, and to that end he'd flown to the estate of the Duke of Hamilton. As far as we know Hess has never met the duke, but he's convinced that the Duke of Hamilton is a Nazi sympathizer or, perhaps, the leader of an opposition party that's trying to remove Churchill as prime minister. His claims are preposterous, of course, at least at face value. The duke is a Wing Commander in the Royal Air Force, and he's responsible for the aerial defense of Southern Scotland and Northern England. Does that sound like a Nazi to you? Also, other than the fascist collaborators whom we've interned for the duration of the war, we know of no other German sympathizers here in Britain. And as for this opposition party that wants to unseat Churchill, I'd be hard-pressed to think of one person who'd want to be a member of such a motley crew, let alone its leader.

"Now, here's where you come in. Hess flew here entirely on his own initiative. As a consequence, Hitler has issued a communiqué stating that Hess is 'delusional'—his word, not mine. Adolf doesn't want his allies to even think that he's secretly opening peace negotiations with us.

"The *Abwehr* agents in Britain, however, have heard quite a different story. Hitler is well aware that Hess knows all sorts of highly sensitive information that could change the outcome of the war in our favor. The *Führer* is concerned that Hess will pass on to us what he knows, either while talking to people he thinks he can trust or under interrogation if we arrest him. Accordingly, over the past few days

Admiral Canaris, the head of the *Abwehr*, has forwarded a message from Hitler to his agents in Britain informing them that Hess is, and I quote, 'a traitor' and ordering them to find him. They are to drop whatever they're currently doing in order to give the highest priority to this task. As soon as one of them locates Hess, he has to kill him. If the agent is unable to do so personally, for whatever reason, then he must send a radio message to Berlin stating where Hess is being held so that the *Abwehr* can dispatch assassins to kill him there. The messages were in Code Haydn, one that we've been able to read since January 1940, unlike the book code used for the transmissions to Germany last night and the night before."

Always quick on the uptake, Lieutenant Wallstead interrupted yet again. "And you think, sir, that those two messages were from sleeper agents who've been lying low near Oban and in the Norfolk Broads but have found out something about Hess?"

"Exactly, Wallstead. And those two agents pose a possibly fatal threat to the Double-Cross System. Yes, they both seem to be located in out-of-the-way places and as a result the risk that they'll transmit information to the *Abwehr* that contradicts the disinformation that our double agents are sending is small. But now that they're no longer sleepers, the spy in Norfolk may move to London, and the man in the Oban area might well go to Glasgow or Edinburgh."

"On the other hand, sir," Wallstead said, "they seem to be well aware that it's a lot safer for them to broadcast where they are. We're unlikely to allocate our limited supply of direction-finding receivers, fixed or mobile, to areas of low population density."

"True. But maybe they'll travel to a big city to gather information and then return to their bases in the deserted countryside to transmit. That would be the worst of both worlds for us."

Wallstead nodded in agreement.

"Well, gentlemen," Pankhurst asked, "what do we do now? How do we lay our hands on the two *Abwehr* agents before they can transmit another message to Germany?"

There was a long silence. Then a Royal Navy lieutenant commander slowly raised his hand.

"Yes, Chulmleigh?"

"Sir, we know that Admiral Canaris has written off several of the *Abwehr* agents he's sent to Britain. The ones who committed suicide, the spies that we've put in prison, and those we hanged obviously don't send messages to him, and he doesn't send messages to any of them. We know all the receiving times for transmissions from Berlin that the *Abwehr* assigned to the double agents before they left Germany. Did Canaris send out the message from Hitler at any other times? That is, did Canaris send out messages that were intended for agent OBAN and agent NORFOLK, if I may name them that way?"

"How stupid of me to miss that! I'll be right back." And the air commodore quickly left the room.

The seven men sat in companionable silence until the air commodore returned a minute later. "Here are the days and times that our radio operators received the transmissions from Berlin with instructions to kill Hess, and this is the list of the receiving days and times for our double agents. Wallstead, you call out the receiving times, and Chulmleigh can tick them off on the list of messages from Canaris."

A minute later an ashen-faced Chulmleigh announced: "Sir, there are two times on this list that Wallstead didn't call out."

"Let's look more closely at the data," Pankhurst ordered. "When was that first message sent?"

Chulmleigh scanned the list. "On Monday, May 12th, at 21:30 hours, sir."

"And agent NORFOLK transmitted his message on Tuesday, May 13th, at 21:30 hours, exactly twenty-four hours later. So, agent NORFOLK has his dinner, listens to the evening news at nine o'clock, and then receives or transmits at half past nine. Now, what about that second message?"

"Tuesday, May 13th at 23:15 hours, sir."

"Thank you, Chulmleigh. Agent OBAN sent his message on Wednesday, May 14th at 23:15 hours, again exactly twenty-four hours later. He has to stay up a little later, until a quarter past eleven, before his communications with Germany begin.

"Gentleman, I think we can safely conclude that we have two *Abwehr* agents at large in Great Britain. One we think is in the approximate area of Oban, the other is probably somewhere in Norfolk or thereabouts. What do we do now?"

Johnson spoke up. He was tall man with fair hair parted on the left, an elongated face with a pointed chin, and brown eyes with long fair lashes. "Air Commodore, where's Hess now?"

"Why d'you ask?"

"Well, sir, Hitler told Canaris to order his *Abwehr* agents to kill Hess. Usually when we put a man in prison, the main job of the jailers is to prevent the prisoner from getting out. But here we have a situation where we have to protect a prisoner against someone from outside getting in and killing him. After all, we should be able to extract a gold mine of useful information about the Third *Reich* from the Deputy *Führer* of Nazi Germany, provided we can keep him alive. Hess is presumably being held in the vicinity of Glasgow; Oban is only about a hundred miles from there. That means that we're holding Hess within striking distance of agent OBAN."

"What do you suggest?"

"Sir, it's not completely clear in my own mind yet, but I have an outline of an idea. Plan A is that, when the Prime Minister announces that Hess has been arrested, he should state that Hess is being held in the Tower of London."

"Why?"

"It's common knowledge that the Tower is currently being used as a prison for captured enemy soldiers. In addition, the Tower is part of one of the three groups of buildings that form the last-ditch defenses of the capital in case of a German invasion, so it's strongly fortified. Those two *Abwehr* agents we're trying to locate are therefore likely to believe us if we announce that he's there. They'll then tell Canaris where Hess is, and the MI8 people will pick up their radio transmissions.

"My guess, sir," Johnson went on, "is that Plan A won't work. All the newspapers will soon have banner front-page headlines that'll read something like 'Hess Parachutes into Scotland, Held in Tower of London.' The two sleeper agents will immediately realize that the *Abwehr* will learn about Hess being in the Tower via other routes, and that they'd be extremely foolhardy to risk giving away their locations by sending information that everyone, including Canaris, already knows. So we wait a few days, and then we go to Plan B. We start a game of Hare and Hounds."

"When I was at school we used to play that game," Squadron Leader Harkness said. "One boy was the hare. He'd tear up sheets of paper, then he'd run through the forest next to the school grounds, leaving a trail of pieces of paper. About an hour later, the rest of us, the hounds, would race along the trail that he'd left, the winner being the boy who got back to school first. The challenge was that the wind would blow the bits of paper, sometimes making it hard to find the trail."

"Yes, we played that one at my school, too," added Captain Marks of the Royal Army Medical Corps, "only we called it Paper Chase. Jolly good fun!"

"I'd appreciate it if you two overgrown schoolboys would stop reminiscing for a minute," the air commodore said, "and let Johnson continue explaining his plan for catching the two *Abwehr* agents."

Marks blushed, and Harkness looked abashed. The other officers seated around the table barely managed to keep a straight face.

"Go on, Johnson."

"Well, sir," Johnson said, "as I said, I don't think that the two *Abwehr* agents will reveal themselves. So, first we move Hess from where we're holding him now to a secret location, probably a military base far from both the West Coast of Scotland and Norfolk. Hess is easy to recognize with his shock of black hair and large black eyebrows, so on the way we arrange for a hairdresser to trim his eyebrows down to almost nothing and bleach his hair and eyebrows blond."

"Now just a minute, Johnson," said Pankhurst, a steely note in his voice. "Unlike the Nazis, we British scrupulously observe the Geneva Convention for treating prisoners of war. Such behavior would violate tenets of the Convention. We'd need Hess's permission if we were to do something like that."

"Sir, I'm sure that Hess would agree if we make it clear to him that his life is in danger—perhaps we could show him Hitler's message that Canaris sent to all his agents here. Hess knows the *Führer* very well indeed. Hess was part of the Beer Hall Putsch in 1923, he was jailed with Hitler for his role there, and while they were in prison together, Hitler dictated *Mein Kampf* to Rudolf Hess. Consequently, when we show him a copy of Hitler's assassination message, he'll be only too eager to have his appearance changed. And we'll give him a false name, too."

"That's fine. Now, let's suppose that we've spirited Hess away to a secret location where no one knows who he is. What then?"

"We start the game of Hare and Hounds," Johnson continued. "We make use of the double agents. We instruct them to send messages to Berlin telling Canaris that we've taken Hess out of the Tower of London and that they're trying to find out where he is. Then they tell Canaris that we keep moving Hess from one location to another for his safely. Or, better still, let's use agent PICKFORD and his network. For some reason, the *Abwehr* often have initial doubts about the information the double agents transmit to them, but they immediately accept whatever they learn from agent PICKFORD's crew of subagents, the ones whose code names are all characters from Dickens."

"Who's agent PICKFORD?" Lieutenant Wallstead asked.

"You remember him, surely?" Harkness said. "He's the British traitor who doesn't exist."

"Yes, you're quite right," Air Commodore Pankhurst said. "In June or July 1937, I don't remember the precise date, we sent a package to the German consul in Edinburgh. It contained the plans for the Muir bombsight. Of course, we knew that they already had the detailed blueprints; our idea was to plant the idea in the brains of the Nazis that there was a British traitor willing and able to supply Germany with top-quality information, an agent who called himself PICKFORD. Just before the war broke out, we sent a radio message to the *Abwehr*, ostensibly from agent PICKFORD, asking them to send him an assistant. Someone in the *Abwehr* got confused and, in his reply to him, referred to him as 'Pickwick.' That gave us an idea—in PICKFORD's reply, he insisted that his new assistant's code name had to be a character from the works of Charles Dickens. The network has been so successful that the *Abwehr* keep sending subagents to help PICKFORD. They tell him precisely when and where the subagent will arrive, so arresting them is child's play. We interrogate them, and, once we've learned everything that they're prepared to tell us, we hang them.

"Sir, how many subagents does PICKFORD have now?" Squadron Leader Harkness asked.

"Twenty, I reckon," Marks interposed. "I'm sure that—"

"No, there must be more than twenty," Lieutenant Commander Chulmleigh insisted. "At least twenty-five, if not—"

"I'm not sure of the exact number," Pankhurst said. "In fact, there may be as many as thirty by now. The subagents that the *Abwehr* sent here are all dead, of course. And MI5 created the subagents that Pickford recruited here in Britain. So we have a network of nonexistent subagents headed by a nonexistent agent PICKFORD. And they fool the Nazis day after day. Amazing.

"I'm sorry, Johnson, we've interrupted you. Please continue."

"Yes, sir. Well, we'll get PICKFORD to report to Berlin that one of his Dickens subagents saw Hess in the Inner Hebrides. Oban is a bustling ferry port and that will make it easy for the *Abwehr* agent in Oban to follow the paper trail. There are ferries from Oban to the major islands of the Inner Hebrides, and to some of the smaller ones as well. If I may refer to that first map, sir, these dotted lines show the many ferry routes.

"And now, sir, please could we see that second map again? Thank you, sir. Another subagent will tell PICKFORD that Hess is being moved from place to place in the vicinity of Dedham Vale, over here, near Colchester, where John Constable painted so many of his masterpieces. As you can see, Constable Country, as they call it, is quite close to the Norfolk Broads. As a result, agent NORFOLK should be able to participate in that paper trail with ease."

"And what do we use for the pieces of paper that the agents are to follow?" the air commodore asked.

"Doubles, sir."

"I beg your pardon?"

"Doubles of Hess, sir. Look-alikes. It shouldn't be too hard to find two men who look somewhat like him, and a good make-up artist will be able to make the resemblance even stronger. We arrange for the doubles to be transported under guard from place to place each day. We'll tell the MI5 men and plain-clothes police accompanying Hess the details of the route to be followed that day, and they'll be on the lookout for the *Abwehr* hound following the Hess hare."

There was total silence in the room after that. Everyone seated around the table was thinking furiously. Eventually Air Commodore Pankhurst spoke.

"There's a weakness in your plan, Johnson. Where do we find not one but two doubles for Hess?"

"Yes, that's certainly one problem, sir. And another is persuading potential doubles to offer themselves as targets for Nazi assassins. Can someone come up with a solution?"

Carlyle answered. He was nearly a foot shorter than Johnson and stocky. His black hair was slicked back. The snub nose seemed too large for his round face. He could charm people with his ready smile and crinkly lines surrounding his brown eyes. "Sir, what we need is some place with a large number of photographs. Teams of our MI5 people can go through the pictures and identify likely doubles. Then we interview them. Hopefully we can find two people willing to volunteer."

"And where do we find those photographs?" Pankhurst asked.

"How about a newspaper office?" Carlyle suggested. "They must have tens of thousands of photographs stored away somewhere."

"But what about security?" Pankhurst responded. "The newspaper people will quickly discover that we're looking for doubles of Rudolf Hess. And when we start to interview likely candidates, it's going to be even harder to keep everything quiet. And once the secret is out, it'll be hopeless—the hounds will simply sit tight and ignore the hare."

"Sir, I've had an idea," Squadron Leader Harkness said. "What about the books of photographs at Scotland Yard? They call it the rogues' gallery. They've got pictures of everyone they've arrested, and a lot more besides. We could go through the photos without anyone finding out."

"Are you out of your mind?" the air commodore thundered. "Do you seriously think that we should employ criminals to trap the *Abwehr* agents?"

"Why not, sir?" Carlyle ventured. "We could promise them a large remission of sentence in return for their total cooperation. And we don't have to worry about them escaping, because the doubles will have to be under heavy armed guard to convince everyone who sees them that we're holding Rudolf Hess."

The silence this time was even longer.

Until that moment, Major Wilfred Tupman of the Royal Marines had not said a word. But now he spoke up. "Air Commodore, the inspector at Scotland Yard who runs the rogues' gallery has a photographic memory. Ironically, I don't seem to be able to recall his name right now, but we could easily find it out. We can show him a picture of Hess and ask him to give us the names of potential doubles currently in prison. Then we can interview the doubles without anyone learning about it, and without revealing the purpose of our questions. With the greatest respect, sir, I think that Carlyle is correct. If we promise someone who's been sentenced to a long term of imprisonment the possibility of parole in return for their fullest cooperation, they may well volunteer for the job."

"Tupman, I think you and your colleagues are certifiably insane. Hitler announced that Rudolf Hess is 'delusional'—I shudder to think what the *Führer* would say about you lot. But it may just work."

CHAPTER THREE
Scotland Yard, London
Friday, May 16, 1941

"Detective Chief Inspector Westerman?"

"Yes."

"I'm Johnson, and this is Carlyle, my MI5 colleague."

"How do you do, Mr. Johnson? I saw you open the batting for Harrow against Eton at Lord's Cricket Ground. But if my memory serves me correctly, sir, your name wasn't Johnson that day. And Mr. Carlyle, is it? D'you know, sir, you look just like your twin brother. But his name isn't Carlyle, for some unknown reason."

"Detective Chief Inspector," Johnson answered, "we'd heard that you have a photographic memory for names and faces of criminals. Until now, I'd believed that Carlyle and I had led utterly blameless lives. But clearly at some time in the past we've committed a dastardly felony of some sort, perhaps helping a dear old lady to cross a busy road when she wanted to stay right where she was, otherwise we'd never have come under your purview."

"Mr. Johnson," said Westerman with a broad grin, "I never forget a name or face, guilty or innocent. And I specialize in aliases, whether for criminal reasons or national security purposes. Now, how can I help you two gentlemen?"

Johnson responded. "I was going to show you a photograph and ask you if you know anyone who resembles him. But after your display of memory, I think it would better if I simply said that Carlyle and I are looking for at least two prisoners currently serving long sentences who could pass as doubles for Rudolf Hess."

"With or without the services of a make-up artist?"

"Preferably without."

"Let me see, sir."

Westerman got up and opened a drawer in one of the many filing cabinets that covered every inch of wall space in his large office. After a few seconds he took out a photograph.

"Mr. Carlyle, I'd like you to compare this picture with the one that Mr. Johnson decided not to show me."

"Good gracious, Detective Chief Inspector, I could swear it was the same man."

"It *is* the same man," said Westerman drily. "We keep photographs of all the top Nazis in our rogues' gallery; they're the worst criminals in the world. Now let me see if I can help you."

He went to another filing cabinet, took out a large file, paged through it methodically, extracted a photograph and placed it in front of Johnson.

"You know this man, I think."

"Detective Chief Inspector," Johnson said severely, "one joke was fine, but this is ridiculous. Of course I know him. He's Freddy Campbell-White. I was at school with him; he was a year ahead of me. He doesn't look anything like Hess, and he's certainly not a criminal."

"Mr. Johnson, how would your schoolmate look with black hair and large black eyebrows? Pretty similar to Hess, don't you think? And as for your character reference, Campbell-White is currently in Strangeways, the high-security prison in Manchester, where he's serving a life sentence for murder and robbery."

"Are you serious?"

"Perfectly serious, sir. If you think that he's a good likeness, perhaps you'd like to meet with him at Strangeways and hear his story from his own lips."

"Detective Chief Inspector, I apologize."

"No need for that, sir, I assure you. Now you said you need at least two likely candidates. I have another idea; let me get his photo for you. I won't be a minute. Ah, here it is. Please be kind enough to take a look at this man. A good likeness, you'll agree, and no hair dye is needed in his case. This one's sitting in Wandsworth Prison, less than five miles from here. His name is Ernest Worthington. He's a jewel thief. For years he got away with haul after haul. His *modus operandi* was to observe a house for days, weeks sometimes, and then break in when he knew that no one was home. We tried everything we could think of to catch him, but there were two obstacles. We never knew where he would strike next, so laying a trap would have been pointless. And the other problem was that he never sold any of the jewels in England."

"So what did he do with them?" Carlyle asked.

"Worthington made a full confession. He told us that he had a partner, a brilliant jewelry designer in Brussels named Joost van den Beeck. About once a year, Worthington took his haul of stolen baubles across the Channel to van den Beeck. The jeweler removed the stones from their settings, melted down the gold, and used the now untraceable gems to fashion truly exquisite necklaces, earrings, brooches, and the like. Then he hopped across the border into Germany where he sold his creations to the wives of Nazi bigwigs and rich industrialists. When he'd sold his wares, he travelled on to Switzerland. There he deposited his ill-gotten gains in two numbered bank accounts, half the money for himself and half for Worthington. For years we made the lives of every fence in England miserable, ignoring their protestations of innocence and badgering them for information on the robberies, but they really did know nothing about it; Worthington was a master operator."

"How did you catch him?"

"We finally decided that we had to set a trap. We heard that Sir Ambrose Wakesmith, the South African mining magnate, was going to rent a house in Mayfair for the season. With his permission, we secreted a policeman in the house before he and his family arrived from Johannesburg. Sir Ambrose was only too happy to agree to the arrangement; he immediately realized that he'd be the only man in London whose wife's gold and diamonds would be safe. Then, you know those weekly magazines that publish photographs taken at society balls, fashionable race meetings, shooting parties, and charity events?"

"You mean like *The Tatler*?"

"Yes, that sort of publication. Anyhow, we dropped a discrete word here and there, and photographs of Lady Wakesmith, lavishly festooned with jewelry, started to appear in those magazines with monotonous regularity. The society editors of the daily newspapers followed suit, much to the delight of her Ladyship, it seems.

"News of that kind travels quickly, and Worthington soon made it his business to learn the address of the house in Mayfair where he could purloin a gold ring set with a twenty-five-carat square-cut emerald, innumerable heavy gold chains and bracelets, and a pair of earrings with deep-blue diamonds so large that Lady Wakesmith successfully started the rumor that they once had served as the eyes in the statue of the primary deity in a Brahmin temple in southwestern India.

"When Worthington thought that the house was empty, he broke in—straight into the arms of the law. And after we arrested him, we searched his house. It'd been several months since his last trip to Belgium, so we found the proceeds of four major robberies hidden under the floorboards in his bedroom. Such an obvious place—I'd expected something considerably more creative from Worthington. Of course, he had to plead guilty, and the judge sentenced him to thirty years' imprisonment. Harsh, yes, but the sentencing guidelines left him with no alternative."

"And what happened to van den Beeck?" Johnson asked.

"Good question. The short answer is: Rudolf Hess murdered him."

"*What?*"

"Here's what happened," Westerman explained. "We found a letter from van den Beeck in Worthington's home. We tipped off the Belgian police and they arrested the jeweler. Because he had apparently led a blameless life up to then, they released him on bail. Then the European newspapers picked up the story. One morning the wife of a top German leader opened the official Nazi newspaper, the *Völkischer Beobachter* (The People's Observer) and discovered that she was wearing stolen gems. She told her husband in no uncertain terms that van den Beeck had to be severely punished. The next day *Gestapo* thugs crossed into Belgium and kidnapped van den Beeck. The day after that he found himself standing in front of a Berlin judge who sentenced him to a year in prison for selling stolen goods.

"Did you know that, soon after he took power, Hitler instructed Hess to review all court decisions that related to persons deemed enemies of the Nazi Party? He had the power to increase any sentence, and to take "merciless action" if he deemed it appropriate. The furious wife of the Nazi bigwig went to her husband, Rudolf Hess, and demanded justice; of course, what she really wanted was revenge. Two hours later, executioners in Plötzensee Prison guillotined van den Beeck.

"It's none of my business why you're looking for doubles for Hess, but I can put two and two together as well as the next man. And I can tell you that Worthington will be only too willing to cooperate with whatever it is that you've got planned for him."

CHAPTER FOUR
Wandsworth Prison, London
Saturday, May 17, 1941

The Governor of Wandsworth Prison escorted Johnson and Carlyle to the interview room. A wooden table, bolted to the floor, occupied the middle of the room. On one side of the table stood two uncomfortable-looking wooden chairs; a third was on the opposite side.

"Sir Charles, does Worthington know anything about us or our visit?" Carlyle asked.

"I've followed the Home Secretary's instructions to the letter. I'm about to order two of my prison officers to bring him here now, without giving them a reason. No one in the prison, other than myself, has any information at all."

"Thank you very much indeed, Sir Charles."

"Not at all. I'll leave you now. Worthington should be here in a few minutes."

Carlyle turned to Johnson. "Let's try and follow the script as closely as we can. We can't let him know the purpose of our visit until he's committed himself. And remember, we want him to think that we're two half-witted twits, the kind of people who leave valuable jewelry lying around for him to steal."

Two warders escorted Ernest Worthington into the interview room, removed his handcuffs, and told him to sit on the vacant chair. Then they stood behind him.

"Thank you, but we'd like to talk privately with the prisoner," Carlyle said.

The two warders looked at one another and shrugged their shoulders. One left the room immediately without a word. "Bang on the door when you want to leave," the other said. Then he, too, left the room, locking the metal door behind him with a loud clang.

"Worthington, my name is Carlyle, and this is Johnson. We're from Consolidated Life and Property Insurance Company Limited. We'd like to ask you a few questions."

"About what, may I ask?" Worthington asked cautiously. "I believe that, when I pleaded guilty, I answered all the questions that the police asked me."

"As I just told you, we're not from the police."

Worthington said nothing. His face was blank.

Carlyle reached into the briefcase he had brought with him and took out a sheet of paper. "Here's a document bearing the signature of the Home Secretary. These lines at the bottom of the page are where we'll sign to attest that you've answered all our questions to the best of your knowledge. When we've placed our marks there, your sentence will be commuted by five years."

Worthington's face still betrayed nothing. "I take it that you're here in connection with a jewelry claim from one of your clients and that you're going to ask me about some jewels that I may or may not have purloined. But if you ask me about other robberies I may or may not have committed and if I'm stupid enough to tell you about them, I'll get another thirty years. With all due respect, Mr. Carlyle, I wasn't born yesterday."

"Worthington, it states here: 'Nothing that Ernest Worthington says may be used in evidence against him in a court of law or elsewhere.' Accordingly, you may speak quite freely to us. Here, read the document. Take your time."

Carlyle handed over the sheet of paper, typed single-spaced. Worthington glanced quickly through the document and then handed it back to Carlyle. The jewel thief shook his head and sighed. "No matter what it says there, they'll do to me whatever they want. Ask away."

"Worthington, it's our understanding that you took the jewels that you stole to Mr. van den Beeck in Brussels," Carlyle said.

"Yes, I did."

"Why didn't you just put them in a box and post them?"

The question surprised Worthington, but he did his best to answer it without revealing that fact. "There are people who take a job with the Royal Mail just for the opportunity to pilfer packages. And that goes for the Belgian Post and every other mail service in the world, for that matter."

"But you could have sent it by registered post," Johnson insisted.

Worthington was about to smile but quickly thought better of it. Instead, he replied with a straight face, "I would have to give my name and address, and declare the contents and value of the parcel. Just how was I going to explain how I came to be in possession of a quarter of a million pounds worth of jewels?"

"You could have paid a courier to take them to Belgium," Carlyle suggested.

The thief looked fixedly at Carlyle. "Do you know any courier you would trust with a quarter of a million pounds worth of anything, let alone jewels?" he asked.

"I see. So, about once year you put the jewels in a valise and took a cross-channel steamer to the Continent," Carlyle said.

"Yes. I took the Hook Continental." Seeing their blank looks, he explained. "It's a train, run by the London and North Eastern Railway. You go to Liverpool Street Station and buy a ticket to The Hook of Holland in the Netherlands. The train takes you to Parkeston Quay at Harwich. There you connect with the night ferry, which takes you to The Hook. You sail on the SS *Amsterdam*, the SS *Prague*, or the SS *Vienna*—three very comfortable sister ships, especially for someone like me who suffers from chronic seasickness even on those rare occasions when the Channel is calm. And the next morning, you take a train from The Hook of Holland to Brussels, changing at Rotterdam."

"I assume that, when you arrived at The Hook, you didn't declare the jewels in your possession, nor when you crossed the border from the Netherlands into Belgium?" Carlyle asked.

Three years in the toughest prison in Britain had taught Worthington to control his emotions. He said nothing and just shrugged.

Johnson took up the questioning. "I assume that, with all your visits to Brussels, you speak Belgian fluently."

Instead of reacting to the ridiculous question, Ernest Worthington simply replied, "There's no such language, Mr. Johnson. In Belgium they speak Flemish and French."

"And which of those do you speak?" Johnson asked.

"Neither."

"So how then did you communicate with van den Beeck?"

"He speaks fluent English." Worthington paused. "I mean, he spoke fluent English."

"But how did you order your meals in Belgian restaurants?"

"Belgium is a small country and, as a result, the Belgian people have to speak other languages. Many people there speak English."

"Van den Beeck used to sell his jewelry in Germany. You said he spoke English. Is that what he spoke in Germany?"

Worthington replied calmly, "In Germany they speak German. Joost spoke many languages fluently, including English and German."

"I see. So Belgians speak French and Flemish, but they also speak English and German?"

"Many of them, yes."

"Did you ever talk to Belgians in German?"

"I don't know any German."

"Didn't you study any foreign language at school?"

"Just Latin."

"Did you try speaking Latin in Belgium?"

Worthington nearly exploded with laughter this time, but managed to control himself. "Latin is a dead language. The Romans spoke Latin two thousand years ago, but no one speaks it nowadays."

He doesn't speak German, Johnson said to himself. *Pity about that. But at least he doesn't realize that that was one of the things we came here to find out. That's good.*

Aloud he replied, "I see."

Then Johnson paused and Carlyle took over. "Now tell me, Worthington—"

But before Carlyle could complete his question, Johnson suddenly resumed speaking. "Have we met before? You look familiar."

"I don't think so."

"I'm sure we've met."

"Probably not."

"Do you have a twin sister, perhaps? An identical twin?"

"Identical twins have to be the same sex. Two boys or two girls. Otherwise, they're not identical, are they?"

"I suppose you're right. Well, do you have a twin brother?"

"No."

"But I'm sure I've seen you somewhere before."

"It's unlikely."

"I know—you're Rudolf Hess!"

"No, I'm not. I'm Ernest Worthington."

"Yes, of course you are. I meant that you look like Rudolf Hess."

"Do I?"

"Yes, you do. I'm sure that people have been pointing that out to you for years. Have you ever imitated Hess? Or masqueraded as Hess at a party?"

For the first time Worthington lost his composure and was unable to maintain his polite veneer. "Masquerade as a Nazi? You must be out of your mind. And Hess of all people—do you know what he did to Joost?"

"Yes, we'd heard," Carlyle said. "But we've digressed. As you correctly surmised, we're here to ask you about certain jewel robberies that, as you rather delicately put it, you may or may not have committed."

For the next half hour they quizzed Worthington about the details of every jewel theft he had perpetrated. Carlyle painstakingly wrote down the locations of the numerous robberies that Worthington had carried out over the years and details of the jewelry he had stolen. Finally Johnson spoke.

"Thank you, Worthington. You've told us everything we need to know."

Both men signed the document. Carlyle said to Worthington, "We'll give this to the Governor now. Oh, there's just one more thing."

Carlyle reached into his briefcase again. This time he took out a sheaf of papers bound with red tape and red sealing wax.

"I have here an unconditional pardon, signed by His Majesty on the advice of the Lord Chancellor. We have a job that we'd like you to do. If you carry it out to our satisfaction, you'll be a free man. You can change your name and start afresh."

"What's the catch?"

"There are multiple catches. First and foremost, you'll have to volunteer for this task. Obviously, we'll give you enough information for you to come to an informed decision. However, this job falls under the Official Secrets Act 1939, which means that, once you know the nature of the project, we cannot allow you to tell anyone else about it. Therefore, if you're interested and want to know more details, we'll have to move you to a secure site to talk about it. If you then decide not to do it, we'll have to keep you in solitary confinement in some isolated place until the war is over. Then you'll return here to complete your sentence."

"Well, the job is obvious. You want me to impersonate Rudolf Hess, even though I don't speak a word of German."

Johnson and Carlyle were both rendered speechless. Finally Johnson was able to stutter, "H-how did you know?"

"Well, it was obvious from your questions. Here's how I saw the situation. You two received permission to come here and interview me in private. That's unusual to say the least. And that five-year commutation of sentence—why on earth would the Home Secretary agree to such a thing to assist an insurance company? That's not the way that things are done in England; the public sector never involves itself in the private sector in that sort of way. One look at that document told me that you two work for the government—MI5 more than likely. Something odd was going on. That's why I was so careful to answer all your questions as politely as I possibly could and cooperate to the best of my ability, in the hope that you could help me get out of here five years sooner.

"Then you started asking me those stupid questions. There's no way that anyone as moronic as you two pretended to be could possibly get permission to meet with me in the presence of the Governor, let alone in private. Now I knew that something definitely was afoot, and in all probability had to do with your feigned ignorance of European languages."

"So why didn't you speak up earlier?" Carlyle demanded to know.

"Have you any idea how unendurable life here in Wandsworth is? Until you'd both signed on the dotted line I wasn't going to say a word. By the way, yes, I volunteer."

"But you don't know the details. It's a dangerous mission. You could be killed."

Worthington lowered his voice for emphasis. "I'd rather be killed right now in the service of my country than stay here for one more day."

"I still have to inform you about the mission before you volunteer," Carlyle insisted. "It's called 'informed consent'—I have to inform, then you have to consent of your own free will. That's how it works when you're a prisoner."

Worthington rolled his eyes. "Go ahead. I can't stop you."

"A week ago, Rudolf Hess landed in Scotland. He—"

"Yes, yes, I'm aware of all that. Everyone in the prison seems to know about it. I don't know how it started, but the news has spread like wildfire. And a number of the screws, er, prison officers, have told me that I look like Hess. Most of the warders here are sadists, and they like nothing better than humiliating the prisoners. That's how they're trying to demean me now."

"Well, as you surmised, we need someone to masquerade as Hess."

"And as I just told you, I'm more than willing to do it."

"What you possibly don't know is that Hitler has ordered his agents in Britain to kill Hess," Carlyle continued.

"No, I didn't know that," Worthington said slowly. "But it's entirely irrelevant. We're at war. I want to serve my country. Other men are putting their lives on the line, so why shouldn't I? And I'll do anything to get out of here. Now, what do I have to do?"

"There's one more thing we need to know. How well do you know East Anglia? I'm referring to counties like Essex, Norfolk, Suffolk, perhaps Cambridgeshire."

"I know that part of the country well. I worked in London itself, as well as in areas with country houses owned by careless, rich people whose wives store their jewelry in locked drawers that a five-year old child could pop open with a paper clip. Or, more likely, in an unlocked jewel box on top of the dressing table. So, yes, I'm familiar with East Anglia."

"What about Scotland?"

"I've never worked in Scotland. In fact, I've never even been to Scotland. I don't really have the urge to visit Scotland. I find that—"

"Thank you," Johnson interjected. "That's what we wanted to know. We're taking you to a safe house where you'll be fully briefed. But this much I can tell you now. Once we've prepared you for the mission, your job will be to impersonate Hess in the Inner Hebrides, an area of Britain where no one knows you and it's therefore unlikely that anyone will realize that you're not Rudolf Hess.

"The safe house is guarded day and night, inside and out. When you leave there for Scotland, you'll be portraying Hess, and obviously while you're playing that role we're going to watch you even more closely than we're going to watch you while you're in the safe house, if that were at all possible. Please don't even think of trying to escape. For reasons of national security, all your guards have strict orders to shoot to kill and not even bother to ask questions afterwards."

"And I assume that the other reason you're sending me to Scotland rather than East Anglia," Worthington observed, "is that if I do manage to elude your sharpshooting guards, I'm most unlikely to find a former colleague to shelter me there until I can make my way to Switzerland to collect my ill-gotten gains."

"I'm beginning to understand," said Johnson dryly, "how you managed to avoid being caught for so long. And I'm grateful for the fact that, from now on, you'll be fighting on our side. Furthermore, for the first and hopefully the last time since this war started, with you now taking an active role in the conflict, I've actually started to feel sorry for the Germans."

CHAPTER FIVE
Strangeways Prison, Manchester
Sunday, May 18, 1941

"What do you want with White?" Phineas Threadborne barked. "He's a murderer and a thief. No decent person would have anything to do with him. And on a Sunday, too. This is most irregular."

"Mr. Threadborne," Carlyle replied as patiently as he could, "as governor of this prison, you've received a letter from the Home Secretary instructing you to set up a confidential interview for us with Campbell-White. I'm afraid that's all I'm permitted to say."

"The man is a disgrace to the human race. Educated at Harrow, the third son of a viscount, no less. The Honorable Frederick Campbell-White— honorable, my foot. That man doesn't know the meaning of the word 'honor.'"

"As I said, Mr. Threadborne," Carlyle repeated calmly, "we are here to meet with Campbell-White. Are you prepared to set up the interview?"

"Under protest, yes."

"We have noted your protest. Now can we please meet with Campbell-White?"

"I'll arrange for my second-in-command to set it up."

"No, Mr. Threadborne, the Home Secretary was specific in his letter to you. You need to arrange the confidential meeting personally."

Threadborne's already somewhat florid face took on a bright red color. Carlyle and Johnson were concerned that the governor might turn violent, but Thredborne somehow managed to control himself.

"Come with me," he muttered and escorted them to an interview room.

"Wait here," he ordered.

It was close to half an hour later that two prison officers escorted a tall blond man of about twenty-five into the interview room. Despite being handcuffed and in leg-irons, Campbell-White maintained his dignity. When he saw Johnson he was about to say something, but Johnson put his finger to his lips.

"Remove the handcuffs and the leg-irons," Johnson said to the older warder, a plump bald man of about fifty who exuded an air of officiousness.

"Can't do that. Governor's orders," was the response.

Johnson took a sheet of paper out of the attaché case he was carrying, and wrote three sentences. "Take this to the governor."

"Can't do that. Got to stay with the prisoner. Governor's orders."

"Fine. Take the prisoner back to his cell. Then come back here and take me to the governor."

"Not allowed to do that."

54

"Fine. You're under arrest for obstructing a security officer in his duties."

"You can't arrest me," the warder blustered.

"Can't I just?" Johnson said. "Read this."

He took a manila folder out of the attaché case, extracted a letter and showed it to the older warder.

"I'm extremely sorry, sir, I didn't know. We'll remove the cuffs and irons right away, sir."

"And then remove yourselves smartly, lock the door behind you and wait outside. We'll bang on the door when we're ready."

The two prison officers quickly obeyed. When the door was locked behind them, Carlyle indicated to the other two that they should sit. Campbell-White said nothing. He had realized that something highly unusual was happening and that it would probably be in his best interests to obey Johnson's instruction and remain silent. In particular, he had caught on to the fact that he was not to greet his old schoolmate.

"Campbell-White," Carlyle said, "my name is Carlyle; this is Johnson. To begin with, we want to learn from you why you are here. Yes, we've read your file carefully, including the transcript of the proceedings at your trial, but we want to hear your side of the story. You pleaded guilty, and therefore there should be no reason for you to hold anything back or, worse, shade the facts in any manner whatsoever. We expect you to tell us the truth, the whole truth, and nothing but the truth. Depending on what you tell us, we may be in a position to put forward an unusual proposition to you."

"Fine. I've nothing to hide. What do you want to know?"

"You were convicted of murder and robbery. What happened?"

"I'll tell you as briefly as I can. Feel free to ask for more details at any time."

"Go ahead," Johnson said.

"When war broke out," Campbell-White began, "I immediately enlisted. I was given a commission in the Tenth Lancers."

"Otherwise known as the 'The Duke of Exeter's Own Cavalry,' I believe," Johnson interposed smoothly.

"Quite right. Of course, after the First World War the horses went, and we became an armored regiment. But the spirit of the Tenth Lancers is still that of a crack cavalry regiment. I found myself the member of a fast set, considerably faster than I was used to, in fact. The mess fees were steep, and there was gambling. Lots of gambling, much more than I could afford. I'm not very bright. As a result, I don't play bridge or poker at all well, and my debts started to mount up. And soon, all too soon, the time came when I couldn't meet my financial obligations.

"I'm the third son of four. The estate is entailed. And that means that Cuthbert, the oldest, inherits everything—I get nothing at all. And I have nothing.

"When I was given a weekend leave I went home to our country place and asked Father for money. He refused. I politely told him that a gentleman doesn't renege on his debts. He pointed out, equally politely, that a gentleman doesn't gamble with money he doesn't have. And he was right.

"I lay in bed that night, unable to sleep, worrying about what was going to happen to me when my fellow officers started to call in the IOUs I'd so rashly signed. Then suddenly I remembered that there's a safe embedded in the dining room wall hidden behind the Sir Joshua Reynolds portrait of the eighth viscount with his hunting dogs; the painting is mounted on a swivel so that you can rotate it to one side to reveal the safe. I knew that Father is a firm believer in bearer shares."

"Don't you mean bearer *bonds*?" Carlyle asked.

"No, bearer *shares*," Frederick Campbell-White insisted. "Writers of third-rate crime fiction encourage their dastardly villains to steal bearer bonds. The point is that whoever has the piece of paper on which the bearer bond is printed owns that bond—all the bearer has to do is take the bond to the issuing government or company and he gets paid out in full, in cash, without giving his name. Bearer bonds are essentially untraceable. They're great for tax evasion, of course. Also, every country seems to issue bearer bonds these days, and that means that those authors have the freedom to set their scarcely credible stories anywhere in the world they like.

"However, most people are unaware that our Companies Act of 1929 permits British firms to issue bearer shares—I don't know if any other country allows them. Anyhow, the shares aren't registered and the firms that issue them don't track transfer of ownership. The person who holds the share certificate can sell the shares to anyone they choose without any questions being asked. Holding bearer shares is risky, of course; if they're stolen, that's that. And if they're lost or burnt or destroyed, there's no way to get them back. But they're great for tax evasion. Any time my father needs money he sells some bearer shares. He reports nothing to the Board of Inland Revenue, and Father never declares anything like that on his income tax return."

"Why do you think that bearer shares are better than bearer bonds?" Johnson asked.

"Because they're a lot safer. If a thief finds a bearer bond certificate, he'll probably know what it is, so he'll steal it and cash it in. But so few people know about bearer share certificates that if a burglar were to see such a thing, in all probability he wouldn't realize that he could safely sell the shares with total anonymity, just as with a bearer bond.

"Returning to the theft, I sneaked into Father's bedroom after he'd gone to bed. Ever since Mother died last year he drinks himself to sleep every night with a bottle of whisky, and I had no fear of waking him. I took his keys from the table next to his bed and went downstairs. The portrait hangs to your right just after you walk through the double doors leading from the drawing room into the dining room. Between the painting and the doors is a table with a brass lamp. The heavy velvet curtains were drawn, and therefore I felt that there was little risk in switching on the lamp. I swung the picture aside, selected the safe key from the ring and turned it in the lock. The door swung open with a really loud creak, and I immediately realized that I should've oiled the hinges first. Anyhow, it was too late to do anything about the noise. I looked inside the strongbox and saw an inch-high pile of what looked like share certificates.

"I took them over to the lamp and examined the top one. I couldn't believe my luck. There was no doubt—this was a certificate for a large number of bearer shares. And the next three were similar, too. I was holding what appeared to be an inordinate amount of untraceable wealth in my hands. I had no knowledge of any of the companies that had issued the shares, but it seemed to me that half a dozen of those certificates would be enough for me to be able to pay back everything I owed as well as my mess fees for the next several years into the future. In short, I was saved from the ignominy of having to resign my commission and declare bankruptcy.

"And then I heard another creak, somewhat softer than the first. One of the double doors from the drawing room slowly opened. Perkins, our elderly butler, stood there in his nightclothes, a heavy silver candlestick in his hand. He peered cautiously into the dining room. With one glance he could see that I'd shifted the painting to one side, the safe was wide open, and I was standing there with a pile of papers in my hands. Not surprisingly, he immediately realized that I was stealing from my own father.

"I'm not sure for what reason, but I was always Perkins's favorite. I think that was why, instead of calling the police or telling my father in the morning, he just asked, 'Master Frederick, what are you doing?'"

"There was no point in my trying to lie, because Perkins had caught on to what I was doing. 'I need money, lots of money, right now,' I replied.

"'Why, Master Frederick?' he asked.

"'I owe a large sum in gambling debts, and I have to pay it back,' I told him.

"'I assume that you asked your father for money, but he refused, and that's why you're doing this.' I just nodded. 'I can't help you with money,' Perkins continued, 'but I have an idea for covering up what you're doing. We're going to stage a burglary.'

"'What do you mean?' I asked.

"'When your father discovers that items are missing from the safe, he's going to call in the police and suspicion is going to fall squarely on you. You and your three brothers know about the hidden safe and where your father keeps the key, but the other young gentlemen are all fighting overseas. In addition, you need money, so you're the obvious person. We have to make the police think that someone broke into the house. For example, you're going to have to put on a pair of gloves and a pair of gardening boots, go outside, break a window pane, unlock the window and climb inside. Then you go upstairs, take the keys, come down again, unlock the safe and take what you need. Then, leaving the key in the lock, you exit by the window. Don't shut the window completely when you go. You should leave it partially open, as if the burglar departed in too much of a hurry to close it properly.'

"'Perkins,' I said, 'you read too many detective stories.'

"'Yes, Master Frederick, I freely admit it, and that's why I know what we have to do. I'm going to sit down on the chair here at the head of the table. Quick, pull down that curtain cord and tie me to the chair.'

"He put the candlestick on the table and sat down. I gave the curtain cord a sharp tug. Nothing happened. I pulled again. Still nothing. Finally I jumped up and grabbed the cord as close to the top as I could reach. My weight was sufficient to bring down the cord—and the curtain rod and the curtains. Surprisingly, there was only a little noise, because the drapes hit the floor first, and the rod and the other bits and pieces landed on top of the thick velvet fabric. But even if the rod had fallen on the wooden floor surrounding the carpet, the only other person in the house was my father, and he was in a drunken stupor upstairs in his bedroom.

"I tied Perkins to the chair as best I could, trying not to hurt him in any way. Then he said, 'Master Frederick, knock me unconscious.'

"'Why?' I asked.

"'When they ask me to describe the burglar, I'll tell them that he hit me hard on the back of my head and he must have tied me to this chair while I was unconscious.'

"'I can't possibly do that to you,' I insisted.

"'Please, Master Frederick. If you need the money that badly then you have to knock me out. If you won't do that then replace what you took and lock the safe. I cannot face what it would do to your father if you were convicted of theft.'

"I thought about what he said but I just couldn't make up my mind what to do. Then Perkins looked round. 'Use the obsidian ashtray on the table by the door,' he suggested. 'It'll do the trick.'

"'But what about the candlestick?' I asked. 'They'll see that you brought it along as a weapon when you heard a noise in the dining room. How will you explain being knocked out while you were armed?'

"'I'll tell them that when I walked into the dining room, the burglar was probably standing on the right side of the doorway. I walked into the room. He was now behind me. He reached behind him, picked up the ashtray, and he hit me with it. Hard. As I fell, dead to the world, I dropped the candlestick. He picked me up and tied me to the chair.'

"'I'm sorry, Perkins,' I said, 'but I don't think that they'd believe that a burglar would pick you up and seat you comfortably in a chair and then utilize the curtain cord—he'd just tie you up where you lay on the carpet.'

"Perkins thought for perhaps ten seconds, then said, 'You're quite right, Master Frederick. Please untie me. I'll stand holding the candlestick, then you knock me out and tie me up with that curtain cord.'

"The story now seemed reasonably credible. I released Perkins and he got up from the chair. With my hand encased in my handkerchief I picked up the ashtray from the table. Then I said, 'Perkins, there's no way I could possibly knock you out, or even hit you hard enough to hurt you. What I'm going to do is give you a soft tap on your head with the ashtray. You can tell them that the blow I gave you knocked you out cold.' Perkins reluctantly agreed—he'd realized that this was as far as I was prepared to go.

"With the ashtray I gave Perkins the lightest of light jabs on the back of his head and stood back. Perkins stumbled around artistically, pretending to lose consciousness. As he did so his feet tangled in the curtain cord that I had carelessly left on the carpet. He lost his balance and fell forward, smashing his skull on the corner of the table. Perkins collapsed onto the carpet and lay motionless. He was dead; I could tell that instantly. The Duke of Exeter's Own Cavalry were in Northern France and Belgium a year ago, and I saw death there, too much death.

"But that wasn't murder," Carlyle protested. "As far as I'm concerned, at worst what you did was manslaughter; at best, accidental death."

"Yes, and at the time I thought so, too. That's why I called the police at once and told them everything that had happened in the fullest detail without calling in the family lawyer first. Like most laymen, I knew nothing about the rule of felony murder. Had you heard of it before you read my file?"

Both Johnson and Carlyle shook their heads as Campbell-White went on. "As you now know, there's a principle in English law that was first codified in 1716, but probably goes back many centuries before that; believe me, I'm now an expert on all this. In short, the rule states that if an offender kills someone accidentally in commission of a felony, he can be charged with murder."

"I learned about the law in the transcript of the proceedings at your trial," Carlyle said, "but it's ridiculous. You had no intention of killing Perkins. You didn't even want to hurt him."

"Yes, that's true. But the fact is that I accidentally killed him while stealing those bearer shares, that is, while committing a felony. Accordingly, I was found guilty of murder. Because of the circumstances and my services to the country during the war I was spared the rope, but that light tap on Perkins's head has cost me my freedom for the rest of my life. I'll die here in Strangeways Prison."

"Not necessarily," Johnson said. "As I told you, we're here with an unusual proposition. First we need to ask you a series of questions. As Carlyle told you, we expect the truth, the whole truth and nothing but the truth. If you lie, everything's off the table—and there's no second chance."

"I understand."

"For your sake, I hope you do. Up to now you've been open with us, and that openness had better continue."

Frederick Campbell-White nodded. "Ask away."

"Do you speak German?" Johnson asked.

"Not a word, I'm afraid. At Harrow we learned Latin and Greek, and nothing else." As he said those words, he looked straight at Carlyle and studiously avoided glancing at Johnson, his fellow Old Harrovian.

"Can you speak English with a German accent?"

"I can try. But I'm sure that I'll sound like an Englishman putting on a German accent, rather than a German speaking English."

"I see," Johnson said. He turned to Carlyle, indicating that he should take over the questioning.

"What do you know about Rudolf Hess?" Carlyle asked.

"That's an odd thing to ask," Campbell-White answered. "Is this a general knowledge quiz of some sort?"

"Answer the question," Carlyle said sharply.

"I don't know very much. He's a Nazi pooh-bah, I think. That's about it."

"Actually, he's the Deputy *Führer*. Haven't any of your fellow prisoners mentioned to you that Hess parachuted into Scotland about a week ago? I'd understood that prisoners in jail often know more about current events than the people outside."

"Maybe that's how it is, but they ignore me. No one talks to me. I killed a defenseless old man, you see, and they don't like that. Yes, there are worse crimes in their eyes—they beat you up at every opportunity for those. But my killing Perkins accidentally is bad enough for them to send me to Coventry. They ignore me; they pretend I'm not there. I'm the invisible man, as far as my fellow lags are concerned. No one sees me, no one interacts with me. To all intents and purposes, I'm going to continue to be in solitary confinement for the rest of my life."

"Next question," Johnson said. "How well do you know Scotland, and specifically the Inner Hebrides and the area around Oban?"

"Very well indeed. An uncle of mine owns an island, Talbert, in the Inner Hebrides. As a boy, I spent almost all my summer holidays there.

"You mean he owns a home there?"

"No, he owns the island. Did you know that only two hundred and fifty people between them own more than half of the land area of Scotland? My uncle is one of them."

"What about the counties of East Anglia? Essex, Suffolk, Norfolk?"

"No, I've never been there. None of them."

"Not even to Cambridgeshire?" Carlyle asked.

"I didn't go to university. As soon as I left school I travelled to the South Seas. I worked on the island of Guadalcanal, in the British Solomon Islands Protectorate. I ran a copra plantation owned by a distant cousin. I removed the shells from the coconuts, broke the kernels up, dried them in the sun, transported them to the nearest harbor and then waited for a tramp steamer to call and buy the crop. When war in Europe seemed inevitable, I left the plantation and returned home in order to enlist."

Johnson looked at Carlyle, who nodded. Johnson turned back to Campbell-White and continued. "As we've told you, we have a proposition to put to you. If you wish, we'll tell you about a mission, a potentially dangerous mission."

"Why did you say 'if you wish'? Why don't you just tell me about the mission?"

"Because once you know about it, you have two choices. The mission is classified Most Secret—after we've told you about it, we cannot allow you to tell anyone else. As a result, if you decide not to undertake the mission once you've heard the details, you'll find yourself in solitary confinement, probably on an isolated military base somewhere, in Greenland, say."

"Greenland?"

"Or Far Northern Canada. Not much difference, really. They're both inside the Arctic Circle. And when I said 'solitary confinement' I meant the real thing, not what you're going through here. You won't be able to communicate with another living soul until the war is over."

"I see. But why shouldn't I volunteer?"

"Because the mission is dangerous."

"Never mind that. I volunteer!"

"But you haven't heard what the mission is yet. We can't order you to do this because you're no longer in the army. You're a prisoner, so you have to volunteer of your own free will, after we've told you about the risks—it's called giving informed consent."

"I volunteer, sight unseen. I don't give a hill of beans about informed consent. Have you any idea what it's like to be confined in here? This prison is just like being in boarding school again. No, I lie, the food is fractionally better than it was at Harrow, and there's no corporal punishment. But for the rest…"

"Look here, Campbell-White," said Carlyle. "We understand that you're eager to get out of prison.

But there's a right way and a wrong way of doing this. If you want to take part in this mission, I strongly suggest that you keep your mouth shut and let Johnson finish saying what he has to say."

Campbell-White nodded.

"Now," Johnson continued, "I've just told you the consequences of our informing you about the mission and your deciding not to volunteer. Now I'm going to tell you what's going to happen if, after hearing about the mission and the attendant risks, you decide to volunteer of your own free will. If you carry out the mission to our satisfaction, you'll receive a full pardon. Immediately after you have completed the mission, you'll rejoin the army, as a private; you may change your name at that time, if you wish. You'll be transferred to Australia—"

"I thought that transportation of convicts to Australia stopped about a hundred years ago," Campbell-White interposed.

"I would strongly advise you not to try to make any more jokes, unless you want to spend the rest of your life in this prison."

"I'm sorry. So very sorry. Please go on."

"As I was saying before that totally unnecessary interruption," Johnson said in a firm voice, "you'll be transferred to Australia, where you'll be trained as a coastwatcher."

"I've never heard of a coastwatcher. Is that something they do in Australia?"

"You'll be given a radio transceiver and sent back to Guadalcanal. There you will set up a watching post. You'll use your radio to report to headquarters any and all movements of enemy aircraft and ships. And after the war is over, you'll be free to live your life as you see fit."

"Could I come back to England?" Campbell-White asked.

"The unconditional pardon you'd receive after carrying out the mission to our satisfaction would enable you to travel anywhere in the world you wish," Johnson said. "In essence, it would wipe out the past. Completely and utterly. You'd be able to make a fresh start wherever you liked, under your current name or a new name of your choosing."

"That's fine. I volunteer."

"But we haven't told you the mission yet, let alone the risks. Would you kindly stop volunteering."

"Sorry."

"Now, as I was saying," Johnson continued. "You have a choice: Do you want us to describe the mission to you or not?"

"For heaven's sake, yes. Say your piece so that I can agree to it and get out of here."

"Fine. The mission is as follows: We will dye your hair black and glue on large false black eyebrows. A make-up artist will make you look about twenty years older; Hess is forty-seven. You will then closely resemble Rudolf Hess. Your mission is to masquerade as Hess in East Anglia."

Campbell-White's mouth dropped open. He was a man of limited imagination, so during the course of the interview it had not occurred to him to try to figure out what this Most Secret mission might be.

But even if he had thought about various possibilities, pretending to be a top Nazi would never have occurred to him."

"You want me to put on stage make-up and act like Hess?"

"Yes," Carlyle said.

"You mean to entertain the troops? Are you two organizing a variety show?"

Carlyle rolled his eyes. Johnson put his hands over his face. Realizing that he had said the wrong thing, Campbell-White tried to save the situation.

"I know I'm not much of an actor, but I'll do anything you ask to get out of here. And if it means strutting on the stage that's fine with me."

Johnson, his hands still covering his face, groaned. Carlyle closed his eyes.

Terrified that he had blown his chance of leaving Strangeways Prison, Freddy Campbell-White desperately tried a different tack. "I've obviously got the wrong end of the stick," he muttered. "What do you want me to do?"

"Campbell-White," said Carlyle, "I'm going to explain the whole thing to you in very short sentences consisting of words that hopefully are of no more than one syllable. Here goes: Rudolf Hess landed in Scotland. We arrested him. We need someone to pretend to be Rudolf Hess, to sit quietly in a police car and be moved from jail to jail in East Anglia."

"But why would you want me to do that? Why don't you just put Hess in the police car and move him around? Why me?"

"Because Hitler has sent out an order to his agents in this country to kill Hess. We need Hess to stay alive, for obvious reasons; the man is a potential source of invaluable information to us. That means that we're looking for a Hess look-alike to pretend to be Hess in public, while the real Hess is safely somewhere else. The risk is that a Nazi agent will try to kill you, thinking that you're the Deputy *Führer* of Germany."

"Do I look like Hess?"

"Do you know what Hess looks like?" Carlyle shot back.

"Not exactly," Campbell-White admitted. "Actually, I have no idea at all."

"He looks just like you'll look with your blond hair dyed jet black, and with large black bushy eyebrows."

"I see."

"I'm not quite sure that you do see," Johnson said. "Anyhow, now that you've volunteered of your own free will, knowing the risks, we're taking you from here to a safe house to prepare you for your mission. Be warned that security personnel patrol the safe house day and night, both inside and outside. Don't even think of trying to escape. You're in possession of Most Secret information, and consequently all the guards have unambiguous orders to shoot even if they only suspect that you're trying to escape. Is that clear?"

"Perfectly clear."

"Furthermore, you need to realize in no uncertain terms that, if you jeopardize this operation in any way whatsoever, they'll construe it as treason and they'll hang you. Do you understand that?"

"Yes."

"On the other hand, if you obey our instructions, you'll get your unconditional pardon once the mission has been successfully completed."

"I look forward to that."

"Fine," Johnson said. "Now I'm going to bang on the door. Let's hope that at least one of the warders is standing outside."

CHAPTER SIX
MI5 Headquarters, London
Tuesday, May 20, 1941

As always, Air Commodore Pankhurst opened the morning meeting at precisely a quarter past nine.

"How is the training of our two Hess impersonators going?" he asked.

No one said anything.

"Why the silence? Johnson?"

"Sir, Carlyle and I are concerned about one aspect of this operation."

"What's the issue?"

"Well, sir," Johnson said, "first I'd like to report briefly regarding the training we're giving the doubles. The core of Operation OTTAWA is to transfer the two men in police vehicles from one place of confinement to the next, be it a jail, police station, or military base, until we can identify the two *Abwehr* agents. However, when the impersonators arrive at that day's destination, they'll have to get out of the car or van and walk, escorted and in handcuffs, from the street into the building. Consequently, it's essential for them to learn to walk

73

like Hess. Also, there'll be times when they'll be standing still in public, for example while waiting for a door from the street to be unlocked. On those occasions they have to stand precisely the way Hess would stand under similar circumstances, especially the angle of the head—that can be a dead giveaway."

"Go on."

"Well, we managed to get miles and miles of newsreel film showing Hess engaged in a variety of different activities. Then we enlisted the help of two excellent acting teachers from RADA."

"What's radar got to do with it?" Pankhurst asked.

"Not radar, sir, RADA—the Royal Academy of Dramatic Art."

"Oh, I see. Well, what happened?"

"Both our men," Johnson said, "have proved to be quick learners. By lunchtime yesterday the professors of drama were satisfied that Campbell-White and Worthington were almost ready to masquerade in public as Rudolf Hess. Campbell-White in particular holds his head exactly the right away. The expectation is that by tonight they'll both be able to play their roles flawlessly. Speaking is proving to be a little more difficult, however, because neither man knows a word of German.

"The language problem leads to a possible danger. On the one hand, everyone around Hess will be MI5 intelligence officers wearing the appropriate uniforms. They'll be dressed as police officers when they escort the Hess impersonators from place to place, as prison officers supervising them in jails, and as military police when they're in charge of them in military prisons. However, no matter how careful we are, there's always the risk that a genuine policeman or prison warder, someone without any security clearance at all, let alone Most Secret, may approach one of our impersonators, speak to them, and discover that he's talking to an imposter. And if that happens, ideally we'd sequester the offending party until the war is over. But if he's already told his friends, we'll have to abort the whole operation. After all, if the news gets out that Hess is a phony, the *Abwehr* agents will stay well away. Yes, there's press censorship and the like, but the real danger is a local policeman telling his wife about the man masquerading as Hess and the news spreading, eventually reaching the wrong ears."

"And what steps are you taking to prevent this?" Pankhurst asked.

"As I said, neither knows a word of German. That's danger number one. More and more young men these days are improving themselves. They're attending classes at Working Men's Clubs or studying from public library books. We're greatly concerned about what might happen if a prison warder who's teaching himself German decides to improve his language skills by talking to a real live Nazi. The result could be catastrophic."

"And?"

"Well, we've also borrowed a dialect trainer from RADA. She's teaching both men to speak English with a German accent or, more precisely, that's what she's attempting to do. Initially they both sounded like Englishmen on the stage trying to put on humorous German accents and failing badly in the attempt. They're improving, but slowly—much too slowly for my liking. Anyhow, the idea is that, if someone addresses them in German, they are to reply as aggressively as they can in English with their newly acquired Teutonic pronunciation, 'Here in England we speak English.' Hopefully that will do the trick.

"It's going to be harder if someone addresses them in English. For example, a curious young prison officer may come to a look-alike's cell to take a meal tray away and try to engage him in conversation. One or more of our men should always be standing outside the cell precisely to prevent that sort of occurrence, but sometimes things go wrong. We've told the doubles to adopt a superior look and just ignore the question. But who knows?

"There's also a risk that local people may verbally abuse a double, either when he's sitting in a police car or about to enter a police station. That's easier to handle. We've repeatedly instructed them both to ignore anything like that as well, and we've assured them that our men will deal with the situation.

"Accordingly, sir, the bottom line is that we're doing our utmost to enable Worthington and Campbell-White to masquerade flawlessly as Rudolf Hess, but there's always a chance that something unanticipated may happen that blows the whole operation sky-high."

"I see. Well, the training seems to be going satisfactorily. But you mentioned that something was bothering you and Carlyle. What is it?"

"Sir," Johnson said, "we disagree on the men's motives."

"What do you mean, Johnson?"

"In my opinion, Campbell-White and Worthington are learning their parts and cooperating in every respect in order to earn their pardons. They seem to trust us, and they know that if they do what we tell them to do, they won't have to serve the remainder of their sentences. And after the war they'll be able to do whatever they want wherever they like, using whatever name they choose."

"And you, Carlyle? Why do you think they're cooperating with us?"

"I think that they're plotting to escape."

"Together?"

"No, sir. They each have their own individual reasons, and I doubt very much if they've confided in one another. Yesterday at lunch Campbell-White mentioned that, once this is all over, the military authorities are going to send him to Guadalcanal to be a coastwatcher. From the look on Worthington's face, I got the impression that he suddenly realized that he, too, will be subject to conscription as soon as Operation OTTAWA has come to a successful conclusion. So, I don't think we need to worry about Worthington escaping until the mission is over, but after that…

"Worthington is forty-three, four years younger than Hess. It's therefore rather unlikely that he's going to end up somewhere on the front line, but any sort of military service is going to interfere with what appears to be his current objective—"

"Which is what?" the air commodore interrupted.

"He has millions in a bank in Switzerland, the proceeds of a highly successful career as a discriminating and discerning jewel thief; only the most expensive items caught his fancy. I think that he wants to go away and live a life of luxury somewhere on his ill-gotten gains."

"And why does Campbell-White want to escape?"

"He doesn't want to go back to Guadalcanal under any circumstances," Carlyle explained. "He's truly ashamed about what's happened. He wants to change his name and make a fresh start in a far-off place where no one knows him. He was on that copra plantation for nearly five years. The island consists of about two thousand square miles of mostly impenetrable jungle, with a number of copra plantations situated in the same general area. As a result, the planters tend to know one another; it's like a big club out there. And they must all be well aware of the robbery and murder—expatriates in a place like the British Solomon Islands Protectorate live for the months-old newspapers from home that the rusty old tramp steamers bring them. The planters share with one another each issue of *The Times* they receive, and they all read every word. Something sensational like this is likely to have been discussed by every British planter and his wife for months on end. It was probably the main topic of conversation at every dinner party, if not the only one. Campbell-White's reluctance to return to Guadalcanal is therefore fully understandable."

The air commodore nodded. "But you don't concur with Carlyle's views, do you, Johnson?"

"Well, sir, I agree with Carlyle regarding what he thinks the two men would like to do once Operation OTTAWA is over. But both impersonators are well aware that we're fighting a war, and I believe that they want to do anything and everything they possibly can to help defeat Hitler."

Johnson paused, collected his thoughts, and continued.

"And there's another reason why I'm doubtful that they would even consider running away. They realize that if they stay the course, they'll receive an unconditional pardon. On the other hand, they know that we've instructed the guards to shoot them if they try to escape; we've made it unambiguously clear to both Campbell-White and Worthington that they're in possession of Most Secret information that the enemy must never learn. Also, if either of them were to abscond before the end of the operation and therefore before getting his pardon, he'll be an escaped convict. For the rest of his life he'll run the risk of being arrested and returned to prison, with a few years tacked on for escaping. I think they're both intelligent enough to realize that it would be much wiser to wait until our operation is over before trying anything."

"Carlyle?"

"Johnson has touched on another point on which we've agreed to disagree. Regarding Worthington, there's no argument; the man is highly intelligent. Dangerously intelligent, perhaps. But Campbell-White is more problematic. He talks like an upper-class twit, like a character in a P. G. Wodehouse novel. But I think he's no fool. For example, when I tried to tell him that, on completion of Operation OTTAWA, the Army was going to transfer him to Australia for training as a coastwatcher, he interrupted me almost before I had completed the word 'Australia' and quick-wittedly said something like 'But I thought transportation of convicts to Australia stopped a hundred years ago.' A stupid man couldn't possibly have done that. My feeling is that Campbell-White is nearly as intelligent as Worthington, but extremely lazy. That would explain his poor performance at school, as well as why he chose to go off to the South Seas where he could sit around doing nothing all day but occasionally supervising the natives who do all the actual work on a copra plantation."

"And what's your opinion about Campbell-White, Johnson?"

"At school, sir, the general feeling was that he was as thick as two planks, and lazy to boot. Personally, I cannot recall him making any witty remarks or, for that matter, saying or doing anything even remotely clever. On the other hand, sir, I was there when he made that crack about Australia and transportation. Maybe he's heard someone else say something like that, and he stored up the witticism for a future occasion. Furthermore, if he had an ounce of brain cells he must've realized that we were there to offer him a potential lifeline, and interrupting Carlyle with a quip of that kind was particularly stupid; it might have seriously jeopardized his chance of getting out of his life sentence."

"So, is he stupid enough to try to escape?" Pankhurst asked.

"Yes, sir, I think so. I can't see him actively plotting to abscond—he's far too lazy for that—but if a sudden opportunity were to present itself, he might well jump at it."

"So, you both agree that the doubles will probably stay the course until Operation OTTAWA is successfully concluded, but it would do no harm to keep an eye on Campbell-White? Perhaps an additional guard or two at all times?"

Johnson and Carlyle both nodded.

Then Lieutenant Reginald Wallstead spoke up. "Sir, Carlyle has just described the jewel thief as 'dangerously intelligent.' At yesterday's meeting we heard how resourceful the man is. Someone who can successfully elude the police for so many years while pulling off dozens of spectacular robberies is not going to sit back quietly in a safe house; he's going to try to find a way of getting to Switzerland to get his hands on his money. I've never met either of the two look-alikes and everything that I know about them I've learned in this room at these meetings, but in my opinion a man like Worthington could well derail Operation OTTAWA. I've no doubt that, even as we speak, he's plotting and planning, weighing up the pros and cons of various possible courses of action, all of which would be to his advantage, not ours.

"We're sending him to the Inner Hebrides. There are hundreds of islands there. Yes, many of them are just rocks peering out of the sea with a solitary stunted bush the sole vegetation, but there must be close to fifty islands with reasonable populations, and probably another fifty with just a handful of inhabitants. The problem, as I see it, is that the whole area is teeming with boats, the only reasonable way to get around in that part of the world. I was once invited to stay on the Isle of Lumm; it's not too far from Ulva Island. There's just one house on Lumm, where the owner of the island and his family spend two or three weeks a year during the summer. They keep a motorboat at Fionnphort on the Isle of Mull, and use it to get to Lumm and back. But there's a second motorboat tied to the jetty in front of the house. If Worthington could get to Lumm or any of the many similar islands with an available boat, then he's resourceful enough to get to Switzerland from there.

"Sir, I believe that, with his 'dangerous intelligence' and burglarious skills and expertise, Worthington poses the real threat to Operation OTTAWA. I strongly suggest that we watch him closely, too."

"I agree," Pankhurst said. "And I also agree that, to ensure the highest level of security, the police who'll escort our Hess doubles from place to place must be MI5 intelligence officers in police uniforms.

And they must all be armed. I'm fully aware that the members of our police force don't carry guns, except in special circumstances. Well, guarding Rudolf Hess is exceedingly special. We'll issue Webley & Scott revolvers and holsters to all policemen involved in Operation OTTAWA, whether actual members of the police force or our people dressed in police uniforms. And all MI5 intelligence officers in plainclothes will be armed, too.

"Next," the air commodore continued, "what about the morale of the look-alikes? The last thing we want is for them to feel that we're punishing them by keeping them in solitary confinement. I'll concede that we obviously can't allow them to have cellmates, and we have to keep them away from fellow prisoners, especially in the exercise yard. But we need their total cooperation at all times. Accordingly, let's try to make their ordeal as pleasant as possible; we certainly don't want them to brood about the possibility of a German agent killing them.

"To start with, let's make sure that they both get all the books, magazines and newspapers that they want. Also, where possible our people should keep them company in their cells. For example, I've no doubt that Worthington is a first-class chess player. Johnson, you're in charge of putting together the team of intelligence officers for Scotland; try to include a chess fanatic in the squad."

"Certainly, sir. What about Canavan, sir? He's always reading chess magazines."

"I didn't realize that grooming his gigantic handlebar moustache left him any time to play chess. Anyhow, I'm sure he'll do.

"Now, Carlyle," the air commodore continued, "it wouldn't surprise me to learn that Campbell-White's idea of bliss is sitting in his cell, staring into space. I doubt if he plays chess. But there may be some game that he enjoys."

A soft voice said, "Tiddlywinks."

"I heard that," Pankhurst said sternly. "And if Campbell-White wants to play tiddlywinks, get him a set of squidgers and winks, and ensure that he plays as often as he wants. Keep the man happy.

"The doubles don't strike me as being particularly religious men, but if either of them indicates that he'd like to meet with a chaplain, we'll send you someone with the necessary security clearance. Also, when transporting them from place to place, keep the conversation going and do your best to maintain a cheerful mood in the vehicle. And, most of all, make sure that they understand that we really need them. Because we do."

CHAPTER SEVEN
MI5 Headquarters, London
Wednesday, May 21, 1941

"Well, Archie, how's Operation OTTAWA shaping up?" asked Sir William Hartsford-Knipe, the Director General of MI5, known throughout the organization as "D."

"Reasonably well," Air Commodore Pankhurst said. "I assume you saw the photographs of Rudolf Hess arriving under guard at King's Cross Station en route to the Tower of London. The pictures were on the front page of all the papers yesterday."

"Yes, indeed," D said. "You and your men handled that really well. I'd have driven him here from Scotland in a fleet of police cars, but attaching a special carriage to the rear of that troop train from Edinburgh to London was a stroke of genius. Apart from anything else, you saved gallons of precious fuel, a lesson that I'm sure won't be lost on the members of the public who are laboring under petrol rationing. Then, you made sure that everyone on the train knew that Hess was in the last carriage and on his way to the Tower. With any luck they'll tell their friends, and that also should help to get the word out. I noted that you had photographers on hand both at Waverley Station in Edinburgh and here at King's Cross Station, and you made sure that they could take as many pictures as they wanted of Hess handcuffed to a policeman and surrounded by armed guards. Finally, you organized a team of press photographers to take shots of the long line of police cars escorting Hess as they drove through the main gateway to the Tower. Most importantly, there were no photographers on hand at the back gate of the Tower two hours later when just two unmarked cars, crammed with heavily armed Special Forces soldiers in mufti, drove Hess from the Tower to Camp Z—wherever that might be. No, I don't want to know, I've got enough secrets in my head for one lifetime.

"Did your men tell you that, in the car on the way to Camp Z, Hess kept complaining about been squashed by the large soldiers seated on either side of him? He's suffers from both paranoia and hypochondria, and as a result he was terrified of getting germs from his travelling companions. I'm sure you've heard that he took with him on his flight no fewer than twenty-eight different medicines, as well as a variety of homeopathic remedies; the story is doing the rounds. Anyhow, the Special Forces troops knew about his paranoia, and they kept telling him that they were there to take any bullets that might be fired at him. Fortunately that partially reassured him."

"William," Pankhurst said, "I have to tell you that Hess's paranoia is proving to be a problem. We started interrogating him, but all he did was complain that his food was poisoned. He eats with some of the guards, and we encouraged him to swap his plate of food with any other plate on the table that he chose. That worked for a day and a half, and we extracted some extremely interesting information from him—whether he was telling us the truth remains to be determined. But now he's completely clammed up again. He says he won't say another word until we send samples of every morsel of food to a laboratory for analysis."

"You're not going to give in, are you?" D asked.

"Of course not. You'll recall that we assumed that any Nazi leader who'd parachute into Scotland behind Hitler's back to organize an armistice was crazy, so from the very beginning we sent in a team of head shrinkers. Surprisingly, the psychiatrists have come to the preliminary conclusion that he's sane, but mentally unstable. They've advised us to stand firm on the key rules: no radio, no newspapers, and no letters to or from his family back in Germany. They predict that, by isolating him in that way, in a day or two he'll cave in and start talking again."

"I hope they're right about that. Now, Archie, tell me about the doubles."

"We've done the best we could to choose men who can pass for Hess—with one of them wearing stage make-up—and who are willing to take the risk of being shot in return for eventual pardons. They're both quick learners and have picked up Hess's mannerisms. They are slowly learning to speak with genuine-sounding German accents—but apparently more work needs to be done in that regard. All in all, the masquerade training seems to be going well."

"But?"

"Yes, William, there's a but. A serious but. I've known Carlyle and Johnson for about five months. I was so impressed with the way they handled the Helga Ziegler case that I co-opted them onto my team. And their work has been consistently excellent since then, too. Well, Carlyle is concerned about the motivation of our two Hess impersonators; he thinks that they're playing along with us while their real intent is to escape. Johnson disagrees. Had it been anyone but Johnson, I'd have said that the reason he won't entertain even the possibility that Campbell-White might try to escape before Operation OTTAWA has been successfully concluded is because they were at school together. But Johnson isn't like that. On the contrary, I find that he's as objective about Campbell-White as he is about Worthington. What I'm saying is that two of my best people disagree."

"What do you propose to do about it?"

"There's not much we can do other than watch both doubles carefully. For example, suppose we arrange for a guard to approach Worthington and offer to help him to escape in return for a share of the money in Switzerland. Worthington would probably smell a rat and refuse, and we'd learn nothing. On the other hand, if he took the bait and tried to escape, we'd have to return him to prison, and half of Operation OTTAWA would be gone. Worse, knowing him, Worthington might actually manage to get away, in which case we'd have to cancel the whole operation—who knows what he'd tell people? In short, the only thing we can do is to guard them both as closely as the real Rudolf Hess."

"You've told them that the Government has instructed the guards to shoot to kill?" D enquired.

"Of course, and we've explained why. I think they both fully understand that we've shared Most Secret information with them, and we simply cannot allow them to communicate with anyone outside until the operation has been successfully concluded. They've undoubtedly observed that all the guards are armed."

"But surely they realize that, if they try to escape, at worst they'll be shot and at best they'll be returned to jail finish their sentences?"

"There actually is a third alternative—they might succeed in getting away."

"In wartime Britain? With all the measures we've put in place to catch enemy agents?" Sir William asked.

"With all due respect, if agent NORFOLK and agent OBAN, as we've decided to call them, have succeeded in evading us up to now, then Worthington and Campbell-White could also manage to escape and hide somewhere in Britain, or even get on a ship to America or some other neutral nation."

"As you well know, Archie," D said, "if those German agents tell the truth about Hess to just one person, that could be enough to destroy the entire operation. And if that were to happen, the whole

Double-Cross System would be in jeopardy. Those two damned Nazi spies are a serious threat. We have to find them and neutralize them before they can pass on to Berlin anything that contradicts the disinformation we're sending to the *Abwehr*. How soon do you think the two Hess impersonators will be ready?"

"One more day of training should do it," Pankhurst said. "The show starts tomorrow. In the meantime, we've put together two teams of MI5 people who will escort the doubles. We've provided them with a variety of appropriate uniforms, as well as simple disguises—moustaches, spectacles, hair coloring and the like. We've also laid on an assortment of vehicles in East Anglia, and boats in a variety of places around the Inner Hebrides. For the protection of the look-alikes, we want agent NORFOLK and agent OBAN to report that a large number of different people in different vehicles are involved in the operation to move the doubles from place to place—that should deter all but the most intrepid of assassins.

"However, that's not why I came to see you today. I'd like to discuss two other items with you. First, you need to know that some members of my team have raised doubts regarding Operation OTTAWA. In fact, one person in particular whose views I greatly respect feels that the entire endeavor may be doomed to failure. Lieutenant Reginald Wallstead correctly points out that the aim of the operation is to use the doubles as bait in order to lure the two *Abwehr* sleeper agents into revealing themselves. The best way of achieving this would be to parade the Hess look-alikes on foot, bound in chains, across the length and breadth of Britain. But our ostensible reason for taking Hess from place to place is to protect him from Hitler's assassins. And the best way to keep someone safe while in transit is to move him only at the dead of night, with a hood over his head, and with all the personnel involved sworn to secrecy and bound by the Official Secrets Act 1939. As Wallstead put it, and I agree with him, we can't have it both ways. For example, if we were to transport Worthington on a public ferry from Oban to, say, Armadale on the Isle of Skye, we wouldn't be able to convince a watching *Abwehr* agent that we're trying to protect Hess. On the contrary, the agent would immediately inform Berlin that we're up to something and from then on he'd stay under cover. Conversely, if we were to transfer Worthington in a high-speed police launch, then it's highly unlikely that the agent could find a way to follow us and we'd lose any chance of smoking him out. He'll just tell Berlin that Hess has been taken to a destination that's inaccessible to anyone other than a policeman, and that will be that."

"But in both those cases, the agent would have to send a radio message to Berlin. And then MI8 should be able to locate him for us."

"In theory, yes. But what if the agent successfully transmits the message and then manages to elude the large-scale manhunt that will inevitably follow?"

"I see your point. What are you going to do? Abandon the operation?"

"Not at all. We're going to proceed carefully, taking young Wallstead's insights into account. We'll steer a careful course between Scylla and Charybdis, using transportation that an agent can follow, while appearing to do our best to shield Hess from the public gaze. For example, we'll use ferries where possible, but we'll take 'Hess' on board before the ship is open to the public, and similarly wait for the ferry to empty completely before hustling our man into a waiting police car. We'll try to achieve the illusion that any exposure of Hess to the public gaze is accidental."

"Can we successfully do that, or is Wallstead correct that the whole thing is doomed from the start and a waste of precious time and money?"

"After extensive discussions and intensive planning, I've decided that we have a fighting chance, and we're therefore going ahead with the operation."

"Fine. I wish you luck with Operation OTTAWA. And what's the second item on your agenda?"

"I'm starting to suspect that the Germans are up to their old tricks. Something about the whole Hess escapade just doesn't ring true. There's no doubt that Hitler is an absolute dictator and a psychopathic murderer without even a hint of a conscience. Consequently, no one in Germany today dares to do anything without Adolf's express permission, because everyone knows that dissent of any kind is immediately punished by torture at the hands of the *Gestapo*, and then death. But they don't only kill the perpetrator; they send his or her whole family to a concentration camp, or just murder them, too. Hess met Hitler in 1920 when he spoke at a small rally in a Munich beer hall, and for the last twenty-one years they've been inseparable chums. There is no question that Hess knew full well that, if he were to fly to Scotland on his own initiative, Hitler would kill his wife and son, as well as anyone even remotely involved in the plot, including the driver who took him to the airfield, the bodyguards who accompanied him there, the *Luftwaffe* personnel who provided him with the Messerschmitt, the mechanics who fitted the fuel tanks to extend the range of the plane, and even the air traffic controller who allowed Hess's aeroplane to take off. And Hess knew with absolute certainly that Hitler would move heaven and earth to kill even his own deputy because he acted without orders. There's only one possible conclusion."

"Are you saying that Hitler sent Hess here?" D asked.

"Exactly."

"If you're right, that means that Hess is a key player in a Nazi disinformation campaign. And if that's the case, we need to treat everything he says with the greatest suspicion."

***

"Notice how Hess has seated himself in the chair directly opposite us with his back to the mirror," Johnson muttered softly to Worthington and Campbell-White. "That's where he invariably insists on sitting. He thinks that the mirror is a two-way device and that we observe him day and night. As a result, he makes sure that the back of his head is always pointing to the mirror, so we can't see his face.

"Well, we certainly watch him all the time, but we do it through the places in this painting where we've scraped away some of the paint. We placed that chair in front of the mirror so that we'd be able to observe his face when he sits there with his back firmly to the looking glass. And we're listening all the time, especially when he talks to himself. This is your last chance to be 100 percent certain that you can copy Hess perfectly. Watch, listen, and learn. You'll spend tonight here at Mytchett Place, and tomorrow you appear in public for the first time. Under no circumstances whatsoever are you to slip up!"

CHAPTER EIGHT
Duntress Castle, Renfrewshire, Scotland
Thursday, September 9, 1993

"You said that they moved Hess to Camp Z. Where was Camp Z?" Benedict asked. "And what sort of camp was it?"

"To answer your second question first," Hamish said, "Camp Z wasn't a camp at all."

"You've lost me again, I'm afraid," Benedict said. The puzzled expression was back on his pudgy face.

"The name was your father's idea. There's a small village in Surrey called Mytchett, about thirty or forty miles from London. It's quite close to Farnborough, where the Royal Air Force had a research establishment. It's also near Aldershot, the headquarters of the Parachute Regiment during World War II. This meant that Mytchett was located in a military area, which made security somewhat easier. We found a country house, Mytchett Place, and we turned it into a fortress. First, we made sure that Hess couldn't get out. We put bars on the windows and that sort of thing, and a hundred and fifty soldiers were stationed outside."

"That's a lot of soldiers to guard just one man," Benedict observed.

"Yes, but that one man was the Deputy *Führer* of Nazi Germany, and he knew endless vital secrets that we wanted to learn. And there was another reason for those soldiers. We knew that a lot of people wanted to kill Hess, and we had to ensure that that didn't happen. In fact, a Polish group somehow heard about Hess—we still don't know how they found out where we'd hidden him—and tried to break into Mytchett Place to take revenge for Nazi atrocities in Poland. There was a gun battle between the Poles and the guards, and those hundred and fifty soldiers proved to be extremely useful that day. Then we had to prevent Hess from committing suicide. He tried that once, by rushing his guards and throwing himself over the railings of the staircase. He broke his left leg, and we had to make further alterations to the house to ensure that he couldn't do it again. It wasn't enough; he tried to kill himself once more by stabbing himself with a bread knife. And, as you know, he finally killed himself in Spandau Prison in 1987. Lastly, we hid listening devices all over the house. We wanted to be certain that we heard every word Hess said."

"And was he a mine of information?" Benedict asked.

"Certainly not at first. Hess flew to Scotland in the uniform of a *Luftwaffe* pilot. When David McLean arrested him on the farm, Hess claimed that he was *Hauptmann* (Captain) Alfred Horn, and insisted on seeing the Duke of Hamilton. McLean helped Hess to limp to the nearest cottage, and called the Home Guard from there. They took Hess to a military base where his injured foot was treated. The Duke of Hamilton came to see him the next morning. Hess revealed his true identity and demanded to meet with Winston Churchill to propose an armistice between Nazi Germany and Britain."

"And did he see Churchill?" was Benedict's next question.

"Of course not. Such a meeting would have been out of the question. Neither Churchill nor anyone else in the government would have considered any sort of cessation of hostilities against Germany even for a moment. The Duke flew to England to brief Churchill and the War Cabinet. Then Hamilton returned to Scotland with an intelligence officer who tried to extract information from Hess. The problem was that Hess didn't reveal that the real reason behind his proposed armistice was that Hitler was about to open a second front by invading the Soviet Union. The Soviets lost some twenty million people in what they called the Great Patriotic War. If Stalin had learned via Hess that Hitler was about to break the Molotov–Ribbentrop pact and invade Russia, millions of lives might have been saved. Hess was an inveterate Nazi, through and through. He didn't come to Scotland to make peace with Britain; his real intent was to give Hitler a free hand in Europe. Consequently he said nothing about the invasion of the Soviet Union."

"That's fascinating," Benedict said. "But you haven't explained why my father chose the name Camp Z."

"Why don't you ask him yourself?" Hamish suggested.

Benedict turned to Sebastian. "Well, why?"

"May 1941 was a terrible time," Sebastian said. "We were losing the war. Food wasn't getting through to Britain because U-boats were sinking our ships. The *Luftwaffe* was bombing our cities day and night, indiscriminately killing men, women and children. Europe was in Nazi hands. Every night we went to bed expecting to wake up the next morning to find that Hitler had invaded England. Consequently, we had good reason to be concerned that Hitler might drop a battalion of paratroopers to kill Hess. We therefore turned Mytchett Place into an armed camp in a secret location—hence the name, Camp Z. There was another reason as well. If the fact that Hess was being held in a military camp reached Hitler's ears via his spies in England, he may have thought twice before sending assassins."

"And did he?"

CHAPTER NINE
Abwehr Headquarters, Berlin
Wednesday, May 21, 1941

"Colonel Donndorf," said Admiral Canaris, head of the *Abwehr*, to his new aide, "this morning I received a disturbing radio message from one of our agents in England, code name PICKFORD. He's been providing us with information since 1937, when he sent a package to our consul in Edinburgh that contained the plans for the Muir bombsight. He has about thirty subagents who report to him; their code names are all characters from the books of Charles Dickens, a nineteenth century English novelist."

Donndorf nodded politely to indicate that he was familiar with the author.

"Up to now," Canaris continued, "information from the PICKFORD network has proved to be pure gold. Yes, on one occasion we had to order PICKFORD to sever all links with two of his subagents; as he himself pointed out to us, the information they provided was just too implausible. But other than that we know we can rely on the information that he forwards to us from the members of his team.

"However, the latest intelligence from PICKFORD contains an item that's scarcely credible, to such an extent that I was surprised that he even sent it to us. He stated that one of his subagents, EDWIN DROOD if I recollect correctly, informed PICKFORD that the British are terrified that Hitler is going to drop a battalion of paratroopers onto the Tower of London to kill Hess. Up to now, EDWIN DROOD has been an exemplary spy. Had the information come from almost any other subagent, I would've had to consider treating all future reports from him with the greatest skepticism."

"But what he said," Donndorf interrupted, "isn't too unreasonable, Admiral. We certainly could drop paratroopers on the Tower of London and kill Hess. Better still, they could kidnap him and bring him back here."

"Of course. It's the next part of his report that concerns me."

Canaris paused as he thought yet again about the contents of the message, and then went on. "PICKFORD then stated that EDWIN DROOD informed him that the British are unable to come up with a safe location for Hess. To protect him as best they can they're moving him from place to place, every night in a new site."

"I see what you mean. That doesn't make too much sense. How can they interrogate Hess if he's always on the move? And even if they move him a relatively short distance each day, it's still going to disorient him, making it much harder for the questioning to proceed smoothly."

"Donndorf, you may have hit the nail on the head. Is it possible that they deliberately want to confuse Hess without giving him drugs? I've met Hess several times, and he's certainly an unconventional fellow, to put it politely. It's conceivable that the British headshrinkers have advised MI5 that the best way to get Hess to talk is to disorient him, and the way they're doing that is to keep changing prisons."

"Yes, that's possible. By the way, where in Britain is all this taking place?" Donndorf asked.

"That's another thing that bothers me: PICKFORD doesn't say. That's very unlike him. His reports almost always consist of solid facts backed by evidence; he virtually never passes hearsay on to us. But look here at his latest message. About halfway down, see where it says, 'Subagent EDWIN DROOD overheard a sergeant in a pub saying the British are moving Hess from place to place, a different location every night.' That sentence is absolutely atypical of PICKFORD. There are no details of any kind. When did this happen? What pub? In which town? A sergeant in what regiment? But the rest of the message is vintage PICKFORD. He's given us the location of a previously unknown Spitfire factory. I've checked with our aerial reconnaissance people. What they thought was a school proved on closer examination to be a factory with a camouflage net designed to fool us into thinking that it was a school. It's on the target list for tomorrow night. But it's that vague part of the message that bothers me. What's your view?"

Colonel Donndorf thought for a while. Then he said, "As you ordered, I sent out those radio messages from the *Führer* himself to all our agents in Britain, instructing them, as a matter of highest priority, to find Hess and kill him, or at least inform us where the British are holding him. Obviously Hess is at the forefront of all their minds. Perhaps PICKFORD is passing on what is at best a rumor just to keep you happy."

"If it had been any other agent, I might agree with you. But PICKFORD has never acted that way up to now. Just about everything that he's told us has been concrete intelligence that we could independently verify. PICKFORD is to all intents and purposes an espionage machine; he sends us unbiased factual information, whether or not he thinks that we want to hear it. For example, last year Hitler announced that he would invade Britain once the *Luftwaffe* had destroyed the Royal Air Force. A few months later, *Reichsminister* of Aviation Hermann Göring presented figures that showed we'd obliterated almost every British plane. Accordingly, preparations for Operation SEA LION commenced. Then both our bomber pilots and our fighter pilots started reporting that they were encountering a surprising number of Spitfire and Hurricane fighter planes all over Britain. Göring pooh-poohed all that, and categorically informed the High Command of the Armed Forces that his *Luftwaffe* had wiped out the RAF. Next we received a long message from PICKFORD that gave the actual Royal Air Force casualty figures for each day of the Battle of Britain.

It seems that our pilots had grossly exaggerated their number of kills. And Operation SEA LION was called off. That saved our armed forces from unacceptably high casualties when conquering Britain."

Colonel Donndorf looked skeptical. He responded, "It also saved Britain from being invaded and destroyed."

"True, but I doubt that PICKFORD sent us that information to save his country. Everything else he's given us proves beyond all reasonable doubt that he's completely on our side."

Colonel Donndorf nodded politely but said nothing more.

"Well, Donndorf, can you come up with any other explanation of the fact that PICKFORD has now sent us vague hearsay rather than hard facts?"

"Maybe he's sending you the best information he's received."

"But why the lack of details?"

"Perhaps to make you realize that he's been unable to find any solid information, and the best he can do under the circumstances is to send you an unsubstantiated rumor."

Admiral Canaris pondered this explanation. "Donndorf, what you say makes a considerable amount of sense. Perhaps we should wait for PICKFORD's next message before condemning him."

"I agree, Admiral. But irrespective of what we learn from PICKFORD, there's another aspect of this situation that we need to address."

"And that is?"

"I've been looking through the files of our agents in Britain, including those of our best people, the PICKFORD subagents. In my opinion, none of them have a killer mentality. Also, I doubt if more than a handful of them possess a gun or could even acquire one. And, as you know, there's much more to murdering a man in cold blood than merely possessing a weapon—you have to want to kill him. In addition, Hess is indisputably going to be protected by soldiers with loaded weapons. Yes, we certainly teach our people how to kill. But according to their files, none of our agents has taken a course in murdering a man protected by armed bodyguards."

"What you seem to be saying is that, when one of our people locates Hess, we're almost certainly going to have to send in an experienced assassin."

"Yes, that's exactly how I see it."

"Who would we send?"

"That's why I raised the issue. The head of the personnel department tells me that the *Abwehr* doesn't have an assassination squad."

"Correct. We don't. We've never needed one. We are a military intelligence organization. Our task is to gather information and analyze it. Killing is the job of the SS."

"Admiral Canaris, suppose one of our PICKFORD subagents were to send a message tomorrow saying that he's located Hess. If you were to approach *Reichsführer* Himmler, the head of the SS, inform him of the situation and ask him for an assassin, I strongly suspect that he'd insist on taking control of the operation. And I think we both know what would happen after that."

"Yes," said Canaris gloomily. "We'd be giving him the opportunity to first take over PICKFORD and his subagents, and then to take over the entire *Abwehr*."

"Exactly."

"So what do you suggest?"

"I have a contact in the SS," Donndorf said, "who probably doesn't know that the *Führer* himself has ordered the killing of Hess. I could ask him to lend us an assassin for future operations in Britain."

"Would he agree?"

"I have no idea. Would you like me to ask him?"

"We've nothing to lose if you approach him. Go ahead."

CHAPTER TEN
Mytchett, Hampshire, England
Thursday, May 22, 1941

Carlyle woke the two impersonators early. "Today's the day," he announced to them. "Get dressed. Both of you have to wear this body armor under your shirts. It's made of manganese steel plates. Two plates cover your front, and the third one at the back here protects your kidneys as well as other vital organs. It's still a prototype—the first one was made only three months ago—but the soldiers who've tested it are most enthusiastic about it. They all say that it provides great protection while, at the same time, it's reasonably comfortable to wear. Also, our tests show that it doesn't unduly impede mobility, which isn't going to be a major issue for you, because you're going to be sitting in a car or van most of the time. True, it's not going to protect you against a head shot, but assassins are taught to go for the body; it's a much bigger target, and a large caliber round can cause massive internal injuries. That means that you'll be fine if Hitler sends his killers after you."

Neither man said anything in response, so Carlyle continued. "Campbell-White, put on your make-up the way we showed you. You're spending tonight in His Majesty's Prison Norwich."

"I hope that the food's better than at Strangeways. I assume that you've arranged for German delicacies to be on tonight's menu?"

"You know, that's actually a bloody good idea. The whole object of the exercise is to advertise your presence in East Anglia. I'll contact the cook at the prison and ask him to prepare *Eisbein mit Sauerkraut* for you."

"And what's that?" Campbell-White asked nervously.

"Boiled pork hock served with fermented shredded cabbage."

"Actually, Carlyle, now that I come to think of it, I'd really hate to put the cook out. I'm sure that whatever he provides for the other prisoners will be just fine for me."

"No, no, it's important that the news gets out. I'll phone the prison right away. I've no doubt that the cook won't have any trouble coming up with something suitable," Carlyle insisted.

Campbell-White looked extremely worried. Carlyle assumed that Campbell-White was simply playing along with the joke. After all, the look-alike had introduced the subject of German food in Norwich Prison. So he added, "Get used to it, Campbell-White. From now on, you're a full-blooded Kraut."

"And where am I headed for?" Worthington asked.

"We wanted to send you to Inveraray Jail, near Oban, but they closed it last century. Pity—it's a wonderful old prison, with three-foot thick walls. Instead, you're spending the night in the cells at Oban police station."

"And I suppose that I'm getting haggis for dinner?"

"Another excellent idea!" Carlyle exclaimed. "I'm sure that the locals would be honored to prepare the national dish of Scotland for their German prisoner. But I think you're going to arrive at the jail too late for your evening meal. We're driving you to King's Cross Station this morning in time to catch the ten o'clock Flying Scotsman. If everything goes according to schedule, the train should arrive at Edinburgh Waverley Station at about six in the afternoon, and there's a four-hour drive from there past the northern tip of Loch Lomond to Oban. You'll get lunch on the train, served in your compartment, of course; we couldn't possibly allow Rudolf Hess to eat in the dining car, even though we'd love to have as many of your fellow passengers as possible see you. And there'll be sandwiches waiting for you when you get to Oban."

"Haggis sandwiches?"

"Spam or cheese, more likely."

"I am most relieved," Worthington said, and sat back with a broad grin on his face.

But Campbell-White still looked worried and asked nervously, "Were you serious about that German food you mentioned?"

Carlyle suddenly became acutely aware that, unlike Ernest Worthington, the Honorable Frederick Campbell-White hadn't realized that this was all a joke. Remembering that it was vital that the two impersonators stay calm and cooperative, he quickly said, "No, I was just joking. What with all this rationing, it's hard enough to organize any meals anywhere, let alone special meals at Norwich Prison."

The relief on Campbell-White's face was obvious to such an extent that Carlyle now started to wonder why his attempt at humor with the *Eisbein mit Sauerkraut* had misfired that badly. After all, someone like Campbell-White who had spent most of his life in boarding school, army, and prison would hardly be picky about food. Then a thought came to him. Institutional food usually follows the same uniform pattern day after day and the resulting predictability is comforting to some. Perhaps it was the break in routine that had disturbed Campbell-White so much. Carlyle made a mental note to try to keep the Hess double happy by adhering as far as possible to a fixed routine over the coming days.

"We're scheduled to arrive in Norwich at about half past three this afternoon," he said to Campbell-White, "so we'll leave here at ten o'clock sharp. The traffic through London can be fierce, especially after an air raid as bad as last night's."

***

Promptly at ten o'clock, four uniformed policemen levered Campbell-White into a police car. He sat at the back, handcuffed on either side to MI5 intelligence officers in police uniforms; Carlyle sat in the front seat masquerading as a chief inspector. He tried to lighten the mood by discussing topics that he thought might interest Campbell-White but, other than answering direct questions put to him, the prisoner soon lapsed into sullen silence and chose not to participate in the small talk.

The trip to Norwich was smooth and uneventful, other than through London. There the effects of the previous night's *Luftwaffe* air raid were all too obvious. A few buildings in the West End were still burning, and it had not been possible to rescue all the injured in the East End yet, so the streets were clogged with emergency vehicles of all kinds. Crews had been unable to clear the rubble strewn across major thoroughfares where buildings had collapsed, and the police car was forced to make numerous detours on its way through the capital city. Eventually they reached the A11 and were able to arrive in Norwich on schedule just before half past three.

***

All the blinds were lowered in the first-class compartment shared by four uniformed policemen and Ernest Worthington. The jewel thief sat between two police constables in the middle seat facing the engine, a pair of handcuffs linking him to the policeman on his right. Opposite him sat a sergeant and a chief inspector. More correctly, the occupants of the compartment were Worthington and four MI5 intelligence officers wearing police uniforms; the "chief inspector" was Johnson. A fifth man in a police constable's uniform stood outside the compartment. Every hour the three constables changed roles so that no one had to stand for the whole journey.

At eleven o'clock, a dining car steward brought a tray with tea and biscuits. He had been informed that the compartment contained a prisoner with his police escort, but was clearly taken aback when he saw who the prisoner was. The constable on duty outside the compartment noticed the steward's reaction and took him aside as he closed the door and re-entered the corridor. "Not a word to anyone," the policeman said sternly. This warning had the desired effect. When a second steward arrived twenty minutes later to collect the tray, it was obvious from the look on his face that his colleague had spilled the beans. At lunchtime, the first steward returned with a tray of sandwiches. He made sure not to catch the eye of the policeman who had ordered him to say nothing.

The train arrived at Edinburgh on time. The five policemen whisked Worthington away to a police van waiting outside the station; a police car was parked behind it. They unlocked the handcuff on the constable's left wrist, clicked it shut on Worthington's left wrist, and locked him into the back of the Black Maria. Then both vehicles drove as fast as they could toward Oban. They made excellent progress until they neared Loch Lomond. There a shepherd with his flock of over a hundred sheep blocked the road, and only the threat of immediate arrest persuaded him to clear the road for the procession of two police vehicles. After that it was plain sailing again. They sped along virtually empty roads through the glorious countryside bedecked with heather and bracken, arriving at Oban just after ten o'clock.

As they drew up at the police station, four soldiers ran through the open doorway of the charge office, Thompson M1928 submachine guns at the ready. They surrounded the van. Two of the soldiers stood with their guns pointed at the vehicle in case the prisoner tried to escape; the guns of the other two were directed away from the van, to prevent German agents from kidnapping him. Then the front doors of the van opened and two policemen emerged. They walked round to the back of the Black Maria, unlocked the door and helped "Hess" to alight. Once both his feet were firmly on the ground, they rushed him into the police station. The two soldiers guarding the van followed closely behind, their two colleagues remaining outside to ward off a Nazi *Sondereinsatzkommando* (Special Forces unit) that might suddenly appear from nowhere as the sun prepared to set over the sea.

***

"We have to get the timing right in the future," Air Commodore Pankhurst insisted. "It's eleven o'clock at night and we're just starting to put together the report for PICKFORD to send to Berlin tomorrow morning. Once we've agreed on the contents, the document has to be vetted by the team from the Double-Cross System and by the PICKFORD people. As always, both groups will have to check punctiliously that nothing we've said conflicts with any of their earlier messages, even though it's going to be well after midnight before they can get started.

"From now on, we'll do our utmost to ensure that the two look-alikes are in their new locations no later than noon, at worst by one o'clock—that's an absolute deadline. That'll give us time to carefully think through the radio messages to send to the *Abwehr* and still get a few hours sleep at night. It'll also give us a certain amount of leeway in case something doesn't go according to plan. For example, if this afternoon the Flying Scotsman had arrived late in Edinburgh, Worthington might have reached Oban too late for inclusion in today's report. And that would have been problematic—it's essential that we start the paper chase for both agent OBAN and agent NORFOLK right now. As I've said repeatedly, the two German sleeper agents pose an unacceptable risk to the Double-Cross System and we have to lay our hands on them as soon as humanly possible. Now, what are we going to tell

Canaris about today's performances by our stellar cast of two skilled impersonators?"

"Sir," Captain Marks said, "we previously came to the decision that we'd inform him that neither of the doubles were spotted by *Abwehr* agents until they neared their respective destinations. I see no reason to change that."

"Does everyone agree?"

Four heads nodded in unison.

"Go on, Marks."

"Yes, sir. However, we're still faced with the problem of trying to convince the Germans that not just one but two coincidences occurred today. First, it 'just happened' that subagent URIAH HEEP was walking past Oban police station when he saw Hess arrive, and subagent EBENEZER SCROOGE 'just happened' to see a police car in the vicinity of Norwich Prison and followed it. We'll obviously do our best, sir. But we've crossed swords with the top *Abwehr* people for nearly two years now, and we know that almost all of them are highly intelligent and exceedingly hard to fool."

"True, Marks. But up to now the quality of the intelligence we've fed them via PICKFORD has been so high that we may be able to get away with it this time. Anyhow, we'll soon know if we've managed to fool them when we read the next set of messages that Canaris sends to PICKFORD."

CHAPTER ELEVEN
Oban, Argyll, Scotland
Friday, May 23, 1941

"Rise and shine, Worthington!" Johnson called. "It's a beautiful day, and we're off to the isles!"

"Isles?"

"The Inner Hebrides. You're taking a ferry to Mull."

"To mull over what?" the puzzled jewel thief asked.

"No, Mull is the name of the island we're going to. We're taking the Oban–Craignure ferry. By the way, I'm not going to be one of the policemen guarding you today. I'll be on the ferry with you, but I'll be wearing civvies. As soon as the steamer has emptied from its last trip, the other men will rush you on board and into a cabin. All the cabins on the ferry are small. Do you remember the hilarious stateroom scene in the Marx Brothers film, *A Night at the Opera*? Well, with four of you in there, I'm afraid that your tiny cabin is going to be even more crowded than that. After the ship docks and all the other passengers have disembarked, my colleagues will hustle you off the ship and into a police car for

115

the short ride to Craignure police station, where you'll spend the night.

"As I mentioned, I'm going to be on the ferry in mufti, but the other men will all be in uniform, like yesterday. It's unlikely that you and I will bump into one another on the ship, but if it should happen, do not greet me or indicate in any way at all that you know me. Is that clear?"

"Yes, certainly, but why?"

Johnson's initial reaction was to reply: Never mind why, just do it.

Then he remembered that he had to keep Worthington happy. So instead he answered, "You're masquerading as Hess. It would be out of character to greet me."

"True. Hess would be unlikely to engage with a random passenger. He might turn out to be an assassin. Hess would be more likely to steer clear of everyone."

"Quite right. In fact, I want you to ignore me whenever we're in public from now on."

"No problem at all. I'm sure I can manage to do that."

***

"Wake up, Campbell-White!" Carlyle said. "We're off to Colchester."

"Colchester?"

"Yes, it's the oldest recorded town in Britain—it dates back to the Roman days."

"Why are we going there?"

"Because Reed Hall Camp in Colchester has detention barracks. We're leaving in an hour; please get dressed. I'll go and organize some breakfast for you."

***

"Donndorf," said Admiral Canaris, "you were quite right; I should've waited before condemning PICKFORD. This morning a new message arrived from him. Notwithstanding the fuel shortage, his subagents have done their best to fan out over Britain to look for Hess."

"And have they found him?"

"Perhaps. PICKFORD reports that last night, around ten o'clock, subagent URIAH HEEP was walking near the police station in Oban when he saw a police van draw up. It was still daylight because Britain is now on Double Summer Time to give the farmers longer evenings to tend to their crops—the sun was half an hour above the horizon. Four soldiers ran out of the police station and converged on the van, then two policemen got out of the vehicle. They unlocked the back door and escorted a handcuffed man wearing a sports jacket and flannel trousers into the police station. URIAH HEEP thinks that the man could have been Rudolf Hess. However, with characteristic candor, PICKFORD informed us that URIAH HEEP never saw Hess in the flesh back in Germany before the war and relied on a British newspaper photograph he saw a few days ago for his identification of Hess."

"Well, it's potentially good news. If URIAH HEEP or, for that matter, one of our other agents can confirm the sighting, we'll be able to take action."

"Yes, but there's a problem, a serious problem. PICKFORD went on to state that, at about half past three yesterday afternoon, subagent EBENEZER SCROOGE was driving along Plumstead Road in Norwich when he saw a police vehicle two cars ahead of him slowing down and turning into Knox Road. EBENEZER SCROOGE remembered that Norwich Prison is situated at the other end of Knox Road and decided to follow the police car. That probably wasn't the cleverest action for an *Abwehr* agent in a foreign country to take, but that's what he did. He saw the police car draw up outside the prison, so he pulled over to the side of the road and stopped about a hundred yards away. From that distance, he saw a man in a gray suit and open-neck white shirt emerge from the car, handcuffed between two uniformed policemen. The three men walked into the prison, followed by the two policemen who'd been sitting in the front seats of the car. EBENEZER SCROOGE described the man in the gray suit as tall and thin, with sharp features, black hair and a receding hairline over both temples, but was unable to definitely identify the prisoner as Hess.

"That means we have two possible sightings of Rudolf Hess. They took place about six and half hours apart, but Norwich is nearly five hundred miles from Oban, so obviously both men can't be

Hess. In fact, we don't even know whether even one of them was our man; neither of the two subagents provided what I would consider to be positive identification."

"It could be that both of our *Abwehr* agents were so eager to obey *Herr* Hitler and find Hess that their eyes played tricks on them—it happens all the time."

"It certainly does, Donndorf. All we really know is that both our agents saw a tall man with black hair in police custody. What do we do now?"

"Well, Admiral, you could certainly order half our agents in Britain to converge on Oban and the other half on Norwich. But what if both those reported sightings were wrong and Hess is actually somewhere else? We need to keep at least some of our people in reserve to investigate other sightings."

"Quite right. In fact, I'm hesitant to send any more of our people on what might well be a wild goose chase. Or two wild goose chases in the worst case."

"Admiral, if that unsubstantiated rumor that PICKFORD sent us yesterday is true, they'll move Hess to another place tomorrow. Why don't you send a message to PICKFORD telling him to instruct his two subagents to stay in the vicinity of their respective sightings, and observe what happens in the morning?"

"Donndorf, that's an excellent suggestion, but we have an insurmountable problem. There's no direct communication between PICKFORD and his subagents."

"What? How can that be? How does the network operate?"

"They communicate via dead-letter drops and accommodation addresses. For example, EBENEZER SCROOGE is based in London. When he has information for PICKFORD, he mails a letter for PICKFORD to a local newsagent—many British newsagents provide accommodation addresses. Then EBENEZER SCROOGE phones a number we gave him. After a fixed number of rings, five I think, someone picks up the phone but doesn't say anything. At that point EBENEZER SCROOGE says the agreed code sentence and hangs up. Somebody then retrieves the letter from the newsagent, usually a different person each time, and delivers it to PICKFORD."

"But sending a letter can take weeks. What about urgent information?"

"Donndorf, the Royal Mail is amazingly efficient. If you and I are in central London, and I write a letter to you and put it in a post box before nine o'clock in the morning, a postman will deliver it to you before noon. And if you write a reply after lunch and post it back to me before two, I'll get your answer before five. There are two mail deliveries a day, and the whole system works surprisingly well."

"That's central London. But further afield?"

"Yes, you're right, you won't get three-hour turnaround, but it's still extremely efficient. Consequently, we've provided accommodation addresses in London for all the Dickens subagents. Obviously they don't address their letters to

PICKFORD; we've given each subagent their own pseudonym for PICKFORD, a *nom de guerre* if you wish, that they use for their letters to him.

"And PICKFORD uses a similar system to communicate with his agents. For example, if PICKFORD has an order for EBENEZER SCROOGE, he leaves a letter for him at another newsagent, and someone then phones EBENEZER SCROOGE and speaks a code sentence that informs him that he has a message to pick up."

"But what about urgent messages?"

"Tell me something, Donndorf. Before you became my aide, you worked in other departments of the *Abwehr* for three years—or was it four?"

"Nearly four years, Admiral."

"And during that time, how often did a message come in from an agent somewhere in the world that you considered to be such an emergency that had to be dealt with right away?"

"Perhaps a handful. At most."

"And what about urgent messages, as opposed to true emergencies?"

"Not too many, Admiral."

"Precisely. And that's why almost all our agents in Britain have one transmission time a week and one reception time. It's extremely rare that something happens that requires instant communication in one direction or the other. And when a report comes in from one of our agents abroad, isn't it correct that, almost all of the time, it's soon enough if we analyze the information and then act within a few days?"

"Yes, you're quite right, Admiral. But occasionally a genuine emergency does arise that requires immediate action."

"I agree. And here's how it works with the PICKFORD network. For information that's not truly urgent, the subagents use the Royal Mail and the accommodation addresses we provide to communicate with PICKFORD, and he does the same. But we also give each subagent a telephone number to use in a genuine emergency. We've instructed them to phone that number and leave a message for PICKFORD with whoever answers the phone. Somehow their messages get through to PICKFORD—we still don't know how. There's certainly at least one intermediary, probably more than one; there's no way that PICKFORD himself answers those phone calls. Furthermore, we now know that even emergency messages don't reach PICKFORD immediately. We suspect that he obtains the information via an assistant who picks the message up from a dead letter drop at a London newsagent after it has passed through the intermediaries. PICKFORD changes the emergency number every thirty days, even if no one has used it that month. And he doesn't give the new emergency number to any agent who has misused it for a routine report that wasn't urgent.

"That's how PICKFORD has stayed safe for more than four years—no one in the network has ever seen him. There's no photograph of him in his personal file. In fact, he has no personal file."

"No personal file? How can that possibly be?"

"There would be no point; we know nothing about him. Your predecessor, Colonel Tobler, once told me that he believes that PICKFORD is a woman. When I asked him for evidence, he just shrugged his shoulders and said, 'Intuition.' Of course, that's not how the *Abwehr* works. But the fact remains that we know nothing about PICKFORD, other than that he's a mine of invaluable information. Perhaps that's not quite the correct way to put it. Maybe I should've said that he manages a network of *Abwehr* agents in Britain, and those agents are providing him with unparalleled intelligence, which he then forwards to us."

"What about emergency communications from PICKFORD to his subagents?"

"That's not possible. We set up the network in a way that would keep PICKFORD safe, but also to ensure that his subagents stay safe, too. No one in the network, not even PICKFORD himself, knows how to directly contact any other member. All the subagents keep their addresses and telephone numbers secret. But the price that we have to pay for this security is that immediate communication between members of the network is simply not possible. The fact of the matter is that the structure of the network has never caused a problem until this Hess situation arose.

"Now that I come to think of it," Canaris added, "we do know one thing about PICKFORD: He transmits from north London."

"Do we even know that, Admiral? Apparently he has people to answer the telephone and collect letters and drop them off; he doesn't do any of those tasks himself. Isn't it possible that one of his associates actually does the radio transmissions?"

"Yes, we've wondered about that. But his 'fist' hasn't changed since he started sending us messages in 1937. After all, the way we send Morse is like our handwriting—the characteristics stay the same. So, there's no question that the same person has been sitting at the Morse key for the past four years tapping out PICKFORD's messages to us. If you're right, that would mean that he had at least one associate working with him in Britain before we started sending subagents to help him. As you know, the British have rounded up and interned all known Nazi sympathizers. It's a miracle that PICKFORD has escaped the net up to now. If someone else is doing the transmitting, then the two of them have somehow managed to elude MI5 for two years before the beginning of the war and then for two years more."

Colonel Donndorf suddenly had an idea. "Admiral, is it possible that PICKFORD is actually a British agent sending us disinformation? That would explain why the British haven't arrested him."

"We've discussed that possibility *ad nauseam* for the last four years. Yes, it's undoubtedly possible. But PICKFORD has provided us with material that, time after time, has proved to be reliable. That in itself means nothing, of course; any competent double agent could do that. The key point is that he—or perhaps she—has sent reports that no British agent would possibly send, starting with the plans of the Muir bombsight. If PICKFORD is a British agent sending us disinformation, then long may he continue to do that because, far from giving us disinformation, he provides more genuinely useful information than any ten other spies we have in Britain. No, Donndorf, PICKFORD is unquestionably on our side. If he happens to be an MI5 intelligence officer, that would certainly explain how he obtains some of his information. But if he is, he's been extraordinarily lucky that his colleagues haven't caught him. As I said, we've thrashed this over and over, but we always come to the same conclusion: PICKFORD is working for us, not for the British."

Donndorf thought about this for a while. Then he said, "Admiral, can we please return to something you said before? If I recall correctly, you told me that EBENEZER SCROOGE communicates with PICKFORD by mailing letters to a certain London newsagent. But EBENEZER SCROOGE was in Norwich; did he use the emergency number?"

"I have to assume that he did. There was no other way to get the information to PICKFORD that quickly. And information in response to a direct order from the *Führer* is incontrovertibly a genuine emergency."

"But aren't all British phones tapped?"

"Well, that's what we've heard from some of our agents. But with numerous calls to check, it was probably safe. Particularly if EBENEZER SCROOGE used one of the many red telephone boxes that dot the whole country—it would be hard to listen in on all the calls that are made from those phone booths."

"Admiral, you just informed me that PICKFORD cannot give urgent instructions to the members of his network. For example, it's my understanding that there's no way he can tell EBENEZER SCROOGE to watch the jail tomorrow morning and see if Hess is transferred to a new location."

"Correct. That's the whole problem. He can't. There's no way PICKFORD can communicate with EBENEZER SCROOGE while he's in Norwich."

"How has this worked in the past? With great respect, Admiral, it seems rather inefficient."

"Donndorf, we've sent each Dickens subagent to Britain to perform a specific task, such as checking on the shipping in Liverpool Docks or reporting on the damage our air raids over London have caused. In other words, one-way communication is all that we've needed up to now; the subagents obtain information and send it to PICKFORD, and PICKFORD forwards that information by radio to us. And it's worked extremely well. As I told you yesterday, the information from those subagents has almost always proved to be pure gold."

"Is there no way at all that we can communicate directly with our agents in Britain?"

"What I've just told you applies to only the subagents of the Dickens network. You recently sent radio messages to all our other agents in Britain. We've provided them with radio transceivers. They transmit messages to us and we transmit messages to them, generally once a week."

"I understand," Donndorf said. "But can't we send an instruction by radio to one of those other agents to go and observe Norwich Jail, and order a second agent to wait outside Oban police station and see if they move Hess to a different site?"

"Our agents listen for radio messages at only specific times, usually just once a week. Suppose there's an agent in London who'll be listening half an hour from now for instructions from us. We can certainly send him a message, but can he get to Oban in a few minutes' time to see if they move the prisoner and determine if he's really Hess? It's impossible. On the other hand, we do have people in Scotland, but are those agents scheduled to listen for a message right now, ready and waiting to rush over to Oban immediately? Probably not. And there's severe fuel rationing in Britain—each person gets only enough gasoline to drive two hundred miles each month. A London-based agent can almost certainly get to Norwich by train and he can walk from the railway station to Norwich Prison or take a taxi if it's too far, but without a car he can't follow if they take Hess to a different prison. My guess is that EBENEZER SCROOGE has somehow acquired black-market fuel coupons, or even forged coupons—how else can he drive from London to Norwich at the drop of a hat?"

"What's to be done?"

"As far as I can see, we have no choice. We're going to have to rely on URIAH HEEP and EBENEZER SCROOGE. After all, they're both fully trained *Abwehr* agents, and they know what to do. If we get a positive identification later today from one of them, we'll send radio messages to all our agents to converge on the relevant area."

"Will that be of any use, Admiral? I understood you to say that, in response to *Herr* Hitler's order, our agents have fanned out all over Britain to try to find the Deputy *Führer*. So how will they receive a radio message from us? It seems that, even with the other agents, the ones with radio transceivers, we essentially have one-way communication, too—they can send a radio message to us at their scheduled transmission time, but we have no guarantee that they'll be by their radios at their reception time to receive instructions from us. And there's an added complication. That last message we sent out, the one in which you instructed all our agents to drop everything and locate Hess, contained a direct order from the *Führer* himself. It wouldn't surprise me if our agents keep looking until they locate Hess. Yes, the Dickens subagents may well send reports by mail to PICKFORD to forward to us, but the others will almost certainly be away from their radios, searching the country as we explicitly instructed them."

"Donndorf, I'm sorry to say that you're probably correct. But we may be lucky. Once we know where Hess is, we'll send messages to all our people in Britain in the hope that someone will be at their radio at their reception time. After all, our agents aren't stupid, and they surely realize that they need to be back at their transceivers to report progress and receive new orders."

"I hope you're right, Admiral."

"So do I, Donndorf, so do I. Now tell me, have you spoken to your contact in the SS?"

"Yes, Admiral. As I suspected, he hadn't heard about the order to kill Hess, and he seems totally unaware that *Reichsführer* Himmler has been trying for years to incorporate the *Abwehr* into his organization. On the contrary, my contact seemed to think that both you and Himmler are on excellent terms, and that lending you an assassin would ingratiate him with Himmler."

"Is everyone in the SS that stupid?"

"Their chief interest in life is killing people, and that means that the answer to your question is probably yes."

"The SS assassin who's about to join us—who is he?"

"His name is SS-Major Helmut Kirchgässner. I've read his file. He has a rather unusual approach to assassination."

"Oh, yes?"

"It seems that he manages to get close to his victim by dressing as a woman."

"He's not a sexual deviant, is he?"

"Definitely not, Admiral. The SS would have thrown him into one of their many concentration camps if they even suspected anything like that. No, he doesn't get erotic pleasure from dressing as a woman. And he certainly doesn't sleep with men— quite the contrary."

"But he does enjoy killing, surely?"

"Yes, of course. According to his file, he's murdered more than thirty people, almost all with an ice pick."

"An ice pick? Isn't that what *die Nadel* (The Needle) uses?"

"No. Henry Faber uses a stiletto."

"Does every SS assassin have his own individual killing method?"

"You can ask Kirchgässner about it when you meet him."

"And when will that be?"

"His transfer to the *Abwehr* is effective at midnight tonight. Do you wish to meet with him tomorrow?"

"Yes. Tomorrow afternoon at two. Arrange it."

CHAPTER TWELVE
Craignure, Isle of Mull, Scotland
Saturday, May 24, 1941

"Good morning, Worthington," Johnson said. "I trust you slept well?"

"Please tell me that we're not taking another boat trip today. It's been more than half a day since I stepped onto blessed dry land, and I'm still seasick."

"How can you say that? My colleagues told me you loved yesterday's little excursion. The sea was as calm as a millpond. And with the porthole open, there was plenty of fresh sea air for the four of you in that tiny cabin. Also you beat Canavan at chess yet again—don't you ever let the poor chap win a game? Canavan loves chess even more than you do, and it would mean a lot to him to win just once, or even draw a game. You played so well yesterday that you couldn't possibly have been seasick then, let alone now."

Remembering that he had to keep Worthington happy, he quickly changed his tune.

"Sorry to tease you, old chap. I know that you suffer dreadfully from *mal de mer*. Do you want me to fetch a doctor? I'm sure he can give you something to make you feel better."

"Thanks, Johnson, but I've tried everything, and nothing seems to work."

"Well, Worthington, I have some good news. Today we're taking you on a bus ride."

"We're on an island. You must be joking."

"Not at all. There's a bus that travels the length of the Isle of Mull, from Tobermory via Craignure to Bunessan, a distance of more than fifty miles. You could also go by police launch from Craignure to Bunessan, but I'm certain you'd prefer the bus."

"How did you guess?"

"Even if I tell you that the road is somewhat bumpy and uneven?"

"How long is the trip?"

"It's about thirty miles, which means that it'll take about an hour and a half. It's more than four hours by sea, because we'd have to sail all the way around the Isle of Iona."

"Thank you for your intriguing suggestion, but I'll take the bus!"

***

"Rise and shine!" Carlyle said to Freddy Campbell-White. "I hope you enjoy beautiful scenery. For the foreseeable future we're going to be driving through Constable Country."

"You mean there are policemen everywhere?"

"No, not that sort of constable. Haven't you heard of John Constable, in the opinion of many the greatest English landscape artist of all time?"

"Not really."

"He painted some of his finest masterpieces in the vicinity of Dedham Vale. And for the next few days we're going to take you from police station to police station in the area, affording you the opportunity to see some of the most outstandingly lovely scenery in Britain. Today you're on your way to Halstead police station. And by the way, even though the first syllable of the word for a policeman rhymes with 'fun,' the 'Con' in John Constable's last name is pronounced the way it's written. That should reduce the confusion between 'Constable' and 'constable' from now on."

"Don't you mean the 'cunfusion'?" Campbell-White quipped.

I was right all along, Carlyle said to himself. *The Honorable Frederick Campbell-White is by no means as stupid as he pretends to be. We need to watch him carefully.*

***

"Donndorf," Admiral Canaris said, "we have a problem, a big problem."

"You mean that neither of the Dickens agents identified Hess yesterday?"

"No, much worse. Both are absolutely convinced that their man is Rudolf Hess."

"But that's impossible, Admiral."

"Of course it is. But that's the situation, and we have to deal with it somehow or other. PICKFORD sent us a message that arrived just after I got to my desk this morning. It contained only two items: a report from URIAH HEEP in Scotland and one from EBENEZER SCROOGE in East Anglia, both insisting that they've located Hess."

"But how can they be that dogmatic?"

"Well, for one thing, neither knows that the other claims to have found Hess. Anyhow, URIAH HEEP dared not stand outside Oban police station from the early hours of this morning, waiting to see if Hess emerged. Instead, he decided to take a chance. He's based in Glasgow, and he therefore knows that Oban is a busy ferry port. He went down to the ferry terminal and sat at a tearoom table by the window watching the ferries arriving and leaving. A ferry arrived from Craignure, a small town on the Isle of Mull. As the last of the passengers walked down the gangway, a police car drove into the harbor area and parked in front of the tearoom. A policeman handcuffed to a tall prisoner with black hair got out of the car and they stood no more than ten feet away from URIAH HEEP, who is absolutely adamant that the man was Hess. Then three other policemen exited from the car. The four uniformed policemen hurried Hess up the gangway and into the Craignure ferry. URIAH HEEP paid his bill, left the tearoom, went to the ticket office and bought a ticket for Craignure. He had to wait for nearly twenty minutes while they prepared the ship for the return trip. Finally he and the other passengers were permitted to board. He explored the ship in an unhurried fashion in order not to draw attention to himself, but he didn't see Hess anywhere. However, in addition to the public areas, there are six private cabins, and a police constable stood outside one of them. URIAH HEEP assumed, probably correctly, that the authorities were holding Hess there.

"The ferry eventually reached Craignure and the passengers disembarked. URIAH HEEP ducked into a restroom and waited until the ferry was quiet. Then he cautiously opened the door a few inches and peered into the passageway. The police and their prisoner were walking towards him, so he quickly pulled back into the restroom, leaving the door open just a crack. As they passed him, he got an even closer look at the man than before. URIAH HEEP is totally convinced that the prisoner he saw is Rudolf Hess."

"Most interesting, Admiral. And what did EBENEZER SCROOGE say?"

"Early yesterday morning he parked his car on the other side of Knox Road. He saw a police car with five men in it, one a civilian, drive past him. He set off behind it. He was careful to keep his distance. The police car headed south on the A12. After about an hour they stopped at a filling station in Needham Market for gasoline; EBENEZER SCROOGE pulled up behind them. While the attendant filled their tank, our agent got a good look at the passenger seated in the back between two constables. He's absolutely certain that the man is Rudolf Hess. The police car drove off. Our man waited a few seconds and then followed; he was worried that, if he put in gasoline too, he'd lose the other car. The police car drove to Layer Road in Colchester, and through the gates leading to the detention barracks in Reed Hall Camp. EBENEZER SCROOGE didn't dare stop there; he just continued driving."

"That's impossible, Admiral. The two men can't both be Hess."

"Obviously not," said Canaris drily.

Colonel Donndorf grinned in acknowledgment. Then he said, "One must be a double. But which of the two? Let me think. Ah, I have it. They transported the one in Scotland on a public steamer, in full view of a number of people waiting at a major ferry port, when they could have used a police launch. But they drove the one in East Anglia from one jail to another by car, and it was just fortuitous that EBENEZER SCROOGE noticed the car in Norwich and picked up the trail. That means that the one in western Scotland is the impersonator, and Hess himself is being moved about in the eastern part of England."

"Tell me, Donndorf, suppose you were in charge of moving the real Hess from one prison to the next in East Anglia. Would you do it in broad daylight? Would you carry it out in such a way that a casual passerby might see him, let alone an enemy agent?"

There was a long silence while Donndorf digested the question. Then the colonel said, "What you're saying, Admiral, is that they're both doubles."

"Precisely, Donndorf. Precisely."

***

"The good news," the air commodore said, "is that it's not even noon yet, and both the look-alikes are safely at their third destinations, Halstead in Essex and Bunessan on the Isle of Mull. The bad news is that we're going to need all the time we have before transmitting the next PICKFORD message to Germany to try to fix Operation OTTAWA.

"The problem is that, as far as MI8 can tell, Canaris hasn't sent messages to any of his agents in Britain regarding the location of the Hess doubles. One possibility is that he's seen through the whole plot—let's hope and pray that's not the case. Another is that he's waiting for additional identification from the Dickens subagents before he acts; that's easy to solve in our next PICKFORD message. A third possibility is that Canaris obviously realizes that both men can't be Hess, and he wants to know which one is the real Hess before ordering his agents to pursue him. There's nothing we can do about that, because we have to find agent OBAN and agent NORFOLK as soon as possible; both our doubles have to be Hess as far as we're concerned. What do we do now?"

Squadron Leader Harkness put up his hand. "Sir, perhaps it will help if you could tell us what Johnson and Carlyle reported to you yesterday."

"That's a good idea," Pankhurst said. "Let's start in Scotland. We had two teams in Oban: the four escorts for the hare, and the seven watchers looking for the hound. The uniformed escorts took Worthington to the Craignure ferry as soon as it docked and all the passengers had left the ship. Three of them sat with him in a crowded tiny cabin; one man stood outside on guard. When the ferry reached Craignure and everyone else had disembarked, they took Worthington to a waiting police car on the quayside and drove him to Craignure police station, one of the three on the Isle of Mull, and locked him in a cell there.

"In order to maximize the chance of spotting agent OBAN while we transferred Worthington from Oban to Bunessan, the watchers split up. One man arrived early at the Oban ferry port and sat at a window table at the tearoom. This gave him a good observation point from which to scrutinize the people in the area. He sat at his table until long after the ferry left, but saw nothing suspicious. He took the next ferry to Craignure and joined the others. Another watcher had taken the last ferry the previous evening and he hung around the Craignure ferry berth waiting for agent OBAN to arrive. Again this proved to be fruitless; it seemed highly unlikely that any of the people who came to the terminal yesterday morning could be agent OBAN. The other five watchers, including Johnson, boarded the ferry separately and spent the hour-long trip looking for agent OBAN. Once more, no hound."

"Unless," Squadron Leader Harkness suggested, "agent OBAN is a master of disguise and somehow manages to look like one of the locals."

"Correct, Harkness," the air commodore said.

"And Carlyle, sir?" Captain Marks asked.

"Again there were four escorts for the hare. They drove him from Norwich to the detention barracks in Reed Hall Camp in Colchester without incident. Again there were seven watchers. One waited in the vicinity of the camp, just in case the news had leaked out that Campbell-White was headed there. Ridiculous, really—there was virtually no way that could possibly have happened—but it's always better to be safe than sorry. The other six split up. Two drove in an unmarked car about mile ahead of the police car with Hess, I mean Campbell-White, and the other four, including Carlyle, were in a second unmarked car about a mile behind them. All three cars duly arrived at Colchester. The watchers are all certain that they weren't followed, and they observed nothing suspicious in the vicinity of the detention barracks.

"In short, gentlemen, none of the watchers was able to spot a hound. We've got two hares running around, but no one seems to be chasing them."

Major Tupman raised his hand. "Can't we transmit messages to agent OBAN and agent NORFOLK, ostensibly coming from Canaris, telling them where to find their respective hares?"

"The problem is that the messages that they sent to Canaris were in a code that we still haven't broken. They'd get extremely suspicious if we sent them a message in any other code."

"Maybe we can transmit a message to them that's 'accidentally' in the wrong code," Squadron Leader Harkness suggested. "Suppose we send a message in

Code Haydn to agent NORFOLK along the following lines: 'To all our *Abwehr* agents in Britain. We have received reports of a man who might be Rudolf Hess. Thursday night he was seen in Norwich jail, and Friday night in the detention barracks in Reed Hall Camp in Colchester. Tonight he's in Halstead police station. Go to Halstead and find the man. If he isn't Hess, let us know as soon as possible. If he is Hess, follow the order of the *Führer* and either kill him yourself or tell me where he is.' We'd have to transmit it at the same time that the *Abwehr* sent that other message to agent NORFOLK—"

"And that might mean a delay of up to six days in the worst case," Chulmleigh interrupted.

"True," said Harkness. "And when they do send out the message, MI8 will have to use a low-powered transmitter, strong enough for agent NORFOLK to think that it's coming from the *Abwehr* radio center in Hamburg, but not strong enough to be picked up outside East Anglia. And we'll send a similar 'accidentally' wrong message to agent OBAN."

"But they may immediately fire off messages to Canaris asking, 'Did you really send this? It's in the wrong code,'" Marks objected.

"Then the MI8 direction finders will pick them up," Lieutenant Wallstead said. "And we'll have them. That's the whole object of the exercise."

***

Colonel Donndorf ushered Helmut Kirchgässner into Admiral Canaris's office. He seemed to be no more than thirty years old, rather young to already be a major in the SS. Canaris noticed that Kirchgässner was somewhat shorter than average with a slender build. He was carrying a medium-sized suitcase that he placed on the floor just inside the room to the left of the door.

"Admiral, this is the man who was strongly recommended to us."

"SS-Major Kirchgässner," Canaris said, "I understand that you're a highly successful assassin, with numerous successful killings to your name. We need you to travel to England to kill someone."

"Rudolf Hess, I hope, Admiral," Kirchgässner said.

"Naturally."

"I'd be delighted to help you."

"Thank you, but first some questions."

"Of course, Admiral."

"SS-Major Kirchgässner, have you ever been to England?"

"Yes, indeed. I studied at Cambridge University for one year."

"That must mean that you can speak English fluently. Which college did you attend?"

"Caius." Kirchgässner correctly pronounced the name *Keys*. Canaris nodded to show he was familiar with the fact that many proper nouns in England are vocalized in unexpected ways.

The SS-major added, "I read law at Cambridge."

"Were you a lawyer before the war?"

"Yes, I was. I specialized in maritime law, a rather abstruse legal area, I'm afraid."

"I understand that maritime law is sometimes referred to as 'admiralty law.'"

"Yes, it is."

"Well, I'm an admiral. Maybe we'll find a place for you on my staff after the war!"

The SS-major did not smile; Canaris noted that Kirchgässner had no sense of humor.

"Now, SS-Major Kirchgässner, I understand that you have a rather unusual *modus operandi.*"

"Yes, indeed. I'm a female impersonator, quite a convincing one, if I may say so myself. This enables me to get closer to my victims, both male and female, than would otherwise be the case. For obvious reasons, few people think of an assassin as a woman. Of course, there have been many women murderers in history, but they've usually used poison. My weapon of choice is the ice pick. Unlike a firearm, it's easy to hide an ice pick under a woman's clothing. And also unlike a firearm, an ice pick is silent, thereby enabling me to make a quick getaway before the alarm is raised. Of course, I use a gun when appropriate. My favorite is the CZ 27. When we annexed the Sudetenland in 1938, we found ourselves in possession of the Česká Zbrojovka factory. They certainly know how to make wonderful firearms there."

"Just how many people have you killed?" Canaris asked curiously.

SS-Major Kirchgässner smiled proudly and said, "Thirty-one."

Admiral Canaris changed the subject rather abruptly. "Please show us how you transform your appearance."

"Certainly. If you look closely, you'll see that I shaved just before coming here. I'm fortunate in that my hair is blond and my beard grows somewhat sparsely over my face. Nevertheless, I still have to shave closely before every impersonation. Of course, that includes shaving my body—and I have to trim my eyebrows."

"But don't people notice that you have less hair than most men?"

"Normally not. People in general aren't particularly observant. And the fact that my hair is blond helps considerably."

"But when you're in bed with a woman," Donndorf asked, "Surely she asks you why your arms and legs are smooth?"

"Colonel, many men have almost no hair on their bodies. Furthermore," Kirchgässner added with a smirk, "the numerous women I've slept with will tell you that I raise them to such peaks of ecstasy, so far beyond anything that they've previously encountered, that they're totally unaware of mundane details such as whether I recently shaved my legs."

The SS-major went to the door and retrieved his suitcase. "What happens now," he said, "is essentially what goes on in every theatre dressing room. Putting on my clothes will be quick, but before that it's going to take me nearly forty minutes to apply my make-up and adjust my wig. I'm sure you'll want to get on with your work while I'm doing all that; perhaps there's another room I could use to change in?"

"Of course. Donndorf, please escort the SS-major to the small conference room. I don't think anyone's using it right now."

Three-quarters of an hour later there was a knock at the door. A woman entered carrying a wooden block, which she placed on the admiral's desk. Then she walked slowly around the room, talking in a somewhat higher pitched voice than before. The two *Abwehr* officers were astounded. Canaris found his voice first: "You don't just look and sound like a woman; you *are* a woman."

Donndorf nodded enthusiastically and then asked, "But what's that wooden block you've left on the desk?"

In his persona as a woman, Kirchgässner sashayed back to the desk. As he reached it his right arm flashed. In one smooth movement he reached into his left sleeve, drew out an ice pick, and drove the point cleanly into the middle of the wooden block.

CHAPTER THIRTEEN
MI5 Headquarters, London
Sunday, May 25, 1941

"Still nothing," a worried Pankhurst said at the morning meeting. "No sighting of either of the two hounds. No messages from Canaris to either of his sleeper agents or, for that matter, to any other agents in England or Scotland. Nothing even to PICKFORD. We can't send our forged message from Canaris to agent NORFOLK until tomorrow night, and we have to wait another twenty-four hours after that to transmit to agent OBAN. Any ideas for what we might do in the meantime?"

None of the five officers around the table said anything.

***

"The latest message from PICKFORD has just arrived," Admiral Canaris said to Colonel Donndorf. "The impersonator in Scotland is still on the Isle of Mull. Yesterday he left Craignure by bus, and it appears that he's now in Bunessan, in a cell at the police station there. Two days ago agent URIAH

HEEP had to stay on the ferry until the police had left with their prisoner, and consequently he couldn't see what happened when they reached the dockside. He assumed that they'd taken Hess to Craignure police station, which is right next to the pier. Accordingly, yesterday morning he hung around the area of the police station. At about ten o'clock he saw Hess emerge. Four policemen escorted him to a bus that was waiting at a stop about seventy-five yards along the main road. It appeared to be one of the regular buses that travel the length of the island. The five men got onto the bus and sat in the back. URIAH HEEP waited until the bus had left, then went into a village shop near the police station. He found out that the bus went to Bunessan, at the southwestern tip of Mull. He also learned that there's a police station there. He took the next bus to Bunessan, but by the time he arrived at the village there was no sign of Hess's double, of course. URIAH HEEP told PICKFORD that he's going to stay overnight at Bunessan and see if Hess leaves the police station this morning."

"Admiral, as far as I'm concerned, this report confirms my belief that this man is a double who is masquerading as Hess. The British police could've transported him by car to Bunessan, but instead they chose to use a public bus. They could even have used a police launch."

"I agree. The man in Scotland is unquestionably an imposter. And the English 'Hess' was at Halstead police station last night. EBENEZER SCROOGE followed him there in his car from Colchester;

hopefully the police escorting the look-alike didn't spot him. And no one seems to have any idea where the real Hess is."

"But why are the British sending the two Hess impersonators around Britain, making sure that they are observed by all and sundry?" Donndorf asked.

"First of all, who says that there are only two doubles? PICKFORD's subagents have detected only two up to now, but there might be dozens of them."

"Dozens, Admiral? Do that many Englishmen resemble Hess?"

"How hard would it be to find a tall man with roughly the correct features? It's easy to adjust the hairline, color the hair if necessary and stick on large black eyebrows. Look at Kirchgässner—with the aid of make-up he transformed himself into a woman. The British have a thriving movie industry, which means there must be lots of competent make-up artists around who can turn out as many Hesses as the British want."

"But what if someone were to address a double in German? Englishmen learn Latin and Greek at school, not German."

"He won't understand what was said to him, but he'll surely say something appropriate in English in reply."

"With a German accent, Admiral?"

Canaris thought for a moment. "Well, maybe it's not that easy. After all, our experts have spent years training the doubles for our leaders. But anyhow, at least we've established that both the sightings to date are look-alikes, not Hess himself."

"Certainly. But don't you think it's correct to claim that all future sightings that our agents report to us will also be doubles? The real Hess is probably squirreled away in some obscure location where no one would dream of looking for him. And if the British do decide to move him from there for some reason, they'll do it in such a way that no one will be able to observe it."

"Yes, I agree," said Canaris. "And that leads to lots and lots of interesting lines of inquiry. But first let's return to my earlier question: Why are the British moving two, or possibly more, doubles of Hess around?"

"To put us off the scent? To get us to order our agents to chase all over Britain in places that are as far as possible from the actual location where they've hidden Hess? To make us think that we've spotted the real Hess so we won't look any further?"

"Perhaps. And what are we going to do about EDWIN DROOD?"

"I'm not quite sure what you mean, Admiral."

"We received a message from PICKFORD that began by stating that the British believe we're going to kill Hess—PICKFORD sent us a report to that effect from EDWIN DROOD, one of his subagents. Do you remember the second part of that report?"

"The second part, Admiral?"

"The second part was that they can't find a safe location for Hess and in order to protect him to the best of their ability they're moving him around on a daily basis."

"Yes, that's correct, Admiral. But we found that suspicious, didn't we, but we couldn't quite put our finger on it, could we?"

"No, Donndorf, we couldn't. But now I can. As far as I'm concerned, the claim that they keep shifting Hess from place to place because they can't find a safe location for him is nonsensical. What about Churchill? Surely Hitler would rather assassinate the British prime minister than Hess? But the British don't move Churchill from place to place every night. And the same applies to the members of the War Cabinet and the top military leaders. I didn't believe that EDWIN DROOD report when we received it, and I certainly don't believe it now. As far as I'm concerned, EDWIN DROOD passed on disinformation fed to him by the British, and PICKFORD sent it on to us."

"Should we tell PICKFORD to cut all ties with EDWIN DROOD?"

"Absolutely not, Donndorf. The more disinformation we get from EDWIN DROOD, the better for us. After all, if you know for certain that what you're reading is disinformation, that tells you a lot. In fact, sometimes you can discover as much from disinformation as from correct information. For example, we'd learn something if we could work out why the British want us to think that they're moving Hess from place to place. There's clearly some sort of plot afoot here, but I can't seem to work out what it is. Can you?"

"Unfortunately not, Admiral."

"In that case, what are we going to do now?"

"We're in a quandary, Admiral. We've transmitted *Herr* Hitler's order to all our agents to fan out over Britain and locate Hess. But we've just realized that if they think they've located Hess, it's actually going to be a double; the real Hess is well hidden. On the other hand, we dare not countermand the *Führer* and tell them to stop looking."

"Are you saying that there's nothing we can do and that we should just let our spies run around Britain on a never-ending fool's errand, instead of gathering vital information for the German military?" Canaris asked.

"I can see no alternative. Can you, Admiral?"

The steel blue eyes under the craggy white eyebrows suddenly sparkled.

"I've thought of something. Suppose we send a team of paratroopers to Britain to kill one of the imposters, it doesn't matter which. We can then report to the *Führer* that Hess is dead. The British won't be in a position to contradict us, for obvious reasons. Then we can tell our agents to get back to their assigned tasks."

"Admiral, where will the paratroopers land?"

"As I just told you," Canaris said, "I don't think it matters. The islands of the Inner Hebrides are sparsely populated so there's no air defense there, and probably almost no enemy troops in the area either, so our men can land unopposed on any suitable drop zone. Alternatively, we could drop them in Fen Country; that's pretty deserted, too, no trees and flat as a pancake, ideal terrain for paratroopers."

"That's not quite what I meant, Admiral. We're currently receiving radio messages from PICKFORD at about the time we arrive at work. That's because of the somewhat crude communications network we have, with a whole chain of intermediaries. But once we discover where the double spent the night, we can inform the military authorities right away. They then have to organize the parachute drop, and that takes time. After all, you can't drop paratroopers in the middle of a town; you have to find a suitable open place for them to land. And you have to provide the men with maps. As a result, even if the paratroopers are already sitting in a plane in northern France when the information comes through, by the time we drop them onto England, the bird will certainly have flown the coop and be on his way to the next destination."

"And once we've dropped them," Canaris said, "we'll have a troop of German paratroopers on the ground in England or Scotland, waiting around unobserved for twenty-four hours for the next message. And the British may be stupid, but they're not totally blind—they would definitely notice our paratroopers hanging around the place. No, Donndorf, that won't work. We're going to have to send in Kirchgässner to assassinate one of the doubles."

***

"You went to Cambridge University, so you must be familiar with East Anglia," Admiral Canaris remarked.

"Oh, yes. Almost every weekend I went on a cycling trip in that part of Britain," Helmut Kirchgässner said.

"Do you know Norfolk and the surrounding counties?"

"Very well indeed, Admiral."

"It seems that our target is being moved from place to place in that area. Donndorf, remind me where he's been."

"Yes, Admiral. Thursday night he was in Norwich, the largest city in Norfolk. Friday he slept in Colchester, in Essex. And last night he was in Halstead, also in Essex."

"Thank you, Donndorf. SS-Major, are you familiar with those towns?"

"Yes, I have visited all three of them. British Railways has an excellent network that covers the whole country, including East Anglia. I used to board a train in Cambridge, putting my bicycle in the goods van, and within an hour or two I found myself in a town from which to explore the countryside on two wheels. I know that area well."

"Good. Now, it seems that my staff still have to decide how to get you to England and back here afterwards. Do you have your paratrooper wings?"

"Yes, Admiral, " Kirchgässner said. "I could certainly parachute into East Anglia. Of course, that still leaves the problem of getting back to Germany.

The last time I was in England I went by U-boat and returned the same way."

"Well, it's up to my staff. I'm sure they'll find an optimal way to get you in and get you out. Now, before my people give you a detailed briefing, I need to remind you that you're after a moving target—literally. As I mentioned, each night he's slept in a different location, up to now a civilian prison, a military detention barracks, or a police station."

"That makes sense," SS-Major Kirchgässner stated. "Rudolf Hess is a prisoner of the British, and you'd expect them to house a prisoner in jails and the like."

"According to our information, each morning Hess leaves at about ten o'clock, under heavy guard—generally four uniformed policemen plus some number of plainclothes men in the vicinity. Presumably all the men are armed. You obviously know from your year in Britain that the only weapon British 'bobbies' carry is a stout wooden truncheon, but when the war started they issued firearms to the police to be used if we invaded Britain. They're not allowed to take their weapons with them on routine patrol, but I've no doubt that the police guarding Hess are carrying guns.

"Armed guards take Hess by police car or police van to his next place of confinement. When he arrives, they escort him, yet again under heavy guard, into the next military or civilian prison or police station in East Anglia where, I assume, they guard him night and day. If you can get past the guards, you can kill him in one of four situations: leaving a prison or police station, en route in a police vehicle, arriving at the next prison or police station, or overnight in a prison or police station. Normally, prisoners are guarded to prevent them escaping. In the case of Hess, the British seem to be well aware that the *Führer* has ordered our agents in Britain to kill Hess, so the guards are also there to protect him. In fact, the reason that they're moving him from place to place each day is precisely to make it harder for people like you."

Kirchgässner smiled for the first time.

"In other words," Canaris continued, "you have a challenge that probably is new to you. You cannot plan far ahead because you don't know in advance where Hess is going to be. The police vehicle will draw up somewhere, and that will be that. Once Hess is inside you can kill him there or wait until he emerges the next morning. In the best case, then, you can plan about half a day ahead, but no more than that."

"I understand," SS-Major Kirchgässner said. "Will I have an assistant?"

"Possibly. One of our agents is following Hess. He has a car. The problem is that we have no way of communicating with him. His code name is EBENEZER SCROOGE—"

"The hero of *A Christmas Carol* by Charles Dickens?"

"Well, I wouldn't exactly call him a hero, but I understand what you're getting at. EBENEZER SCROOGE is a subagent of agent PICKFORD, our top man in Britain. EBENEZER SCROOGE is on the scene and sending us daily reports of Hess's movements. We'll show you a photograph of EBENEZER SCROOGE, and hopefully you'll be able to make contact with him."

"Is there a sign and countersign?" Helmut Kirchgässner inquired.

"No. We sent EBENEZER SCROOGE to England to gather information, not to take part in an active operation like this. You'll have to use your best judgment in deciding how to make contact with EBENEZER SCROOGE when you see him or, more correctly, if you see him. Yes, he's a fully trained *Abwehr* agent but no, he's never taken part as an active agent in any operation. Will he be more of a help or a hindrance to you? That's up to you to decide when you meet him."

"Admiral, if I can't make contact with EBENEZER SCROOGE, which it seems might well be the case, my task without a suitable back-up will be considerably harder. I really do need an assistant, preferably one with extensive operational experience. Could you transmit a message to PICKFORD to send one of his subagents to East Anglia to help me?"

"Yes, I'm sure we can arrange that," said Canaris.

He turned to Donndorf. "Contact PICKFORD. Inform him that the assistant will need to know when to listen for PICKFORD's transmissions to us. And PICKFORD will have to provide him with wavelength information, of course."

"Pickford has evaded MI5 all these years precisely by not sharing information of that kind with his subagents. Will he cooperate?" Donndorf asked.

"I'm sure he will. And I'm equally sure that he'll change his wavelength and transmission times just as soon as SS-Major Kirchgässner has completed his mission. Agent PICKFORD is fanatical about security."

"One other thing, Admiral," Donndorf said. "How will the assistant be able to decode the messages PICKFORD transmits to us?"

"PICKFORD will tell him that he uses Code Haydn, like all our other agents in Britain. Even our agents who use a book code can decrypt messages sent in Code Haydn."

"And I've just thought of something else," Donndorf added. "Will the assistant have a sufficiently powerful radio receiver?"

"Well, if he doesn't, PICKFORD will surely be able to provide him with one. He'll arrange for an underling to deliver it to the appropriate newsagent, securely wrapped and labeled as something innocuous, and the assistant will pick it up from there. As always, the newsagent won't realize a thing."

Canaris turned to the SS-major. "I believe that will take care of your assistant. Is there anything else you need?"

"Admiral Canaris," Kirchgässner asked, "Have you discovered why the British are sending Hess around the country?"

"Not yet. We have some theories, but nothing more than that."

"But you would agree, Admiral, that this is part of some MI5 plot?"

"Possibly. It could be that they're just trying to disorient Hess to make it easier to extract information from him. In that case, it's essential that you kill him as soon as possible, before he gives away vital state secrets that could cause us to lose the war. But you may be right. This could indeed be a plot of some kind on the part of MI5."

"I'm concerned that one component of that plot may be to inveigle an assassin to come to England, where he'll be captured."

"Yes, it's certainly possible. And if that's the case, how would you want to handle the mission?" Canaris asked.

"I understand that you wish your staff to arrange how, when, and where I arrive in England, as well as setting up contact arrangements with an assistant."

"Of course."

"For a start, I think that it's vital that as few people as possible in England know any of the details of my trip to East Anglia. I would be most grateful if you could phone Commander Schwerin. He's on the staff of Admiral Dönitz, the head of the U-boat section of the *Kriegsmarine* (German Navy). Can you ask him to make arrangements for me to get to and from England? I'd like to come ashore in the vicinity of Clacton-on-Sea."

"Where exactly?" Admiral Canaris asked.

"I have a chart that I'll show to the captain of the U-boat when we get close to Clacton."

"I understand. Yes, I can easily arrange that. Now, how do you want to liaise with your assistant?"

"In addition to the radio, he needs to be accessible by telephone at all times. He'll receive PICKFORD's messages to you on his receiver and pass the information on to me when I phone him. I'll leave for Essex just as soon as PICKFORD provides you with the contact telephone number. And there has to be a sign and a countersign, of course. It would probably be most convenient for me if the assistant were based in Colchester."

"That's fine. Donndorf, take care of it. Anything else?"

"I have my own equipment, but I'm going to need maps of the area, preferably Ordnance Survey maps if you have them—the selling of maps in wartime is forbidden in Britain, just as it is here. And I'll need British money, including lots of coins for public telephones. But there's a question I'd like to ask you, if I may."

"Certainly, SS-Major. Go ahead."

"Admiral, why did you call me in? When PICKFORD tells you where Hess is located, why don't you simply drop a company or two of paratroopers in the vicinity of the jail? They should have no trouble storming a prison and killing Hess or, better still, capturing him and bringing him back alive to be a guest of the *Gestapo*."

"That's the whole problem," Admiral Canaris sighed. "As soon as subagent EBENEZER SCROOGE sees Hess entering the next police station or jail, he phones someone in London. That person is the first in a chain of contacts that eventually leads to PICKFORD. We don't know how the information gets to PICKFORD, but the key point is that it seems to reach him only the next morning, nearly twenty-four hours later, and then he has to compile his report, encode it, and transmit it. We suspect that there's a dead letter drop or something like that in the chain that would explain this slowness. PICKFORD immediately passes Hess's location on to us by radio, but by then it's too late to send paratroopers across the English Channel; Hess is on his way to his next location."

"But is there time for me to get to the prison before they move Hess?" Kirchgässner asked.

"The message arrives here at about nine, British time, and up to now they've moved Hess at ten. Consequently, if you're not too far from the site and you have a fast car, you might be able to get there in time to follow him to his next place of imprisonment."

"I can steal a car—that's no problem. But fuel is another issue entirely. Gasoline is heavily rationed in England. Could you inform PICKFORD that the assistant he's sending me needs to bring me a good supply of fuel coupons?"

"That won't be necessary. Our forgers turn out excellent imitations. We'll provide you with as many fuel ration books as you think you might need, together with identity cards, food ration books, and the like," Canaris assured him.

"That's excellent. With any luck I won't need to have any face-to-face contact with my assistant. If this is an MI5 trap, the fewer people I meet, the better. By the way, how did you get the original gasoline coupons? I assume that you have a route that you use to get agents out of England. If so, could I utilize it?"

"Actually, we found a motor fuel ration book on the body of a British soldier in North Africa."

"But I thought that the British were extremely careful about not letting soldiers take any personal effects abroad that we could use."

"Yes, you're quite right," the admiral said. "But somehow this ration book slipped through. I'm sure that they carefully checked the soldier's wallet before he embarked, but the ration book was in an outside pocket of his battledress. We'll give you ten books. Each person is allowed three gallons of fuel a week, and if you need more than that, as you probably will, you'll have to go to a different filling station with another book of coupons. Just fill in the registration number of the car you've stolen on the cover before you hand the book over. And remember to present your National Registration Identity Card at the same time."

***

"Gentlemen," Air Commodore Pankhurst said, "I had a telephone conversation with Johnson after lunch today. He's in Tobermory, the chief town of the Isle of Mull. This morning they brought

Worthington by bus from Bunessan to Tobermory, with still no sign of agent OBAN.

"Johnson raised an important point. If we continue to run this operation in Scotland the way we're currently doing it, there's no way that agent OBAN could possibly follow Worthington.

"There are four ways to move the look-alike around the Inner Hebrides: by car, by bus, by ferry, and by police launch. Agent OBAN probably doesn't have access to a car on any of the islands, so there's no way he can follow if we transport Worthington in a police vehicle. If we put Worthington on a bus, agent OBAN is most unlikely to give himself away by boarding the same bus. But if he doesn't, how can he find out where we've taken Worthington? Of course, if he knows the location of every police station in the Inner Hebrides then perhaps he can make an intelligent guess, but that's not a good way to play the game of Hare and Hounds. It's worse with a public ferry. For obvious reasons, agent OBAN will have to wait for the next ferry to the same ferry port, and by the time he arrives there we surely will have moved Worthington elsewhere. Finally, following a police launch is impossible without a boat. And in the unlikely event that he has his own boat or can hire one at short notice from a local fisherman, he obviously realizes that he'll inevitably be spotted as he pursues the police launch.

"In short, I informed Johnson that my sending Worthington to the Inner Hebrides was a mistake. He'll have to spend tonight in Tobermory, at the police station in the part of the town on the top of the cliffs. After all, he's there now and it would be a large-scale inconvenience to move him to the mainland tonight. But tomorrow morning we'll move him back to Oban by police launch, and from then on we'll move him by car from location to location on the West Coast of Scotland in the vicinity of Oban.

"Any questions?"

Major Tupman put up his hand. "Yes, Tupman?"

"Sir, I'm sorry to sound negative, but what if agent OBAN doesn't have access to a car?"

"Then Operation OTTAWA will fail, at least in Scotland. It's as simple as that. And, yes, I should've realized that before I approved the operation."

CHAPTER FOURTEEN
Tobermory, Isle of Mull, Scotland
Monday, May 26, 1941

"Good morning, Worthington! Rise and shine! You're on your way to Oban again," Johnson said.

"Oban? Back to the mainland? I thought I was going to spend the rest of my days island hopping."

"Well, we've decided that you've overstayed your welcome in the Inner Hebrides. Instead, we feel that you should broaden your horizons and visit the beautiful area around Oban. The scenery is truly glorious; there are breathtaking views of deep lochs ringed by high mountains, some of them still snowcapped even though it's May. Why, you might even get to see the Loch Ness monster; Loch Ness is only a hundred miles from Oban along the Great Glen."

"Just a minute. Precisely how am I to travel back to Oban? Are you thinking of putting me back on that ferry again?"

"Not at all," Johnson said. "The ferry that you were on sails from Craignure back to Oban. That would mean a bus ride to Craignure, and then the ferry. No, that would be an undue hardship. Instead, we're putting you on a police launch right here in Tobermory. You'll walk directly from here to the jetty and onto the launch, and the helmsman will take you straight to Oban. The whole trip is only about fifty miles; you'll be there before you know it. No more than three hours, maybe just two and a half."

"Three hours in a small boat tossing and turning on the ocean? I don't think I'll last three minutes."

"Come on, Worthington, it's not the open sea. Most of the way you'll be in the Sound of Mull, a narrow passage. Anyhow, you'll survive."

"There are two stages to seasickness. During stage one, you're afraid that you're going to die. During stage two, you're afraid that you're not going to die."

"Enough! It's time for the boat to leave," Johnson said.

Four uniformed policemen escorted Worthington on foot from the police station on Erray Road into Bredalbane Street, then down Back Brae to the port below and onto a police launch. As 'Rudolf Hess' walked through the quaint town, the islanders on their shopping rounds stopped and stared at the prisoner. None of the townspeople seemed to recognize him. The seven watchers, placed at strategic points along the route, looked intensely at everyone, but there was no one whom they thought might possibly be agent OBAN.

***

"Good morning, Campbell-White! Rise and shine! You must have slept ten hours or more last night. As you did the night before, and the night before that."

"Well, Carlyle, there hasn't very much to do since leaving that house where the real Hess is living. What's it called it again?"

"Mytchett Place."

"Yes, that's it. What I do now is sit and chat to your colleagues when they're kind enough to come to my cell to amuse me. The rest of the time, I just sit. And when it's night, I go to sleep."

"We can get you any reading matter you want: newspapers, magazines, books. Just let me know."

"Carlyle, the fact is that I'm not really one for reading. But I do enjoy listening to the radio. Would it be possible to have a radio in my cell for the times when you and your colleagues have better things to do than visit a Hess impersonator in his cell? I'll keep the volume down, of course."

"Certainly! I'll organize a radio and a really long extension cord as soon as we get to today's destination, which is Chelmsford, by the way," Carlyle said.

"Now tell me again where I am now."

"You're in the police cells at Thorpe-le-Soken."

"That's what you said yesterday. I didn't believe you then, and I don't believe you now. There can't possibly be a place with a name like that."

"I've brought you a map of Essex. Look, here it says Thorpe-le-Soken. We're just a few miles from Clacton-on-Sea."

Campbell-White peered disbelievingly at the map that Carlyle had brought him.

"What does the name mean?"

"You asked me that yesterday, and I told you I didn't know. You'll be delighted to hear that I've taken the trouble to find out for you. 'Thorp' is a Middle English word meaning a small village. And a thousand years ago, when the Anglo-Saxons were ruling this area, the word 'soke' denoted an area that had some special privilege granted to it. And the special privilege Thorpe-le-Soken was granted was to have you as its guest last night.

"Now please get dressed. Chelmsford awaits. I'll organize a breakfast tray for you. And before we leave at ten, make sure you're wearing your body armor. You're too valuable to Britain for you to take any chances.

"Oh, one other thing. You're doing a great job with the make-up and the stick-on eyebrows, but I noticed last night that the blond roots of your hair are starting to show. You need to apply that black hair dye every single day."

***

"Admiral Canaris," Colonel Donndorf asked, "what if Kirchgässner recognizes that the man he's about to kill is actually a double?"

"Is that likely, Colonel? At the instant when he's about to draw his ice pick from his sleeve and plunge it into his victim, the SS-Major is unlikely to be concerned with minor differences in appearance."

"True, Admiral. But what if the impersonator is talking as the assassin approaches his target? It doesn't matter if the man is speaking German with an English accent or English without a German accent, Kirchgässner will instantly realize that he's about to kill an imposter."

"That could be a problem, Donndorf. I hadn't thought of that possibility."

"My guess, Admiral, is that he won't kill the double, which would put us in a bind."

"And my guess, Donndorf, is that Kirchgässner loves killing so much that he won't lose the opportunity.

"In any event," Canaris continued, "as far as I'm concerned, a more pressing issue is what SS-Major Kirchgässner will do to us if he discovers that we've arranged to send him to England to kill an imposter who's impersonating Rudolf Hess. I freely concede that it's not a good idea to trick an assassin, especially one who by the time he returns will have successfully murdered thirty-two people with his ice pick and his handgun, a CZ 27 if I recollect correctly. But I think we'll be able to convince him when he gets back that we had no idea that his target was a Hess look-alike. After all, how could we possibly have known that the man was a double?"

"I just hope you're right, Admiral. I have no desire for you and me to be numbers thirty-three and thirty-four on Kirchgässner's list of victims."

***

The three cars drove through the heavy rain along Victoria Road, Chelmsford, about half a mile apart. As the leading car made a left turn into New Street, the driver noticed that workmen had dug up a strip of the road directly in front of the police station, so he turned right into Legg Street and parked there. In turn, the other two drivers did the same. The watchers got out first and spread out in the vicinity. When they were in position, the four policemen escorted Campbell-White back to New Street and into the police station.

The area was deserted. When the storm began, the members of the road gang quickly took shelter in the pub situated diagonally across the road from the police station, and the local inhabitants had sensibly decided that they would do their shopping after the weather had improved somewhat.

***

"Gentlemen," Air Commodore Pankhurst said, "I've called you together this afternoon because there have been some important new developments. As you know, PICKFORD sends his updates each morning to Canaris by radio roughly an hour before we transport our two Hess impersonators to their next location. We do it that way so that it's too late for the Germans to arrange for a plane-load of paratroopers to descend from the skies onto the jail or the police station housing one of our lookalikes; by the time the Nazi troops could get here, the doubles will have moved on. But there's sufficient time for the two hounds to pick up the scent of our hares.

"However, Canaris seems to have found a way around our stratagem. Earlier this afternoon he told PICKFORD that he's sending an agent from Germany to East Anglia, code name BROCKEN. BROCKEN will communicate directly with Canaris using his own radio, bypassing our deliberately slow and cumbersome PICKFORD network. Unless we can find a way to get our hands on BROCKEN, we could be facing German Special Forces troops in East Anglia. Perhaps our navy can sink the U-boat bringing him to England, or the air force can shoot down the German plane before BROCKEN can drop by parachute, or maybe MI8 can locate the radio transmitter he uses to send messages to Berlin. But if we can't lay our hands on him, we could be in big trouble.

"Another aspect of Operation OTTAWA: Agent BROCKEN says he wants an *Abwehr* agent in Britain to assist him, someone with extensive operational experience."

"What about sending EBENEZER SCROOGE?" Major Tupman asked.

The other officers all started laughing.

"Of course, I know that we hanged EBENEZER SCROOGE soon after he arrived in Britain, like all the other PICKFORD subagents that the *Abwehr* sent here," Tupman protested indignantly. "What I meant was: Someone in MI5 could pretend to be EBENEZER SCROOGE."

"That's not going to work," Wallstead objected. "The *Abwehr* people must have given agent BROCKEN a physical description of EBENEZER SCROOGE, and probably a photograph as well. Also, EBENEZER SCROOGE is a German, and we all know exactly what happens when we try to train an Englishman to impersonate a German."

This remark also drew gales of laughter.

"Couldn't one of the tens of thousands of German refugees who fled to Britain before the war play the role of EBENEZER SCROOGE?" Harkness asked. "Surely there's someone who resembles the man in the photograph?"

"There's not enough time for that," Pankhurst insisted. "We'd have to find someone who's capable of carrying off the deception—looking alike isn't enough. And what about the issue of security? And we'd have to train the double thoroughly, including decryption of messages in Code Haydn. No, we have to provide BROCKEN with an English-speaking assistant, someone working for PICKFORD."

"What does the assistant have to do?" Lieutenant Commander Chulmleigh asked.

"Canaris didn't specify. All he said was that the assistant needs to be ensconced somewhere in Colchester in a room with a telephone to enable BROCKEN to contact him, and with a radio so that he can pass on to BROCKEN all the information that PICKFORD sends to Germany. He instructed PICKFORD to provide the assistant with wavelength and transmission time information and to tell him that he uses Code Haydn for his radio transmissions to Germany.

"Now that I come to think of it," Pankhurst continued, "that's rather ironic. In January 1940, the *Abwehr* sent subagent BARNABY RUDGE to England in a U-boat. They gave him a package to give to PICKFORD. It contained a document that provided the details of Code Haydn."

"Wasn't that exceedingly foolhardy?" Captain Marks asked. "Surely they realized that subagent BARNABY RUDGE might be arrested?"

"Of course. That's why they printed the entire document using water-soluble ink. If a Royal Navy vessel were to intercept his inflatable dinghy as he paddled to shore from the U-boat, all he had to do was drop the package into the sea. They also put some sort of incendiary device inside. If the security people arrested BARNABY RUDGE and found the package, unless they opened it exactly the right way it would explode, and the document would quickly incinerate. Finally, they gave him a hand grenade with a pull fuse. Subagent BARNABY RUDGE was a fanatical Nazi who had repeatedly declared his willingness to give his life for his *Führer*. If all else failed, BARNABY RUDGE would pull the pin, and the grenade would instantly destroy him and the secret document.

"The *Abwehr* considered every eventuality—or so they thought. However, the submarine landed BARNABY RUDGE at the wrong place in northern Devon; MI5 agents were waiting for him on a different beach more than five miles away. Abandoned and friendless on enemy soil—or so he believed—he lost his nerve. He went to the first house he saw and asked the way to the nearest police station. There he declared to the constable on duty that he was a German spy. He handed over the package to the stupefied policeman, while repeatedly warning him that it was booby-trapped. The next day, PICKFORD sent a message to the *Abwehr* in Code Haydn, informing them that BARNABY RUDGE had arrived safely. And since then we've been able to read countless encrypted messages that the Germans have sent to their agents all over the world.

"Anyhow, when I next speak to Carlyle, I'll tell him that he's BROCKEN's assistant. We'll set him up in a room in Colchester and have a phone installed. He doesn't need a radio—we can tell him everything by telephone, of course, before the radio operator masquerading as PICKFORD transmits it, in encoded form, to Germany. Of course, we'll tap the phone line and trace any incoming calls. And we'd better assign a man to follow Carlyle if BROCKEN orders him to go somewhere."

Everyone nodded. Then Lieutenant Wallstead asked, "Sir, shouldn't we give Carlyle a radio just in case BROCKEN comes to his room, with or without an invitation?"

"Good point, Wallstead," Pankhurst said. "Also, bearing in mind that PICKFORD transmits in Code Haydn, we need to provide Carlyle with all the materials that he would need to be able decode the messages. Of course, the radio must stay tuned to the frequency that PICKFORD uses. And while on the subject of taking precautions, do we need to warn Campbell-White that a Nazi assassin is on his trail?"

"What good would that do?" Major Tupman asked. "The man's a sitting duck and he's well aware of it, body armor or not. If we tell him about BROCKEN it may throw him into a state of panic."

"Does everyone agree? Fine. Anything else about BROCKEN?"

Lieutenant Wallstead spoke up. "Is the word *Brocken* significant in any way?"

"I looked it up in our library before the meeting," the air commodore said. "Brocken is the name of the highest peak in Northern Germany. I'm not sure how that helps us. It's in the Harz Mountains. Again, that doesn't tell me anything. Any ideas?"

There were mutterings of "No" and shakings of heads.

"There's another thing. I know we all learned the Greek myths at school, but the Germans have their legends, too. Brocken Mountain, it seems, is associated with devils. And it's the meeting place of witches on Walpurgis Night, a traditional spring festival in mainland Europe. Some versions of the Faust legend have scenes on Brocken. Anything at all?"

This time there was just silence.

"One final idea. Are there any mountaineers in the room?"

More silence.

"Well, I learned that when climbing a mountain on a misty day, a climber's shadow can create strange optical effects. A Brocken Specter is a huge shadow of the climber, cast onto the mist, but the magnified size of the shadow is actually an optical illusion. There's a detailed explanation of the phenomenon in *Encyclopedia Britannica*. However, as you all know, science is entirely beyond me. Apparently a Brocken Specter can occur anywhere, but it's frequently observed on Brocken because of the numerous mists on the mountain, hence the name. Still nothing?"

No one said anything. Then Lieutenant Wallstead spoke up. "I wonder if the 'optical illusion' is at all significant. That is, maybe when you look at the agent you see one thing, but it's actually an illusion—the reality is something else."

"That may be just a little far fetched," Pankhurst answered. "However, it's the only suggestion we have up to now. Of course, the other possibility is that the name was simply the next one on a list, the same way we came up with Operation OTTAWA—that ensures that we don't give any clues to the other side. Let's move on.

"I've informed the Chiefs of Staff Committee that Admiral Canaris is sending an agent to East Anglia. Because he's not a PICKFORD subagent, we have no idea how he's coming or when he's scheduled to arrive. In the best case the military will be able to capture him when he gets here, but a lone parachutist descending into the Fen Country or a U-boat quickly landing a man by boat on a deserted beach and immediately submerging again can be hard to prevent. We can't expect them to bring the entire air force and navy to bear against BROCKEN, nor can we ask the army to flood East Anglia with troops. I think that the best we can do is to alert the seven watchers and four 'policemen' that, in addition to agent NORFOLK, they need to be on the lookout for BROCKEN.

"There's one final item this afternoon. Tonight we're sending the message ostensibly from Admiral Canaris to agent NORFOLK, and tomorrow night a similar one will go to agent OBAN. If they don't spot our forgeries, both hounds should be in play by Wednesday morning."

"Together with BROCKEN?" Captain Marks asked.

"If the military don't capture him first then, yes, together with BROCKEN."

CHAPTER FIFTEEN
Chelmsford, Essex, England
Tuesday, May 27, 1941

The door to the police station opened and two policemen emerged, followed by another two handcuffed to Campbell-White on each side. The five men moved in the direction of Legg Street where their car was still parked.

A young man was lounging near the corner. He saw Campbell-White and did a double take. Then he bent down and picked up a stone lying in the pile of gravel that the workmen repairing New Street had dug up. As he flung it at the Hess look-alike, he yelled, "That's for my father, you Nazi bastard," and ran past the members of the road gang in the direction of Victoria Road. Two of the watchers moved in, blocked his path and collared him.

The sharp stone hit a nerve on Campbell-White's right hand. The sudden severe pain made him shout, "Bloody hell, that hurt!" in an upper-class accent that unmistakably revealed that Campbell-White had been educated at one of England's most exclusive boarding schools. A man in a tweed jacket stood unobtrusively in the shadows at the entrance to

Cottage Place, virtually across the road from the police station. When he heard Campbell-White cry out, he started to walk slowly down the one-way street toward where he had parked his car. He drove to Colchester, obsessively watching his speedometer in built-up areas to be certain that he stayed below the limit of thirty miles per hour.

***

In view of the fact that Johnson had told him that there would be no more journeys by water, Worthington decided not to mention that he was still suffering from the after-effects of the launch trip the previous day along the Sound of Mull. Adding to his discomfort was the sense of déjà vu that had haunted him all night, brought about because he was locked in the same cell in the police station in Oban as four days previously.

Each day before they moved him to his next destination, his escort had meticulously checked that he was wearing his tungsten steel body armor. However, his head and his limbs were exposed. The MI5 guards would sometimes try to reassure him by making remarks like "That armor will keep the bullets out" or "Don't you worry, Worthington, the Jerries are notoriously bad shots—why, they couldn't hit the side of a double-decker bus at ten paces." But everyone involved in Operation OTTAWA, including Worthington himself, was acutely aware that, in addition to protecting only his torso, the body armor would be of little use if a Nazi spy tossed a hand grenade at the Hess look-alike.

While he was in the safe house learning how to impersonate Hess, the realization that he was no longer in Wandsworth Prison, the toughest jail in Britain, crowded all other thoughts out of Worthington's mind. His visit to Camp Z was the turning point. Seeing the captive Rudolf Hess sitting in front of him, oblivious to the three watchers behind the painting, brought the reality of his situation home to Worthington; he had simply moved from one sort of prison to another. Yes, there were many significant differences. The physical location of his place of confinement now changed from day to day, and the guards treated him with respect and kindness at all times. Nevertheless, Worthington was intelligent enough to realize that this new form of imprisonment was, at heart, no different from the old; he was still deprived of his freedom. And in addition, he was a sitting duck, a target for an *Abwehr* killer. Perhaps that was why the MI5 people were always really nice to him.

"It's going to be a short run today," Johnson told him. "We're taking you to the police station at Fort William."

"Named after William the Conqueror, I suppose. I never realized that he conquered Scotland, too."

"He didn't. They named the settlement after William of Orange, who around the year 1700 simultaneously became King William the Third of England and King William the Second of Scotland. Then over the next fifty years they changed the name of the town three times before calling it Fort William again, this time after Prince William, the Duke of Cumberland, whom some Scots call 'Butcher Cumberland.' And the reason I'm telling you all this is so that you'll know that there's a tradition here in Scotland of going round in circles while irritating as many people as possible, achieving exactly nothing and then getting right back to where you started in the first place. Which is why you're here in Oban again, precisely where you were four days ago.

"Get your body armor on, please. We're about to leave for Fort William."

***

The sun was setting as the company of soldiers circled Bowens Farm on Halstead Road, just outside Colchester. Four police vehicles swooped down on the farmhouse.

An officious police inspector hammered on the door with his clenched fist.

"Open up!" he demanded.

A small woman opened the door and saw the police arrayed outside her home. "Yes?" she said timidly.

"Mrs. Bowen?"

"Yes."

"We'd like a word with your husband," the inspector said, pushing his way past the now badly frightened woman and shouting to the men behind him, "Handcuff her and put her in the car."

The inspector rushed into the house. A plump man of about fifty was asleep in an easy chair. He was wearing reading glasses, and a newspaper had fallen from his lap onto the floor. The inspector shook him awake.

"Clive Bowen?"

"Yes? What is it? Who are you and what are you doing here?"

"Clive Bowen, I arrest you under the Treachery Act 1940."

"Treachery? What are you talking about? I haven't committed treason—I'm a farmer!"

"Where's your radio transmitter? MI8 picked up a coded message sent from this farm not half an hour ago. Where's the radio?"

"My radio is on the table over there. We listened to the news at nine o'clock and then I must have fallen asleep reading the paper. Since when is it treason to listen to the BBC?"

"Not that radio, man. Where's your transmitter?"

"Transmitter? What are you talking about? I don't have a transmitter. What would I do with a transmitter? This is my radio, my only radio, and that's it. And if you don't believe me, you can search the farm. Go ahead, look everywhere; I don't care. And don't forget to look in the barn and the guest cottage and in the pigsty. And search the dogs, too. They're outside. You can hear them barking their heads off. And you can search the sheep pen and the—"

"Just a minute. What guest cottage?"

"We have a guest cottage at the back that we rent out. There's a foreign gentleman staying there now. I'm sure he won't mind if you—"

But the inspector had stopped listening and was leading a posse heading for the cottage. They had drawn their revolvers; arresting a local farmer was one thing, but a "foreign gentleman" was quite another.

A burly constable drew his leg back, about to kick the door open with his steel-toe boot. Inside the one-roomed cottage, agent WÜRZBURG was pacing up and down, deeply worried that the *Abwehr* might not have received his urgent message. Tall and thin with sharp features, he was still wearing his tweed jacket. Ever since he had discovered earlier in the day in Chelmsford that the man the constables were escorting from the police station was an imposter, the German agent had become obsessed by the thought that his hero, Adolf Hitler, would be humiliated beyond all measure if one of his spies killed a Hess look-alike in place of the genuine Deputy *Führer*. The British would splash the disaster on the front page of every newspaper, with humorous banner headlines like "Hitler's Halfwitted Hitman Dumbly Dispatches Double" or "Adolf's Asinine Agent Assassinates Actor." No, the *Abwehr* had to learn of the deception and call off the killers at once.

Suddenly the door of the cottage burst open, and a troop of armed police rushed into the room. Two men grabbed agent WÜRZBURG and cuffed him with his hands behind his back.

"Where's the transceiver?" the inspector barked.

Unable to use his hands, the terrified agent pointed with his head in the direction of the suitcase under the bed. The inspector gestured to a constable who pulled the suitcase out, placed it on the bed and opened it, revealing an SE 85/14 radio.

"Take him to Colchester police station," ordered the inspector, "and get MI5 here right now."

"And what about the farmer's wife?" an elderly sergeant asked.

"You'd better release her," was the embarrassed reply. "And tell Clive Bowen that he's no longer under arrest."

***

"You're going to have to make your mind up quickly," Carlyle said. "Either you're going to totally cooperate with us from this moment on, or we're going to hang you without delay. I need some answers from you right now, not tomorrow or even in an hour's time. If you're not prepared to help us immediately just tell me, and I'll organize your execution on the spot."

"I'm prepared to cooperate to the best of my ability," said the spy in a frightened voice. "But could you remove the handcuffs, please? They're hurting my wrists." His English was fluent, with hardly a trace of an accent.

"Answer a few questions first," Carlyle said, "and then we'll see. Now, what's your name?"

Even though he was terrified out of his wits, the spy hesitated. Abhorrence of betraying the Fatherland started to overcome his dread of summary execution.

"You need to make your mind up this instant, one way or the other," Carlyle insisted. "Tell me your name without the slightest further delay, or we're going to hang you for espionage right now."

Hearing the word *hang* for the second time overwhelmed what little courage the German agent had managed to muster. Blind panic set in, and words started to pour out of his mouth.

"My name is Hermann Leichtal. I'm an *Abwehr* agent. My code name is WÜRZBURG—there's an *umlaut* on the first 'u.' I arrived in England in October 1938. I travelled here on the ferry from the Hook of Holland to Harwich. My papers are forged; they're in the name of Herbert Lampert. My orders were to find an isolated house in The Fens and lay low there until ordered into action by radio."

"Your English is excellent, and you speak it with only a slight accent. Have you lived here before 1938?"

"No. The *Abwehr* language teachers are first rate. My superiors informed them that I would probably be a sleeper agent for some time, and so it was vital for the locals to accept me as someone who has lived in England for many years. A new arrival from a foreign country always arouses suspicion, especially someone with a heavy German accent."

"Where did you live?"

"I rented a house on the outskirts of a tiny village in Norfolk named Brideford Parva."

"What was your occupation there?"

"Nothing. I was given several valuable postage stamps confiscated from Jews in Germany. Any time that my funds ran low I went to a philatelic dealer in London and sold a stamp or two."

"What orders have you received and when did you receive them?"

"Please can you remove the cuffs?" Leichtal was on the point of tears.

Carlyle summoned a policeman, who unlocked the handcuffs with obvious great reluctance.

"Now answer my question, or the cuffs go back on. What did Admiral Canaris tell you to do, and when did he do it?"

At the mention of the head of the *Abwehr*, Leichtal looked even more terrified than before. "I received a message about two weeks ago."

"On what date?" Carlyle asked.

"I have to stand by to receive radio transmissions every Monday night at half past nine, local time."

"And today is Tuesday, May 27th."

"Thank you." Leichtal counted on his fingers. "That means that I received the message on Monday, May 12th."

"And when did you reply to that message?"

"My transmission time is exactly twenty-four hours later. So I replied on Tuesday, May 13th at half past nine."

Both dates and both times are correct, Carlyle said to himself. *This man may be telling the truth to try to save his miserable neck.*

"What did you say in your message?" Carlyle asked.

"Before I left Germany they gave me a book code. They told me that messages they transmitted to me would be in that code, and I was to reply in the same code. But the message they sent to me on May 12th was in Code Haydn. That confused me. To sort the matter out I sent a message back in the book code asking if the order from the *Führer* sent in Code Haydn was genuine."

You stupid fool, Carlyle said to himself. *You were a sleeper agent, instructed to observe total radio silence until activated and to send a message only if a matter of the very highest importance arose. But you revealed yourself when you received a message in the wrong code just because it contained an order from Adolf Hitler himself. And how ironic that we uncovered you because someone in the* Abwehr *forgot to use the book code.*

Aloud he said, "And did they reply to your query?"

"Yes. Six days later Admiral Canaris confirmed that the order was genuine."

"And when did you last receive a message?" Carlyle asked Hermann Leichtal.

"Last night. It was a Monday. It came through promptly at half past nine."

"Tell me what the message said."

"It was sent to all *Abwehr* agents in Britain. I assume that was why it was also encrypted using

Code Haydn instead of the book code. In his message, Admiral Canaris gave us the location for the last five days of a man who looks like Rudolf Hess. He instructed us to find the man and determine if he's Hess. If he isn't, Admiral Canaris ordered us to report that fact to him as soon as possible. But if he really is Hess, then the admiral instructed us follow the order of the *Führer* and either kill Hess ourselves or inform Berlin as to his current location. We were told that, in addition to our weekly transmission time, we could send a message any night at half past nine on our usual wavelength. And we had to listen in at nine every night in case there was a message for us."

"Do you recall where he said Hess had been?"

"Yes, I do. It was a series of police stations and jails. First in Norwich, then Colchester, and finally in three towns in the vicinity of Colchester: Halstead, Thorpe-le-Soken, and Chelmsford."

"And did you reply to the message?"

"Yes, I did."

"When?"

"This evening at half past nine."

"What did you say?" Carlyle asked.

"I acknowledged receipt of the message sent to all agents. I told Admiral Canaris that I drove to Chelmsford early this morning. I saw four policemen closely escorting a man who looked like Hess out of the police station. Then some young ruffian threw a stone at him—the hooligan shouted something like, "This is for my father." The stone must have hurt the man a lot, because he yelled out in pain. But he spoke in the unmistakable accent that characterizes the aristocratic Englishman. In other words, the man is definitely an imposter. There's no possibility that the real Hess could have talked that way."

"And that's what you told Admiral Canaris?"

"Yes. And then I told him that I relocated to Colchester because you've been moving the look-alike from place to place in the vicinity of that town. I wanted to be close by, just in case I received further orders with regard to the double. I looked for a room on a farm from where I could send messages without anyone hearing me tapping my Morse key. I was lucky to find Bowens Farm, where I had my own cottage."

"So you sent the message to Canaris. What then?"

"I was concerned that it might not get through—sometimes there are problems in the ionosphere. So I was waiting until half past ten to retransmit, just in case. But a few minutes before I could do that, the policemen broke into the cottage and arrested me."

"I see. One last question for now: What book is the basis for your code?"

"Robert Southey's *The Life of Horatio, Lord Nelson.* I keep it in full view on a table in the sitting room of my home in Brideford Parva to show that I'm a true-blue patriotic Englishman, but I brought the book along with me so that I could communicate with Berlin. You'll find it in my suitcase next to the radio."

CHAPTER SIXTEEN
Abwehr Headquarters, Berlin
Wednesday, May 28, 1941

"Donndorf," Admiral Canaris said, "last night we received a message from agent WÜRZBURG, the second one since we activated him. He said that he received the message you sent on Monday night to all our agents. You stated that the imposter was in Chelmsford. But how did you know that he was there before PICKFORD reported it yesterday morning?"

"Admiral, what message was that?" Colonel Donndorf asked, looking confused.

"Didn't you send a message to all our agents on Monday night?"

"No, Admiral, I did not."

"And did you know then that the double was in Chelmsford?"

"No, Admiral, I certainly didn't. How could I?"

"Contact our listening station in Hamburg at once. Find out if they heard anything two nights ago."

Donndorf rushed from the room, returning about ten minutes later grim-faced. "Well, Admiral, at least we now know why the British are sending the Hess doubles around the country. They want our agents in Britain to tell us where Hess is. I'm certain that they've set up direction finders all over Britain to locate our radio transmitters. They've laid a clever trap to arrest our agents, utilizing the genuine transmission we sent to them about two weeks ago. I know what the *Führer*'s orders were, but I strongly suggest that you send a message to all our agents in Britain calling off the search for Hess. And we also have to stop SS-Major Kirchgässner."

"Colonel, it's too late. He's already left for England. And as for your insane idea of countermanding *Herr* Hitler's order, do you realize what you're saying? The penalty for even hinting at something like that is an agonizing death for you, your family, and probably most of your friends as well. I didn't hear what you said, and I strongly suggest that you didn't say it."

***

"Worthington, tonight you're sleeping in Mallaig. It's a major fishing port and it's another important ferry terminus. In fact, you'll probably be able to see the harbor from your cell. But don't worry, you're not going anywhere by boat."

"I'm most relieved to hear that, Johnson."

***

"Gentlemen," Air Commodore Pankhurst said triumphantly, "we've captured agent NORFOLK!"

Cries of "Congratulations, sir!" and "Well done, sir!" echoed through the room.

When the hubbub had died down, Major Tupman asked, "What happened, sir?"

"The short answer is that on Monday night he fell for our forged message hook, line, and sinker. The fact that we'd used Code Haydn didn't bother him in the least because our message stated that the *Abwehr* was sending it to all its agents. And he had no way of knowing that PICKFORD didn't tell the *Abwehr* about Chelmsford until Tuesday morning.

"He drove to Chelmsford this morning. Outside the police station he saw our men moving 'Hess' to Basildon. A young man whose father was killed at Dunkirk was passing by and saw Campbell-White. He threw a sharp stone at him, screaming 'This is to revenge my father, you German swine!' or something along those lines. The stone must have pinched a nerve against a bone, because it really hurt Campbell-White. Because of the pain he forgot to use the Germanic English that we'd laboriously taught him and he cried out in his normal accent instead. Agent NORFOLK heard the way he spoke and sent a message to Canaris to tell him that Campbell-White is an imposter. We detected the transmission and caught agent NORFOLK.

"Also, we've managed to decrypt the two messages that agent NORFOLK sent to Berlin. Yes, it's a book code, and we have his copy of the book. Unfortunately, we've discovered that agent OBAN is using a different book code; that's a new problem that we're going to have to solve. But at least we can close the file on agent NORFOLK."

"Air Commodore, would it be possible for you to tell us more about how you caught him?" Major Tupman asked.

"Certainly. MI8 picked up his transmission to the *Abwehr* last night. For two weeks they've been listening fruitlessly to the airwaves, but finally they heard a message in a code similar to the one they picked up a fortnight ago. Only this time, MI8 had direction finders all over the place and the message was lengthy. They soon homed in on a farm outside Colchester. They summoned the police and a company of Royal Engineers who were on a military surveying and cartography course on a nearby farm. The sappers surrounded the farm while four carloads of armed police raided the farmhouse, terrifying the farmer's wife and confusing the farmer, whom they woke from a deep sleep. Then they learned that a foreigner was staying in the guest cottage behind the farmhouse. They rushed over to the cottage and caught agent NORFOLK, transceiver and all. His name is Hermann Leichtal, code name WÜRZBURG. We've taken him to a safe house to interrogate him in depth. As soon as I know any more, I'll let you know."

Everyone was smiling as Pankhurst concluded his report. Then Chulmleigh asked, "Does this mean that we can release Campbell-White now and send him off to Australia?"

"By no means," said Pankhurst sharply. "We can't allow him to tell his story until we no longer need Worthington to play his role. But more importantly, we now have to use Campbell-White as bait to catch agent BROCKEN. And don't try to tell me that that isn't in Campbell-White's contract. We're at war, total war."

"Do we tell him that we've got agent NORFOLK?" Squadron Leader Harkness asked.

"Definitely not," the Air Commodore said. "When we first learned about agent BROCKEN, we decided not to tell Campbell-White because we didn't want to unnerve him. At that time, if someone came after him, it might be agent NORFOLK just wanting to find out if he was the real Hess, or it could be agent BROCKEN determined to kill him. Now that agent NORFOLK is out of the picture, there's a 100 percent chance that an *Abwehr* agent who approaches Campbell-White is a trained assassin. If Campbell-White were to discover that fact, he may refuse to cooperate any further or even try to escape. No, gentlemen, Campbell-White has to stay in his state of blissful ignorance until we've captured BROCKEN, too.

***

That evening Johnson was feeling lonely. He walked from Mallaig police station along Station Road and from there to Highland Street. He stuck his head into the first pub he saw. At first glance, the men and women in the Beehive Inn did not seem to be too sociable, so he continued up the hill. The Thistle looked rather plain and ordinary from the outside, but when Johnson walked in, a number of the locals seated at round tables greeted him in a friendly manner. Johnson noticed that he was the youngest man in the room by many years, as a consequence of conscription he thought, but there were two tables of women in their thirties.

He walked up to the old wooden counter and said to the heavily bearded barman, "A wee dram of Laphroaig, please."

"I'm glad ye didna ask me for a 'whisky' or a 'glass of Scotch' or suchlike," the gray-haired barman said with a broad smile. He walked slowly to where the bottles of single malts stood on the glass shelves at the back of the bar; his left hand shook slightly as he filled the jigger to the rim and then poured the measured tot of whisky into a glass. Johnson judged that the barman was about sixty-five years old.

Johnson paid for his drink, raised his glass to the barman and said, "*slàinte mhath* (good health)." He deliberately spoke loudly enough to be heard by some of the men and women seated at the tables and was gratified to hear a chorus of *do dheagh shlàinte* (your good health) coming from behind him.

He turned round to acknowledge their response. As he did so, he saw a handsome woman of about twenty-five walk into the room. She was tall and muscular, with shoulder-length, honey-blonde hair. She wore a white Aran honeycomb-pattern sweater and a long plaid kilt skirt; Johnson did not recognize the tartan.

Every person in the bar stood as she walked confidently from the door to the counter. The barman greeted her politely. Then he turned, picked up the right-most bottle on the bottom shelf and poured a generous quantity of whisky straight from the bottle into a glass. She raised her drink, turned to the company and said, "*Air ur slàinte* (To your health)." Everyone in the room chorused in unison "*Slàinte agad-sa* (To your health as well)." Then they resumed their seats.

Johnson moved toward her. "Good evening. My name's Johnson," he said with a broad smile.

"I'm Lady Alison," she said. She spoke with an upper-class English accent; there was no trace of a Scottish burr.

The helpful barman added, "The Right Honorable Countess of Mallaig is also The MacRobson of MacRobson."

"Ah, a countess *and* the Chief of Clan MacRobson. How do you do?" Johnson said.

"Good evening, Mr. Johnson. Welcome to Mallaig."

"Thank you, Lady Alison. You live in a beautiful village."

"Yes, indeed. The arrival of the railway at the turn of the century could have ruined the place, but the local council ensured that Mallaig retained its roots as a fishing village. We owe much to their foresight."

"Yes, we certainly do."

They sipped their whiskies in silence. Then she asked, "Mr. Johnson, I was going to ask you what brings you to our village, but I understand that one ought not to ask such a question these days."

"Quite right, Lady Alison, one probably shouldn't. In view of the fact that the powers that be have all but banned travel for pleasure, a visit to Mallaig might well be on government business."

The conversation flagged again. Then Johnson saw that her glass was empty. "May I buy you a drink?" he asked.

"Thank you, but I drink only Lochervan, and it's not for sale here. I'm afraid that the bottle that Fergus MacRobson is kind enough to keep over there is for my personal consumption only. But I do have a bottle of the eighteen-year old in my home, just around the corner. There's something I'd like to discuss with you. It's a confidential matter—this isn't the place. And in any event, it's nearly ten o'clock, and at twenty past ten sharp Fergus will enforce the wartime licensing hours for this district and toss us all out, incredibly politely, into the street."

The barman smiled as broadly as before.

"Lady Alison, I'd be delighted to accept your kind invitation," Johnson said.

"Excellent! Goodnight Fergus, I'll see you tomorrow night. Come with me, Mr. Johnson."

Everyone respectfully stood again as Lady Alison walked to the door, which Johnson held open for her. She led the way to a cottage two streets away.

"Come in, Mr. Johnson."

He looked around. The cottage was exceedingly plainly furnished, with none of the trappings that he associated with a member of the aristocracy or the chief of a Scottish clan.

"Did you expect me to live in a castle?" she asked archly. "Well, in peacetime I do. I converted Castle Robson into a convalescent home for the duration of the war and moved into this cottage. Take a seat on that sofa—it's the only comfortable piece of furniture in the room. Let me get you a drink."

She went to the kitchen and came back with two glasses of eighteen-year old Lochervan, a single-malt whisky that was distilled only a few miles from Johnson's home. Seating herself next to him on the two-seater couch, she handed him his drink. He raised the glass and gave the same toast as before. From his perfect Gaelic accent, Lady Alison correctly deduced that Johnson was a Scotsman.

"I gather that you come from these parts?"

"Yes."

"May I ask from where?"

Before joining MI5 as an intelligence officer, he would have answered "Duntress Castle, Renfrewshire." Furthermore, as the eldest son of a Scottish earl, he would have introduced himself to her in The Thistle as Hamish, Master of Duntress. But for the past two years he had put his ancestry behind him. He was now in every respect an MI5 intelligence officer named Johnson. Accordingly, he fended off her question by replying, "Not too far from here. There are Johnsons from all over Scotland."

"Mr. Johnson, may I speak frankly?"

"Of course, Lady Alison. That goes without saying."

"You were in Fort William last night. The previous night you stayed in Oban. That was your second visit there; the first was six days ago. For three days you were on the Isle of Mull; you stayed in Craignure, Bunessan, and Tobermory. You're part of a travelling circus consisting of four policemen who probably aren't policemen, seven men who continuously scrutinize all of us the way a cat watches a mouse, plus the star of the circus, a man who may or may not be Rudolf Hess. And, yes, we can easily see through your silly disguises. That tall, thin plainclothes man with the huge handlebar moustache—his name is Canavan, I think. He can color his hair to his heart's content and wear as many different pairs of spectacles with plain glass as he likes, and he can stick those silly false beards onto his chin, but he just looks like the same tall, thin man with a huge handlebar moustache trying to look like someone else.

"Those of us who live in this part of Scotland do nothing but talk about you and your men. The members of your team can't move an inch without someone noticing them and telling the rest of us all the details, especially their latest disguises. We've decided that you're all from MI5, but we can't possibly imagine what you're trying to achieve."

"Lady Alison, you're quite right. We are indeed a travelling circus. And what we're trying to achieve is what all circus entertainers do: We're doing our level best to amuse the crowd. From what you've just said, I think we're succeeding."

Johnson stood. "Thank you for the whisky and for your hospitality, but I think I need to return to my fellow clowns. Goodnight, Lady Alison."

It was only when he had almost reached the single men's quarters at the police station where he was spending the night that Johnson suddenly realized what Lady Alison had said.

***

The U-boat rose to periscope height. "*Herr* Blau," Lieutenant Hörtel said, "take a look through the sighting periscope. We're off the coast of Essex. That light you see is in Clacton-on-Sea. There's supposed to be a blackout, but someone has been careless tonight with the heavy curtains."

"Most helpful for us," SS-Major Kirchgässner remarked.

As the U-boat started to submerge again, Kirchgässner handed a chart to Hörtel. "Lieutenant, our destination is only about five or six miles away. Look at this chart. Do you see this large tidal island just off the coast?"

"Yes, *Herr* Blau."

"It's separated from the mainland by the narrow causeway over here. At low tide you can just wade across; at high tide you have to use this bridge. That's Clemford Island. It's about five miles from east to west, and three miles north to south. Here's the village of East Clemford, and there's West Clemford. Between them lies a nature reserve—do you see it there near the center of the island? It consists of a low-lying marsh with ditches, ponds, and sand dunes. Over here in the middle of the southern shoreline is a wide sandy beach; it fronts the nature reserve. Can you position your boat offshore from the beach? As you can see from the chart, the water is quite deep there."

"I daren't go much faster than two or at most three knots, *Herr* Blau. There are underwater mines that aren't marked on your chart, and the British have laid submarine nets in places. And destroyers continually patrol British coastal waters."

"Of course. Take every precaution, Lieutenant."

Three hours later, Lieutenant Hörtel cautiously raised his attack periscope.

"*Herr* Blau," the Lieutenant said, "I think I've found your beach."

"I know it's some hours before sunrise, Lieutenant, but the moonlight may be adequate for you to see a war memorial made of white marble in the center of the beach, roughly where it adjoins the dunes of the nature reserve. Can you see it?"

"It looks like an obelisk with a cross on the top."

"That certainly sounds like it, but let me take a look." Helmut Kirchgässner peered through the eyepiece. "Yes, that's it. As you must have noticed, they've covered the shoreline with the usual anti-invasion barriers that they laid on all the beaches on the south and east coasts of England last summer. There seem to be two lines of anti-tank cubes here.

In front of them, along the low water mark, they've erected a row of anti-boat and anti-tank tubular steel obstacles, what the British call 'Admiralty scaffolding.' And I can see barbed wire. There are coils of concertina wire everywhere. They're no longer terrified that we're about to send an invasion force of thousands of troop barges across the Channel onto their beaches, so hopefully they've made a gap in the coils of wire so that the English can let their dogs play in the ocean. Yes, I can see a gap now; it's just to the right of the obelisk. I'll be able to get to the nature reserve without having to use my wire cutters."

"Aren't you worried about land mines, *Herr* Blau? After the fall of France, the British didn't have enough troops to defend all their beaches, so they laid mines everywhere."

"If there's a gap for the locals to walk their dogs, there won't be any land mines. Lieutenant, once you're satisfied that there are no hostile forces in the vicinity, surface and get me to the beach. Make a careful note of the location. I'll send a radio signal to your base at Bremerhaven on the usual wavelength when I'm ready to return. Be here at two in the morning on the following three nights. I'll be standing on the platform next to the obelisk and when I see you surface I'll signal with my flashlight: short–short–long–short repeated twice. Is that clear?"

"Perfectly clear, *Herr* Blau."

Lieutenant Hörtel methodically scanned the shore for some minutes. "*Herr* Blau, the beach seems to be deserted. I looked for Home Guard patrols, but unless they're hiding in wait behind those large reinforced concrete anti-tank cubes, there's no one out there, which is not surprising in the middle of the night with no imminent threat of invasion. I'm bringing the boat to the surface. Good luck!"

Three crewmembers clambered into an inflatable dinghy and helped SS-Major Kirchgässner in. Members of the U-boat deck crew handed him his large knapsack. The four men started to paddle toward the sandy beach. As the dinghy neared the water's edge, they steered carefully toward the gap in the barbed wire. The SS-major climbed out of the dinghy onto the beach. He turned back and waved cheerfully to the others. Then, hoisting his knapsack onto his back, he slipped through the opening and strode up the beach to the dunes. Nearing the war memorial he turned left and walked along the edge of the nature reserve in the direction of West Clemford.

His immediate need was to find a safe hideout from which he could operate. It had to be sufficiently deserted for him to be able to operate his radio without detection; a landlady hearing him tapping away at his Morse key would immediately call the police. But there was a second reason why he needed isolation: Kirchgässner had to be able to change into women's clothing without anyone noticing. That precluded hotels, boarding houses, furnished rooms and the like. He needed to be the sole occupant of a house situated far from other dwellings.

The *Abwehr* had provided him with two sets of forged papers, one for each of his two personae. The documents included ration books, but in order to use them to purchase food he first had to register with the shops of his choice; the Ministry of Food supplied shopkeepers with only enough food for their registered customers. To avoid any possible problems in that regard, he had brought a three-day supply of foodstuffs with him; food would therefore not be an issue initially. But there had to be a red telephone box within a reasonable distance of his accommodation, preferably situated in an area with relatively few passersby, so that he could call his assistant and find out where his target was currently to be found.

After about half a mile the beach came to an end, and Kirchgässner found himself on a narrow road. In June 1940, a German invasion of England appeared to be inevitable. In the hope of confusing the enemy, the British removed all street signs near the coast. But Kirchgässner had no need to consult one of his maps to find out where he was—he knew that this was Estuary Drive, a dead-end street on the perimeter of West Clemford. On his left lay a low grass- and reed-covered bluff overlooking the North Sea. To his right was a row of six holiday cottages; the marshy nature reserve continued behind the dwellings. While Helmut was at Cambridge, a fellow law student of his named Harvey Pettigrew had invited Helmut and four other Caius College students to spend a weekend at the cottage owned by his uncle. Harvey had mentioned to Helmut that wealthy friends of his uncle owned the other cottages, but that none of them were usually used more than one or two weeks a year. In particular, Harvey had permission to use his uncle's cottage whenever he liked. *What with the war,* Kirchgässner said to himself, *there's no way that anyone is taking a seaside holiday in West Clemford at this time; all of the cottages have to be empty.*

Kirchgässner looked around carefully. Not surprisingly, he was alone in the dim moonlight. The street was deserted and the cottages seemed neglected; it appeared that no one had stayed in any of them for a long while. The gardens in front of the cottages were unkempt, with dead plants in the flowerbeds and long grass everywhere.

The SS-major could have chosen any of the six, but for old times' sake he decided to establish his hideout at Harvey's uncle's house, Number One, at the end of the street closest to the center of the village. It had been a wonderful weekend, the most enjoyable part of his year in England. Soon after they arrived in West Clemford they all went around the corner to The Mitre, a local pub, for a beer. There they met several attractive young women who agreed to accompany them back to the cottage. He could not remember all the finer details—at one stage he had overindulged in Harvey's uncle's stock of Napoleon brandy—but he would never forget the glorious time that he had had there.

As he reached Number One, Kirchgässner realized that something was wrong. The wooden gates from the street leading up the short gravel driveway to the garage were open. The garage doors were open, too, and a sports car was parked in the garage. It looked to him like an MG TB roadster. The gate leading to the front door was also wide open. No lights were glowing dimly at the edges of the blackout curtains in the front room, but this was not surprising in the middle of the night.

Kirchgässner took every precaution. He walked through the garage gates, kept to his left and skirted the house. When he reached the paved back yard, he slowly tried the handle of the kitchen door. It was locked. He reached into a pocket, took out a small metal tool and inserted it into the lock. Within seconds there was an almost inaudible click, followed by a soft creak as he opened the door as quietly as possible. The kitchen displayed evidence of recent use—a half-empty bottle of whisky graced the large wooden table in the center of the room, and two glasses lay on their sides in the sink. Then he heard a noise.

Kirchgässner's first instinct was to leave Number One immediately and choose a different cottage for his base. But he quickly realized that it would be extremely risky to stay in any of the other five homes if there were people living in this cottage. They might see him as he walked past, and that would jeopardize his mission. He carefully took off his knapsack and laid it on the kitchen floor. He drew his CZ 27 pistol, fitted the silencer, and crept as quietly as he was able into the passage. There he heard another noise, similar to the first. It seemed to be coming from the master bedroom. The door was shut. With his left hand he turned the handle as soundlessly as he could, then slowly opened the door, using the jamb to shield as much of his body as possible. He peered into the dark room. The curtains were open. Even though the moon was about to set, there was enough light for him to see a couple making love. Before they could react, Kirchgässner fired his handgun twice. The silenced pistol emitted two dull pops. The lovers twitched, then lay still. Kirchgässner turned the naked bodies over. The man was Harvey Pettigrew; Helmut had never seen the woman before.

He closed the blackout curtains and turned on the light. The crumpled pile of clothing on one side of the bed turned out to be the hurriedly torn off uniform of a flight lieutenant in the Royal Air Force. The clothing on the other side revealed that his second victim had been a flight officer, the equivalent rank in the Women's Auxiliary Air Force. He knew that officers of their rank were often company commanders, so the Air Force might come looking for them sooner rather than later. How many other women had Harvey brought to the cottage? Would one of them suggest to the Royal Air Force Police that Harvey might be absent without leave in his love nest in West Clemford?

Once again, his first instinct was to leave the area right away. However, he had to have a secure hideout for the assassination. The six cottages were ideal for his purpose, but it would not be safe to stay in Number One. Helmut Kirchgässner had stayed alive by thinking of every conceivable risk and mitigating as many of them as possible.

He carefully wiped down the surfaces he had touched, hoisted his knapsack, took the two glasses and the whisky bottle, and left the way he had come. He walked along Estuary Drive until he came to the last cottage, Number Six. As before, he entered via the locked kitchen door. This time the cottage showed no sign of having been entered for years. Satisfied, Kirchgässner left his knapsack in the kitchen and returned to Number One. He searched Harvey's clothes for the keys to the MG roadster. He was about to go to the car when he had an idea. He picked up all the clothes strewn around the bed and took them to the car. If he wore the uniform of an Air Force officer, he reasoned, it might make it easier for him to get close to Hess. He laid the clothes on the passenger seat of the red two-seater.

Then he thought again. The CZ 27 fires a 7.65 mm Browning cartridge. Suppose a pathologist extracted the bullets from the hearts of the two people he had just killed—wouldn't the doctor immediately conclude that they had been fired from a German pistol? Were there any British handguns that used the 7.65 mm Browning? Maybe there were, but offhand he could not think of one. And why had he not thought of that before coming to Britain armed with a CZ 27?

There was no question that he had to move the bodies to prevent anyone finding the bullets. But where? What about the other cottages?

SS-Major Kirchgässner unlocked the kitchen door of Number Four. Returning to Number One he took off his clothes to ensure that they would not be stained with blood. He laboriously carried the naked body of Harvey Pettigrew to Number Four, where he dumped the corpse onto the bed in the master bedroom. Then he did the same with the dead woman. Returning to Number One, he wiped his body down with a damp bath towel and dressed again. He stripped the bloodstained bedding off the bed and turned over the mattress to hide the bloodstains. Next, he took the sheets, blankets and pillows to Number Four and dumped them on the floor of the bedroom there next to the two corpses, together with the towel that he had used.

Then he locked the back door of Number Four. Kirchgässner moved the MG TB Roadster to the garage at Number Six, walked back to Number One and closed the garage door and both gates. A final inspection of the premises reassured him that, to all but a trained investigator, there was no sign that anyone had been in the cottage for a good while.

Walking back to Number Six, Kirchgässner remembered that Harvey Pettigrew had been an impecunious student, whereas he now owned a bright red MG sports car. Where did the money come from? Perhaps his rich uncle had died, leaving him the cottage and pots of money. If Harvey had given the cottage as his home address to the Royal Air Force, a search for the missing officer might include Number One. Kirchgässner realized that, from now on, he had to take the greatest care while walking in Estuary Drive. Also, he should drive the car as little as possible. Its color made it conspicuous, and MG had made only a few of that particular model before war broke out. At least he had access to essentially an unlimited supply of gasoline—the forged books of petrol coupons would see to that.

He closed the garage and both gates at Number Six and went to bed in the second bedroom, willing himself to wake two hours later at six o'clock. He woke precisely on time. He shaved meticulously, then went to work in front of the mirror with his cosmetics and then the wig. Finally he put on the tailored linen blouse, woolen cardigan, tweed skirt, and flat shoes that he had brought with him in his knapsack, and Kirchgässner was ready. He remembered seeing a telephone booth in the vicinity of the pub that he had gone to at the start of his prewar visit to West Clemford with Pettigrew and his other friends. He consulted the relevant map to refresh his memory, then walked the length of Estuary Drive, turned right into Gladstone Road and left into Omdurman Avenue. Halfway along he saw the red telephone box. The mature plane trees that lined the street on both sides largely sheltered it from view.

He asked the exchange to put him through to the number that Colonel Donndorf had passed onto him before he'd left Berlin. The call went through quickly. Depositing the requested coins, he gave the sign, "Is your mother still suffering from pneumonia?"

Immediately he heard the countersign, "Only in her lower left lung today."

"Where is he?"

"Can you phone me back in two hours?" Carlyle said.

He heard BROCKEN terminate the call before it could be traced, not realizing that the operator in West Clemford might remember putting the call through to Colchester.

CHAPTER SEVENTEEN
MI5 Headquarters, London
Thursday, May 29, 1941

"Gentlemen," the air commodore said, opening his quarter past nine meeting, "notwithstanding the best efforts of our armed forces, agent BROCKEN has arrived in East Anglia. He phoned Carlyle about two hours ago wanting to know where Hess is. Unfortunately, BROCKEN hung up before we could trace the call."

"And what did Carlyle reply?" Chulmleigh asked. "Did he tell BROCKEN that Hess spent the night in the cells at Maldon police station?"

"No, that would have made BROCKEN extremely suspicious. Up to now, PICKFORD has sent his messages to Canaris at around nine every morning. If Carlyle had given the information two hours earlier than usual, BROCKEN might have smelled a trap.

"Carlyle was careful to ask BROCKEN if he could call back in two hours. That should be about now. I've told my staff to interrupt this meeting and tell me if Carlyle phones in with a report. We've caught

Hermann Leichtal, but we still have an *Abwehr* agent in play in Essex: BROCKEN.

"And now some good news," he continued. "Operation OTTAWA may have had some success in Scotland. Johnson phoned me last night with some interesting information. Ah, that knock on the door must be Captain Nicholas. Come in, come in. Did Carlyle report?"

"Yes, sir, he did. I've written down the message."

The captain handed a sheet of paper to Air Commodore Pankhurst who read it, smiled and then announced to his team, "BROCKEN phoned again, and Carlyle told him that Hess is in Maldon police station. Gentlemen, the game's afoot! Nicholas, telephone Maldon, tell them to delay Hess's departure for Witham until eleven o'clock. Let's give BROCKEN plenty of time to get there."

As Captain Nicholas left the conference room, the Air Commodore continued where he had left off. "Last night, Johnson met the Countess of Mallaig in The Thistle, a pub in Mallaig. There's no Earl of Mallaig, by the way; Lady Alison inherited the earldom when her father died, together with the chiefship of Clan MacRobson. It seems that both can be passed down the female line. It's not all that common, but the crown charters of some peerages have that provision, and the clans make their own rules.

"At closing time she invited him to her war-time home, a cottage in Mallaig, for some Lochervan whisky. There she referred to our Operation OTTAWA team in Scotland as a 'travelling circus.' She correctly enumerated the number of policemen and watchers, declared that they were all from MI5, and accurately reeled off the locations where Hess had slept for the previous six days.

"But then she slipped up—maybe. She referred to Worthington as 'a man who may or may not be Rudolf Hess.' Why would she say such a thing unless she wanted to find out from Johnson if the man he's escorting around Scotland really is Hess? Which possibly means that either she's agent OBAN or she's associated with agent OBAN."

Captain Marks raised his hand.

"I know what you're going to ask me, Marks. You want to know if the meeting in the pub was purely fortuitous. Right?"

Captain Marks grinned sheepishly. "Right, sir. You know me only too well."

"Well, if it makes you feel any better, that was my question to Johnson, too. But he doesn't know the answer. He says that there are only three pubs in the village; perhaps Lady Alison tried them all in turn until she located him. Or maybe she had no idea that Johnson decided to spend an hour relaxing in a friendly pub and she dropped into The Thistle the way she does almost every night. Apparently she keeps her own bottle of whisky there."

The next question came from Lieutenant Wallstead. "Sir, is the countess of German extraction?"

"As of now," Pankhurst said, "we know very little at all about her. But Johnson says that she speaks the King's English better than the King does.

There's no question that she was born and bred here. Maybe she spent some time in Nazi Germany—that we'll have to find out."

Now it was Major Tupman's turn. "Sir, I have a question concerning the radio message we sent to agent OBAN. Was the message similar to the one we sent to agent NORFOLK? In other words, did it state the places where Worthington had been for the previous six days?"

"Yes, that was what we agreed."

"And Lady Alison rattled off those same six locations in her question to Johnson?"

"Yes, I believe that she did."

"Sir, I understand that the message was sent on Tuesday night at a quarter past eleven, too late for her to meet with Johnson. But the very next evening, Lady Alison invited Johnson home for a whisky and asked her question about Hess. I find all that more than a little suspicious."

"Suspicion doesn't constitute proof, Tupman. But I have to agree that it's a strange coincidence."

Now Squadron Leader Harkness had a question. "Sir, this is unprecedented. We've arrested a number of *Abwehr* spies, that is, Germans who have been trained and equipped by the *Abwehr* and sent here. And we've also arrested hundreds of British subjects who are Nazi sympathizers, such as supporters of the British National Socialist Party and all too many members of the aristocracy. They've aided and abetted the enemy, but most of them have never been to Germany, and none of them have had transceivers that the *Abwehr* has supplied to them.

What Johnson seems to be alleging is that an Englishwoman, a peer of the realm or more correctly, a peeress, is an *Abwehr* agent. And—"

"Let me interrupt you there, Harkness. I don't think it's correct that Johnson has gone quite that far. At least not yet. Anything else?"

Lieutenant Commander Chulmleigh raised his hand. "Sir, do we have enough evidence to search Lady Alison's cottage? If she's agent OBAN, then she must have a transceiver hidden somewhere."

"Chulmleigh, we have no evidence at all. All we have to date is a remark she made to Johnson regarding the identity of a man whom we've moved around the West Coast region of Scotland. But I can see where you're going with this.

"Gentlemen, I think we need to investigate the Countess of Mallaig. I'm sending a man to Mallaig, and I'd like Harkness to find out everything about her that he can from here in London.

***

Earlier that morning it had taken SS-Major Kirchgässner about five minutes to walk from Number Six to the telephone box in Omdurman Avenue for his seven o'clock phone call to Carlyle, five minutes that might make the difference between making contact with Hess or missing him as he left his current place of imprisonment. Accordingly, at two minutes to nine he drove the sports car to Omdurman Avenue. He parked near the red booth and at exactly nine o'clock asked the operator to put him through to Colchester.

He gave the sign, received the countersign and asked, "Where is he?"

"Maldon police station."

Kirchgässner immediately terminated the call and rushed to the red sports car. He knew that Maldon was less than twenty miles away, and that even if he scrupulously observed the speed limit in built-up areas, he could easily arrive there before ten o'clock, the time that they had always moved Hess on to the next location. He took out the map he had placed in the glove box, unfolded it, checked the route and drove off in the direction of Maldon.

Just before he reached the village of Tolleshunt D'Arcy, he encountered a barrier that Home Guard soldiers had erected across the road. The previous night, a Royal Air Force Spitfire fighter plane had badly damaged a Junkers Ju 88 bomber on its way back to its base in occupied France after a raid on the oil depot at Saltend, just outside Hull. The pilot of the Junkers had crashed while attempting an emergency landing on a straight portion of the roadway and there was no way Kirchgässner could drive his car through the wreckage. It was obvious to him that, even if a team of road workers arrived right away, it would be some hours before the road could be cleared, and he started to make a U-turn. Not realizing that what he thought was the firm verge of the road was actually part of a salt marsh, he reversed a little too far, and the rear wheels of the car stuck in the mire. He tried to use the powerful engine of the MG TB to propel the rear-wheel-drive car out of the morass but he pressed down too hard on the accelerator. The wheels spun and sunk deeper into the marsh and he had to walk to a nearby farm to get help. Artfully playing the role of a helpless female, he was able to persuade the farmer to use some of the precious rationed fuel in his tractor to pull the red MG TB back onto the road. As the farmer fastened a rope from the back of his tractor to the front axle of the car, Kirchgässner heard him muttered under his breath, "Women! They shouldn't be allowed to drive. And they certainly shouldn't be allowed to drive red sports cars."

SS-Major Kirchgässner was careful not to let even the merest trace of a smile cross his face. Nor did he grimace when he glanced at his watch and realized that there was now no way he could possibly reach Maldon by ten.

***

"The Headmistress will see you now," said the School Secretary, a large woman of uncertain age, with a mop of unruly hair piled on top of her head and held in place with a variety of metal clips.

"Thank you," said Squadron Leader Harkness as she ushered him into the headmistress's study.

A small birdlike woman rose from behind the desk to greet him. Miss Raynor, who had built Evesdon College into one of Britain's leading schools for girls, was widely known and respected for her views on education.

"How can I help you, Detective Inspector Clarke?" she asked politely.

"Thank you for seeing me this afternoon on such short notice, Miss Raynor. One of your former pupils is being considered for a position that requires a security clearance, and I was hoping that you wouldn't mind answering a few questions about her. Here's my letter of authorization from the Home Secretary."

"Thank you, Detective Inspector. I hope it's not one of his daughters that you've come to ask me about! No, I see it's Lady Alison, now the Countess of Mallaig. Well, I'm delighted that she wants to work for our side again."

"I'm not sure I quite understand you, Miss Raynor. Did she work against us?"

"After the accident, I mean."

"What accident? I'm afraid that I know almost nothing about Lady Alison. You're the first person I'm interviewing about her."

"Let me start at the beginning, then. Lady Alison is the daughter of the late Earl of Mallaig. She came here in 1929, I believe, and left in 1935. She's blessed with brains, poise, maturity, leadership skills, and great sporting ability—we were all hoping that she'd be chosen to be a member of the British equestrian team for the 1936 Olympic Games in Berlin, but unfortunately she wasn't selected. Not surprisingly, when she reached the Sixth Form I made her Deputy Head Girl. She did not disappoint me.

"In 1935 she went up to Oxford to read economics. All five women's colleges would have accepted her, of course. She chose St. Anne's; I'm not quite sure why. During the summer after her first year she went to Berlin for the Olympic Games to cheer our equestrians on. Unfortunately, all we managed to win was the bronze medal for team eventing—that's dressage, cross-country, and show jumping.

"Alison had two older brothers whom she adored: Callum and Giles. In early August, while Lady Alison was at the Games, her brothers went to a ball at Murchison—that's the Duke of Salisbury's country house. At about two in the morning they left the dance in Callum's car; they were staying at the home of a friend of their sister's, Petronella Carbondale. The facts are a little sketchy, but it seems that as they reached the Army Training Estate on Salisbury Plain en route to the Carbondales' house they saw a sports car with four attractive young ladies turn into the military training area. Ordinarily, that particular gate is not open to the public, but in view of the impending arrival of the young women, certain young officers had prevailed on the guards on duty that night to leave the gate open and discreetly disappear for a short time. Remember, this was in 1936, and we were by no means as security conscious as we are now.

"The brothers decided to follow the sports car. A thick hedge prevented their seeing the ladies' car turn sharply to the right after passing through the gate, so Callum drove into the training area and continued straight on. He ignored the notices forbidding entry and, unfortunately, the many signs warning about unexploded shells and mortar bombs.

"As I'm sure you know, the Royal School of Artillery uses the Army Training Estate for live firing. I believe that the site is also used for weapons testing. So any reasonable person would know that one should never ignore any signs in the Estate that warn of unexploded ammunition. Sadly, it appears that the two young men were somewhat under the influence of alcohol, and they drove on. Eventually they realized that they were lost, so Callum turned onto a side road. It seems that, in his haste to find the young women, he sped up. The car swerved from side to side, veered off the road and hit an unexploded land mine.

"Alison was devastated. She worshipped her older brothers, especially Giles, and their deaths affected her badly. She went into what I suppose was a state of shock of some kind; perhaps 'nervous breakdown' would be a better description. Her mother, Lady Felicia, had to fly to Berlin to bring her home for the funeral. Alison just sat in a chair in Castle Robson, day after day, not moving, never speaking a word; they virtually had to force-feed her. Various eminent physicians and psychiatrists came to Mallaig to try to improve her condition, but without success.

"Then one day, about four months after the tragedy, she suddenly snapped out of it. She announced that the government was responsible for what had happened, and that she would take her revenge. Clearly her mind had become unbalanced.

"On the death of her brothers she became the heir apparent to the earldom of Mallaig. It certainly would've been prudent for her to take the opportunity to learn as much as possible about the management of the huge estate she would eventually inherit. Instead, she left home, moved to London and joined the British National Socialist Party, the greyshirts. She wore the BNSP uniform at all times; she even carried an autographed photograph of Adolf Hitler in her blouse pocket. She had not yet inherited the estate, but what little money she had she donated to the cause. She moved in with Forbes Penthwick's sister; Forbes was the founder of the BNSP and the unchallenged party leader. Alison even stood for Parliament as a BNSP candidate in a by-election; she received so few votes that she lost her deposit.

"Then Alison traveled to Germany and was photographed with Hitler at Berchtesgaden; the picture appeared in *The Times*. Soon afterwards something happened in Germany, I have no idea what, but there were plenty of wild rumors, none of them credible in my opinion. The upshot was that she had another nervous breakdown, and her mother had to come to Berlin a second time to take her home. That was in late 1938, if I remember correctly.

"Just after the war started her father died, and Lady Alison inherited the earldom. In her condition, she was unable to run the estate; her mother, the dowager countess, took over. And that's all I know. I try to keep in touch with my girls and their families, but the war makes it hard. I hope I've been of some use to you, Detective Inspector."

"Yes, indeed, Miss Raynor. I'm most appreciative of your time, and for the detailed information you've provided, all of which will be treated in the strictest confidence, of course."

She nodded. Then Miss Raynor said, with a broad smile on her face, "Would you please give my warmest regards to your sister, Detective Inspector?"

"My sister?"

"Yes. Annabel Harkness is your sister, is she not? As I recall, you came here for Speech Day in 1937 when we presented her with the Prize for Acting. And kindly tell her from me that I think she's a much better actor than you are, 'Detective Inspector Clarke.'"

With a twinkle in her eye, she escorted him to the door. As she opened it, she asked him, "What's Annabel doing, if it's not secret?"

"She's a flight officer in the WAAF, the Women's Auxiliary Air Force."

"You probably don't know where she's posted, and if you do you're not allowed to tell me, but my guess is that, with her brains, they've posted her to that special unit for the best and the brightest just outside West Clemford."

***

"Doctor Finlayson, I wonder if you might ask you a few questions about Alison, Countess of Mallaig. She's being considered for a confidential role, and I'm involved in obtaining her security clearance."

"Captain Rees, I'm sure you realize that doctors are not permitted to give any information about their patients."

"Doctor, I'm not asking you about medical matters. Anything like that is strictly between you and her."

"What do you want to know, then?"

"I gather that you've known the Countess of Mallaig for many years."

"Yes, that I can tell you. I set up my practice here in Mallaig about three or four years before she was born. And that means that I've known her all her life."

"And have you been her medical practitioner all that time?"

"As I'm sure you've found out, I'm a general practitioner, and the only GP here in Mallaig. As a result, Lady Alison, like almost everyone else in the village and the surrounding district, consults me in the first instance."

"I understand. Now, without crossing the line into medical territory, how would you describe Lady Alison?"

"Describe her? You mean physically?"

"No, that's not what I mean. As I stated, she's being considered for a position that requires a security clearance. What can you tell me about her that would be relevant? For example, would she keep a secret?"

"If she wants to, she'll be silent as the grave. But if she's ordered to keep something secret, that's a different kettle of fish. Since the accident that killed her brothers, the Countess of Mallaig has changed; she does only what she wants. She takes orders from no one, unless she chooses to do so."

"Does she ever choose to take orders?"

"Yes. Sometimes. Did you know that she was a member of the British National Socialist Party? That scoundrel Forbes Penthwick founded the party; I gather he's in jail or perhaps an internment camp, together with the rest of his gang of Nazi supporters. Well, Alison worshipped Forbes, and I used that word correctly. Everything he said or wrote was holy writ for her, to such an extent that she ended up in Germany with his hero, Adolf Hitler. That's when things started to fall apart again for her."

"Do you know what happened to her in Germany?"

"She's never told me directly, but in the course of my treating her she's occasionally let slip certain remarks. I've come to a specific conclusion, but I regret that I cannot share it with you."

"Because it's based on what she's said to you in your capacity as her doctor?"

"Precisely, Captain Rees."

"Well, can you tell me this? Let's suppose that you've correctly deduced what happened to her in Germany. In your opinion, would that disqualify her from being given a security clearance?"

"You put me in an extremely difficult situation. Let me try and think of a way of explaining the situation to you without breaking medical confidentiality. In view of the fact that you're considering giving Lady Alison some sort of security clearance, I think you need to know that nothing actually happened to her in Germany."

"Then why did she have a major nervous breakdown?"

"Perhaps I can explain it this way. The accident that killed her two brothers brought about her first nervous breakdown. But then, too, no one did anything to her. An event took place, something terrible, that affected her deeply, but she was just an innocent bystander, if you will.

"I can see I'm not getting through to you. Let me try again. Sometimes awful things happen and we say to ourselves, if only I hadn't done this or if I had done that, everything would have been fine. In contrast, in both cases, Lady Alison was in no way an instigator or a participant of any kind. And although both events affected her greatly, it would be wrong to label her a victim. What happened on Salisbury Plain wasn't aimed at her, nor was the incident in Germany. Yes, the two incidents affected her greatly, but in both instances she was simply a passive observer."

"I think I understand what you're getting at. For example, she might have been an accidental witness to an inhuman Nazi atrocity of some kind. Is that the sort of thing you mean?"

Doctor Finlay looked Captain Rees straight in the eye but said nothing.

Captain Rees continued. "One final question, doctor, if I may. As a layman, it seems to me that the Countess of Mallaig is conflicted. On the one hand, she's strongly anti-British as a consequence of her interpretation of the accident that killed her brothers. On the other hand, she's strongly anti-German after what happened there. Would you agree with that analysis?"

"Yes, Captain, I would. And I'd like to say something more about that. I know Lady Alison very well indeed, better than any other patient in my practice. And yet I couldn't tell you whether her anti-German sentiments are stronger than her anti-British."

"Doctor Finlayson, we've both used the phrase 'anti-German' rather than 'pro-British' and similarly with 'anti-British.' It sounds to me like the Countess of Mallaig is someone whose primary emotion is hatred rather than love."

"I would have to agree with you there, Captain Rees."

***

"Good evening, Miss Carbondale. I don't know if you remember me, but Annabel Harkness is my younger sister."

"Of course I know you—we've met several times. Won't you come in? I'm sorry about the washing hanging everywhere. There are six of us WAAF officers living in this house, and the mess is truly astounding. They say that men are untidy, but I'd challenge any six men to even remotely approach our appallingly low standard. There's a bottle of gin somewhere here. At least I think there is. I saw it yesterday. Or was it the day before?"

"Don't worry about it. I shouldn't drink anyway—I'm here on official business. You look as if you're about to go back on duty, but may I quickly ask you a few questions?"

"Of course, though I can't imagine why you're here."

"Thank you. What can you tell me about Alison MacRobson?"

"That's an easy one. She's a real bitch."

"Could you be a little more specific perhaps?"

"Certainly. She's an arrogant, self-opinionated, bossy, vindictive, authoritarian bitch."

"I see."

"May I ask you why you're asking these questions? And why are you asking me? I was two years behind Alison at school, but your sister Annabel was in the same form as her; she knows Alison much better than I do."

"I've no idea where I can get hold of Annabel, but your mother gave me your address when I telephoned her."

"And why all these questions?"

"If I say 'official business' will that satisfy you?"

"Not in the least."

"I thought not. Well, she's being considered for a job that requires security clearance, and I'm one of the people who are vetting her."

"No, you're not. There's no way on earth that anyone would offer her any job of any kind. The truth is that she's done something evil and you're investigating her. I hope they lock her up and throw away the key."

"Miss Carbondale—"

"When you danced with me at the Kitcheners' ball, you called me Petronella. And later you tried to seduce me in the conservatory, behind the large lemon trees."

"No, I did not."

"Oh, really? What exactly were you trying to do, then? You were disgustingly drunk at the time—that's probably why you don't remember."

"Miss Carbondale, I mean Petronella, I'd be most grateful if you could tell me why you dislike Alison so much?"

"I don't dislike her. I hate her, I abhor her, I despise her, I detest her, I—"

"Did she do something particularly nasty to you?"

"Miss Raynor made the worst mistake of her life when she appointed That Bitch to be Deputy Head Girl. Alison was bossy and domineering from the day she came to Evesdon, but when she had real power it went to her head. Words that come to mind include controlling, dictatorial, tyrannical, overbearing, and pushy. And did I mention despotic, arrogant, and domineering? Also, a word that I may just have used before was bitch. As you well know, life at boarding school is like being in jail, only worse. But Alison managed to turn life at Evesdon into a living hell."

"You know she joined the British National Socialist Party?"

"I hadn't heard, but it doesn't surprise me in the least. Alison was the *Führer* of Evesdon. And now I really have to go. Give my love to Annabel when you see her.

"Oh," she added, "one final thing. You most definitely did try to seduce me at the Kitcheners' ball."

Petronella paused, and then added with a smile, "You should come back and try again sometime. Bye!"

***

Before presenting his ration card to storekeepers the next day, agent BROCKEN wanted to familiarize himself with the shops in the village. He preferred to do his food shopping in side streets rather than on High Street, the main thoroughfare of West Clemford—the fewer people who saw him, the better. On returning to Number Six after his abortive attempt to get to Maldon in time, he took off his wig and his woman's outfit, meticulously removed every trace of make-up, and caught up on much needed sleep. Waking in the late afternoon, he put on the men's clothes he had worn when he landed on the beach early that morning. As soon as it was dark outside, he spent an hour walking through the deserted streets, noting the position of the post office, the police station, the two filling stations, the public library, and the schools, as well as the various shops. If the situation were to go out of control, detailed knowledge of the geography of the village might mean the difference between a death sentence and escaping back to Nazi Germany in a U-boat.

CHAPTER EIGHTEEN
West Clemford, Essex
Friday, May 30, 1941

Dressed in the woman's clothes he had worn the previous day, Helmut Kirchgässner stood in the telephone booth in Omdurman Avenue. He heard a nearby church tower clock chiming nine o'clock as he asked, "Is your mother still suffering from pneumonia?"

"Only in her lower left lung today," Carlyle said.

"Where is he?"

"Police station in West Clemford."

What irony, Kirchgässner thought. My target is sitting in a police station that's an easy five minutes' walk from here.

Agent BROCKEN instinctively realized that it would be exceedingly unwise for him to hang around the police station for an hour. Instead, he got back into the car and drove back to Number Six. He decided that at a quarter to ten he would walk from the cottage to the news agency diagonally across the road from the police station, buy an *Essex Chronicle*, and pretend to read it in the shop while keeping an eye on the police station. Signs of activity there would signal the imminent departure of Rudolf Hess for his next place of imprisonment, which he assumed would occur promptly at ten o'clock, as previously. He had no way of knowing that Pankhurst had changed the routine; his men were now to move Hess one hour later than before, to give Kirchgässner time to travel to where Hess had slept the previous night.

When agent BROCKEN got back to the cottage, he came to the conclusion that it would be best if he wore the uniform of the WAAF flight officer he had killed in Harvey Pettigrew's cottage. That would allow him to get close to Hess, and would make his getaway easier; everyone would think that a uniformed soldier running away from the scene of the killing was chasing the assassin. He remembered the conclusion that a British Air Ministry committee had reached the previous year regarding the WAAFs: "No work should be done by a man, if a woman could do it or be trained to do it." He smiled grimly to himself.

He quickly took off his clothes, checked his make-up and wig, and donned the WAAF outfit. Carefully examining his appearance in a full-length mirror, he was surprised to see how well the officer's uniform, made of barathea wool in air force blue, fitted him. After checking that the safety catch was on and the magazine was full, he put his CZ 27 in the right side-pocket of the tunic. He put his ice pick in the left side-pocket, together with a spare eight-round magazine and the silencer for the CZ 27. Finally he remembered that WAAFs were required to carry their gas masks with them at all times, so he slung the gas mask bag over his shoulder.

What about his money, maps, fuel coupons, and two sets of identification papers? He didn't want to leave them in the cottage, just in case a sneak thief broke in. So he stuffed them into the gas mask bag. Then he left the cottage and walked briskly to the newsagent. There was a short line of people waiting to buy cigarettes and newspapers, and he quickly reached the counter. Clutching two pennies in his right hand, he glanced down at the pile of copies of the *Chronicle* lying there.

Two familiar faces stared up at him from below a banner headline: "Missing Air Force Officers." The captions under the pictures read Flight Lieutenant H. Pettigrew and Flying Officer E. Duxton. He handed his money to the newsagent, took the newspaper and walked over to the shop window in order to be able read the front page while observing the police station.

Kirchgässner read the article carefully. It said the two officers had left their base just outside West Clemford on Wednesday night and no one had seen them since. There was no mention of foul play, nor did the article hint at any sort of relationship between the two of them. The last paragraph stated that the Royal Air Force Police had sent reinforcements to the Essex area, and that they would be questioning Air Force personnel in the vicinity regarding the missing officers.

He lowered the newspaper slightly and was disconcerted to see that, while he was reading the article, two RAF policemen had placed themselves directly outside the shop. As he watched, he saw them stop two airmen who were walking toward the door of the news agency, perhaps to buy cigarettes. The military police carefully checked their identity cards, asked a few questions, then allowed the men to enter the shop. Two other RAF policemen stood on the other side of the road, blocking the sidewalk there. Each of the four policemen wore a white webbing belt. The belt supported a heavy black wooden truncheon on the left hip and a white holster containing a sidearm on the right hip. The MPs had apparently spent many hours applying blanco compound to their cotton webbing, because their belts and holsters gleamed like freshly fallen snow. The muscular policemen made Kirchgässner think of four large stone statues, painted air force blue, that a powerful crane had deposited pair-wise on either side of High Street.

SS-Major Kirchgässner discretely unbuttoned the left breast pocket of his uniform tunic and took out a small cardboard folder that proved to be Form 1250, the Royal Air Force identity card. It was in the name of Emily Duxton, and the photograph inside bore no resemblance to him.

Helmut Kirchgässner tried to think of a way that he could bypass the military police to get within shooting distance of Hess. No solution came to him; his mind obstinately stayed a total blank. Then he tried to imagine the situation that would soon occur when four armed policemen brought Hess out of the police station. There would be plainclothes officers in the area as well, perhaps six of them. All ten men would be armed, but one policeman would have his left wrist handcuffed to Hess's right wrist, which might make it hard for him to shoot accurately. That left nine policemen and four military policemen.

If he had worn his civilian woman's clothes he would definitely have tried to kill Hess when he emerged. After all, Kirchgässner would have had the advantage of surprise. No one would have been concerned if they saw a woman walking in front of the police station; the thirteen handguns would undoubtedly have remained in their holsters, especially the side arms belonging to the MPs. But Kirchgässner was dressed as a flying officer in the middle of a village whose inhabitants were searching assiduously for Emily Duxton. The moment he exited from the newsagent's shop, the four RAF policemen would be keenly on the alert.

Dressed as a WAAF officer, the odds were strongly against him. Worse, he was trapped in the news agency until the MPs left, which might be many hours from now. He thought quickly, then approached the newsagent.

"Ma'am," he said, trying hard to hide his German accent while raising the pitch of his voice, "there's a man outside that I'd prefer not to bump into. Could I please go out the back door?"

The middle-aged newsagent smiled sympathetically. "A former boyfriend, I suppose?" she asked.

"Yes, I'm afraid so. I'm very glad that you understand."

"Don't worry, dearie, I've been in the same situation. Come round to my side of the counter. Now go through that doorway there into the passage and out the door at the end. You'll find yourself in a lane that leads to Acton Street."

***

"Gentlemen, based on the report from Captain Rees in Mallaig and what Harkness has just told us this morning, we may have slipped up," Air Commodore Pankhurst said. "Soon after war broke out, the government passed Regulation 18B of the Defense (General) Regulations 1939. It allowed us to imprison British citizens who were German sympathizers. We arrested only about twenty people, all of them hard-core Nazis. Of course, they included Forbes Penthwick, one of the most dangerous men in England. But we left his followers in peace, because they were considerably less of a threat.

"In May last year the authorities became concerned that there might be a fifth column in England. We rounded up tens of thousands of enemy aliens and brought them before alien tribunals. The tribunals found the overwhelming majority of them to be 'friendly aliens' and released them. We also arrested and interned or jailed about a thousand British citizens under Regulation 18B, almost all of them from the far right, including many members of Penthwick's British National Socialist Party.

"We didn't detain the Countess of Mallaig. Our purpose was to arrest everyone who, in our opinion, posed a threat to Britain. But a woman sitting motionless all day and every day in a chair, never saying a word, having to be cajoled to eat, could hardly perform traitorous acts.

"What we overlooked was the possibility that Lady Alison might recover to the extent that she could once again resume her pro-Nazi activities. Johnson is perspicacious, as we all know, but when he met her two nights ago he never detected anything in her manner that might lead him to suspect that in the past few years she's had two serious nervous breakdowns. And the fact that she's apparently now fully recovered means that Lady Alison is once again on the list of potential targets of Regulation 18B.

"Now, I'm certainly aware that interning her on grounds of 'hostile origin or associations' may send her over the edge again. On the other hand, the safety of Britain is paramount, and must take precedence over everything else. Our country gave the world Magna Carta and *habeas corpus*. But we currently have internment without trial here. Why? Because our very survival as a people is at stake. And the secret of the Double-Cross System is a vital pillar of our defense against Nazi Germany. We cannot take the risk of agent OBAN sending radio messages to Berlin that contain facts that might contradict the disinformation that our double agents are sending, especially PICKFORD's subagents.

"We have two matters to discuss now. Firstly, do we recommend to the authorities that they intern Lady Alison under Regulation 18B? And secondly, is she agent OBAN? On the basis of what you've learned about her, Harkness, what do you think?"

"Sir, the problem for me is that Lady Alison is not one individual but many. The car accident and the incident in Germany both changed her personality dramatically, in a different direction each time, to such an extent that she went through a nervous breakdown on both occasions. I'm not sure if anyone, not even Dr. Finlayson, could give us an accurate picture of what's currently going on in her mind. I'm certainly not a psychiatrist, but it seems to me that, as a consequence of what she's been through, she's somewhat unstable and may suddenly change again; solid information about her today may be totally incorrect tomorrow.

"And regarding whether she's agent OBAN, we have lots of damning circumstantial evidence, but no hard facts. We haven't even tried to find out where she was on the night of May 14th, when MI8 detected that radio transmission from coming from the West Coast area of Scotland, perhaps from somewhere outside Oban. Yes, we could ask her, but if she's agent OBAN that would tip her off. Or it could tip her into a third nervous breakdown, perhaps permanently this time, and we'll never know the truth.

"What concerns me, sir, is that we have no choice—we must uncover agent OBAN. Suppose that it's Lady Alison. If we lead her to suspect that we're on her trail, she'll just do nothing for a few months, waiting for us to drop the investigation. And when we eventually decide that she's no longer worth watching, she'll resume her pro-Nazi activities."

"Are you suggesting that we should intern her right away, and never mind the possible consequences to her?" Pankhurst asked.

"No, sir, that's not what I mean," Harkness said. "Suppose that Lady Alison isn't agent OBAN after all. Arresting her would alert the real agent OBAN that we're onto his trail. To protect himself he'd go underground for a few months, and then resume his activities, with potentially extremely dangerous consequences for Britain. As I said before, we have to unmask agent OBAN as soon as possible. I have two ideas that I suggest we try next."

***

"Group Captain Arbuthnot," Detective Chief Inspector Liddell said, "I'm here with some information about your missing officers."

"What have you found out?"

"The news is not good. I believe that they were both victims of foul play."

"Foul play? Do you mean murder, Detective Chief Inspector?"

"That is what I think."

"Good heavens, man, tell me everything."

"Sir, I'd like to start at the beginning so that you can see how I arrived at my conclusion."

"Go ahead."

"Soon after eight o'clock yesterday morning you learned that the two officers were not at their posts. You knew that Flight Lieutenant Pettigrew lives close to the base and that he and Flying Officer Duxton are romantically involved. You consider them both to be excellent officers so you decided to handle the matter as confidentially as possible, particularly because nothing like this had ever happened before. First you decided to wait until ten. When they still had not shown up by then, you dispatched your flight sergeant to Pettigrew's home in your car."

"Yes, Flight Sergeant Perkins. He's been with me for more than ten years, first in India before the war and now here. I trust him totally and I rely heavily on his discretion."

"I see. Perkins arrived at Number One, Estuary Drive. He knocked on the door, but there was no answer. In one room the curtains were open. He peered into the house but it appeared to be deserted. He looked through the garage window; Pettigrew's red sports car wasn't there. Perkins drove back and reported to you. At this point you called us in."

"Yes. The RAF Police are excellent at dealing with drunks and fights and petty theft. They're a fine bunch of men, but I'm afraid that they're not detectives."

"We made inquiries," Detective Chief Inspector Liddell continued, "and we discovered that Pettigrew and Duxton had left the base together on Monday night around eight o'clock in Pettigrew's MG TB. There's a public house, The Mitre, around the corner from Pettigrew's cottage. I went there and showed the licensee photographs of the two missing officers. The publican immediately recognized them. He said that Pettigrew had been coming to The Mitre for five or six years. It seems that a bachelor uncle of his used to own the cottage where Pettigrew now lives. He gave his nephew free run of the place; Pettigrew stayed there about one weekend a month. Then his uncle died, leaving everything he had to Pettigrew, including the house. When war broke out, Pettigrew was posted here, and whenever he was off duty he went to his cottage. The publican intimated that over the years there have been many different women before Duxton, but for the last six to nine months she's the only one he's taken to The Mitre.

"On Monday night they drove to The Mitre, where they had one or two beers. The publican admitted that at closing time Pettigrew bought a bottle of Dewar's White Label whisky from him. That's not allowed now, of course, but a licensee will do it for a good customer. Neither officer has been seen since they left The Mitre around ten o'clock on Monday night."

"That doesn't necessarily mean that there's been foul play. They could have drunk their bottle of scotch somewhere else. After all, Pettigrew has a car."

"That's quite correct, Group Captain. However, there's more. When they still hadn't shown up by this morning, I obtained a search warrant for Number One, Estuary Drive—that's Flight Lieutenant Pettigrew's cottage here in West Clemford. My men and I drove up in our car, accompanied by two of your RAF policemen in their own vehicle. I brought them along because I was unsure under whose jurisdiction this matter fell. After all, there was as yet no evidence of any crime, so it was probably still your case, not mine. Nevertheless, I suspected that we might be visiting a crime scene, so I asked your men if they wouldn't mind waiting in the street; I didn't want them accidentally destroying evidence."

"Quite right, Detective Chief Inspector. As I said, they're first-class men, but they do know their limitations."

"Now, it seems that one of your men is an avid birdwatcher."

"A birdwatcher?" Group Captain Arbuthnot asked doubtfully.

"Yes. It seems he saw an erne flying towards the nature reserve."

"A flying urn? You mean he saw a vase in the air?" The group captain seemed totally confused.

"No, sir. He saw an erne, e-r-n-e, a white-tailed sea eagle. Apparently they're quite rare in these parts. So he ran toward the nature reserve."

"He deserted his post to watch a bird? Give me his name."

"I can't quite remember it, sir," Inspector Liddell lied. "I have it written down somewhere."

"Well, be sure to let me have it before you leave. Please continue your report."

"Certainly, Group Captain. As I was saying, the RAF policeman ran toward the nature reserve. And it's a good thing he did that, because when he reached Number Six he saw fresh tire tracks in the gravel drive of the cottage, which otherwise seemed to have been neglected for years. To cut a long story short, I quickly obtained a search warrant for Number Six as well.

"We went inside, and discovered that people had recently been living there. The first thing we saw was clothing belonging to a man and a woman. We also found Flight Lieutenant Pettigrew's uniform there, but there was no sign of Flying Officer Duxton's kit. A half-empty bottle of Dewar's White Label and two glasses were in the kitchen. Pettigrew's red MG TB was in the garage of Number Six. Finally, we found a Telefunken transceiver in one of the bedrooms."

"Do you know what you're saying?"

"Yes, Group Captain, I do. It seems that two German agents have been using Number Six as a center for espionage. We don't know why yet, but for some reason they killed Flight Lieutenant Pettigrew and Flying Officer Duxton, perhaps in their cottage, perhaps elsewhere. We haven't found their bodies yet. But there's enough circumstantial evidence to persuade me that both officers are dead."

"What a tragedy! Two of my finest officers. I'm going to miss them both, and so will everyone else who knew them. Two wonderful young people. What a loss! Giving up your life for your country in battle is one thing, but to be murdered by German spies…"

Both men were silent. Then the group captain asked, "Where do we go to from here?"

"The case is now in the hands of MI5. My men and the military police are both out of it for now. And probably for good, once they confirm that we accidentally uncovered a den of Nazi agents."

"Detective Chief Inspector Liddell, I think I know where the bodies may be."

"Where?"

"Suppose you're a German spy and that you've established your hideout in Number Six. For some reason, you and your female fellow agent have just killed two innocent people in Number One. You don't want to leave the bodies there, because the police may turn up looking for the owner of the house and his girlfriend. On the other hand, it's hard to dispose of two corpses in such a way that no one would ever find them. Where would you put the bodies?"

"I'd bury them somewhere in that large marshy area in the nature reserve behind the cottages."

"Precisely, Detective Chief Inspector. I suggest that you and your men look for them there."

***

Kirchgässner thanked the proprietor of the news agency profusely as he left the shop and walked briskly along the alley to Acton Street. Following a circuitous route to avoid High Street, he made for Number Six. But as he was about to turn from Gladstone Road into Estuary Drive, he saw a police car drawn up in front of Number One. He spun around before anyone saw him and swiftly walked back the way he had come.

What should he do now? It all depended on what the police were doing. If they just wanted to see if Pettigrew was at his home, they would leave in a few minutes, and he could return to Number Six without difficulty. Accordingly he decided to hide in the back yard of what seemed to be an unoccupied holiday cottage in Gladstone Road and wait.

Half an hour later the police car was still there. This was bad news; they must have decided that the two air force officers were dead and were searching for evidence that would help them find the killer. On the other hand, if they were fully occupied at Number One, he could safely make his way through the salt marsh behind the row of cottages and get back to his hideout at Number Six. He found a path leading to the nature reserve. He followed it, but it soon petered out. He went back to Gladstone Road and tried a different path. This one, too, came to a sudden end, but he decided to press on. He had to walk carefully to avoid slipping into the morass. Next he encountered a place where he had no choice but to take off his black lace-up shoes and stockings to ford a muddy ditch, lifting his skirt to keep it clean. As he neared the back of Number Six he had to wade through a shallow pond. He dried off his feet as best he could and replaced his footwear. Eventually he reached the back fence. As he was about to climb over, he heard voices. He ducked down and listened.

"Here's his uniform. But where did they put her clothes? They don't seem to be anywhere in the cottage."

Helmut Kirchgässner was once again faced with a dilemma. He had to have a car to travel to where Hess would next be imprisoned. He needed the clothes in the cottage; he could no longer wear Emily Duxton's uniform in public. And he could not return to Germany unless he had his transceiver to send a message to the submarine base.

He had two choices. He could scale the fence, kill all the police inside Number Six and then those at Number One, load everything he needed into the red car and establish a new hideout somewhere else—with every policeman and soldier in Britain sworn to find him and with Hess safely tucked away behind the high walls of an impregnable prison until the British had captured the mass murderer. Or he could walk away from the cottage still wearing Flying Officer Duxton's uniform; break into a house and steal another set of clothes; acquire a different car, preferably a less flashy model than the red MG TB; kill Hess; and find some other way of transmitting a message to the *Kriegsmarine* to send a U-boat to ferry him back to Germany for his next mission.

SS-Major Kirchgässner remembered the old proverb, "He who fights and runs away will live to fight another day." He clearly had to avoid West Clemford at all costs. So he crouched low behind the back fence and moved parallel to the coast in the direction of the village of East Clemford.

***

"Gentlemen, I called you here this afternoon because there have been critical developments in Essex. As you know, yesterday morning agent BROCKEN phoned Carlyle twice. The second time, Carlyle told him that Hess was in Maldon. We kept Hess in the police station there until eleven o'clock to give BROCKEN time to arrive, but he didn't show up. This morning, BROCKEN phoned Carlyle again. Carlyle told him where Hess was, West Clemford this time. And again BROCKEN didn't show up. I don't understand why he hasn't yet made an attempt to kill Hess.

"But something important has happened. We've found where BROCKEN was staying—in a cottage in West Clemford. He could easily have tried to kill Campbell-White this morning. Instead, it appears that on Wednesday night he murdered an RAF officer and his WAAF officer girlfriend, probably in another cottage in the same street; we found a bloodstained mattress there. As of yet we haven't uncovered a motive, and we haven't found the bodies, either. The police were looking for the two missing officers and stumbled on BROCKEN's hideout. Two German agents were staying there, a man and a woman. We found their radio transceiver and their clothes. But there was no sign of BROCKEN or the woman. We've posted guards in the area in case they should come back for their kit, but it won't help them if they return there—we've brought everything we found in the cottage here for analysis, including the radio transceiver.

"The goal of operation OTTAWA is to locate two *Abwehr* agents: agent OBAN and agent NORFOLK. We've found agent NORFOLK, and we suspect that Lady Alison may be agent OBAN. But now we have two more Nazi spies to capture: agent BROCKEN and agent ESSEX, if I may give her that name. Agent ESSEX is a real mystery. Did she arrive in Britain with BROCKEN? If that's the case, why didn't Canaris inform PICKFORD? And if not, is she another sleeper, like Hermann Leichtal? Or was she born here, like Lady Alison?"

"Sir," Chulmleigh asked, "do we know that the woman whose clothes were in the cottage in West Clemford is an enemy agent? Couldn't she just be a local lass whom BROCKEN picked up?"

"If she is, why did she leave her clothes in the cottage?" Harkness asked.

"Perhaps because he killed her, too," Chulmleigh said.

"But why keep her clothes, then?" Captain Marks asked. "He killed Pettigrew and kept his clothes. He killed Duxton, but he didn't take her uniform. He might have killed this woman to guarantee her silence, but why did he decide to keep her clothes?"

"Maybe we've got it all wrong," Lieutenant Wallstead said. "What if agent ESSEX is wearing Duxton's uniform? Perhaps the two Nazis killed Duxton for her uniform; Pettigrew witnessed the murder and had to be silenced."

"But if agent ESSEX is British, why would she kill Duxton for her WAAF uniform?" Squadron Leader Harkness asked. "They're easily obtainable."

"But who says that agent ESSEX is British?" Marks asked. "Maybe we've got the whole situation the wrong way round. Maybe agent BROCKEN is a woman."

"Then who's the man?" Harkness enquired.

"He's a Nazi sympathizer, born here, who's assisting her," Marks suggested. "Here's how I see it. A Brocken Specter is an optical illusion—we see one thing, but the reality is something else. In this case, the reality is that Admiral Canaris sent a woman here to kill Hess. We're looking for a man, because we're conditioned to think that way. If a man approaches Hess, we instinctively tense up and ask ourselves: Could he be agent BROCKEN? But if a woman walks up to Hess, we relax, because we assume that all assassins are men. But during the French Revolution, Charlotte Corday killed Jean-Paul Marat in his bathtub."

"And in the Bible," Tupman added, "Yael hammered a tent peg into the head of Sisera, the Canaanite general. And Judith beheaded Nebuchadnezzar's general, Holofernes."

"Well, BROCKEN is a woman. And that would explain why we can't find Duxton's uniform—BROCKEN is wearing it," Chulmleigh said. "Now we have to find out who the man is."

"We've known for years that Canaris is a cunning adversary," the air commodore said, "but this latest stratagem is exceptionally clever. He's sent hundreds of *Abwehr* agents to Britain. Only one of them has been a woman: Helga Ziegler. Yesterday we discussed the possibility that agent OBAN may be a woman; today it's BROCKEN. I agree with Marks and Tupman that there's no rational reason why they shouldn't both be women. But based on Canaris's past record, one woman agent is unexpected; we'd never think of looking for *two*. An exceedingly cunning ploy!"

"Sir," Wallstead asked, "Carlyle has spoken to BROCKEN at least three times. Did he ever get the impression that he was talking to a woman?"

"Good thinking. I'll phone him now. I won't be long."

Three minutes later Pankhurst returned. "Carlyle is adamant that the person on the other end of the line was a man whose first language is German. His accent wasn't particularly strong, perhaps because he's lived here for a while, or possibly because the *Abwehr* English teachers are exceptionally good.

"We have to warn everyone involved in Operation OTTAWA to be extremely vigilant if anyone approaches Hess, be it a man or a woman. All of our people need to know that it's possible that we're looking for a female assassin. Or a male assassin. Or both."

***

Kirchgässner was worried. Before he could continue with his mission of killing Hess, he had to find new clothes, food, and somewhere safe to sleep, in that order. During the weekend that he had spent at the cottage while a student at Cambridge he had not visited East Clemford, and he had not been there on any of his cycling excursions. However, it seemed likely that East Clemford was not all that different to the village on the other side of Clemford Island. In particular, he assumed that he could find an unoccupied holiday house where he could stay.

Acquiring food and clothing was a different problem. Even owners of a second home were rarely wealthy enough to possess enough clothes to leave items at their holiday cottage. And with food exceedingly tightly rationed, the chance of finding much to eat in a cottage left empty until the war was over was slight. He would have to break into a house when the husband and wife were at work and steal food and clothing from there.

It was now one o'clock in the afternoon. If he burgled a house, might the householder return home for lunch while he was rifling the cupboards for the items he needed? It seemed somewhat unlikely. After all, during wartime most people did not have the luxury of a long lunch-hour; they probably took sandwiches with them to work. And what about children—at what time did they return home from school? Kirchgässner was ruthless even by Nazi standards, but he drew the line at killing children to ensure that they would not identify him.

The path he was following through the marsh ended at the southeastern corner of the nature reserve. The sea was to his right. In front of him were the remains of a signpost; officials had broken off the horizontal pieces bearing the names of the streets. Consulting his map, he noted that Cavendish Street was the name of the road to his left; the one in front of him was Nelson Way, which fronted the shoreline. On the other side of the road, the corner house looked a lot like the six holiday cottages in Estuary Drive in West Clemford. The street in front of that house, Nelson Way, immediately turned to the left. As a result, Kirchgässner could not see the rest of the houses on that road, but he assumed that they would also be similar. However, he was looking for a house occupied by residents of East Clemford who were away at work. Accordingly, he turned left at Cavendish Street, hoping it would take him in the direction of the center of the village and away from the coast. After walking past a few more holiday cottages, he was relieved to see two-story houses on both sides of the road with well-tended flower gardens and vegetable patches, a sign that their occupants lived there on a permanent basis. Some of the homes had children's toys lying outside on the lawn; he mentally crossed them off his list. The next house that he passed on the left-hand side of the street seemed to fit all his criteria. Kirchgässner tended to rely heavily on his intuition, and he somehow instinctively knew that a childless couple who were both at work lived at this address.

The name of the house painted on the front gate read "Rookery Nook." The wooden gate was ajar. He pushed past it and quickly made his way along the side of the garage to the back of the house and tried the kitchen door. He was not surprised to find it unlocked—in his experience, many people living in villages and small towns were careless about such things. He opened the door about a foot and listened, but heard nothing. He entered the kitchen and walked through to the entrance hall. Again he stopped to listen, but the house was undoubtedly deserted. Agent BROCKEN crept silently up the stairs to the second floor where he found two bedrooms. He walked into the larger one. Facing him were two wooden clothes closets.

He opened the first closet and took out a neatly pressed navy blue suit on its hanger. One glance was enough; the man who lived in this house was nearly a foot taller than he was. He replaced the suit and moved on to the next clothes closet. As he opened it he heard someone unlocking the front door. Kirchgässner slipped into the closet as quietly as he could, leaving the door slightly open in order to be able to hear what was happening downstairs. He checked that his ice pick was still in the left side-pocket of Emily Duxton's tunic together with his spare ammunition clip and silencer. He took his CZ 27 out of the right side-pocket, fitted the silencer and waited.

He heard footsteps walking down the hallway away from the front door in the direction of the kitchen. He guessed that the woman of the house had come home to make lunch, perhaps just for herself or maybe for her husband as well. But the unknown person walked into the front room instead.

Now Kirchgässner heard what sounded like someone opening a cupboard, taking out a bottle and a glass, opening the bottle and pouring some liquid into the glass. The person downstairs drank quickly, refilled the glass and drank again. Next he or she went into the kitchen. The assassin could hear water running; presumably, the drinker was now rinsing out the glass. He heard the glass and the bottle being replaced, the click of the cupboard door as it closed, and then footsteps back to the front door. The whole liquid lunch had taken no longer than five minutes from start to finish.

The house was once again silent. SS-Major Kirchgässner crept out of his hiding place and tiptoed to the window. He managed to just catch sight of a tall thin balding man walking swiftly in the direction away from the sea before he disappeared from view. Agent BROCKEN returned to the second closet. Fortunately for him, the woman of the house was approximately the same size as he was. He helped himself to a complete set of clothing, including a pair of gloves and a handbag of sufficient size to adequately conceal his weapons as well as contain the papers he had crammed into the gas mask bag before leaving Number Six. He took off Flying Officer Duxton's uniform and dressed in the twinset and skirt that he had selected. The shoes were a little tight, but he felt confident that he could manage to walk in them. Finally he put on the gloves. They might look somewhat out of place, but he did not want to leave fingerprints anywhere.

Kirchgässner went downstairs to find a bag for the uniform; under no circumstances did he want to leave Flying Officer Duxton's clothes in the house. In a storage closet he found a suitcase that he took upstairs with him. He now selected a second complete set of women's clothing, the smartest outfit he could find, and placed the items in the suitcase together with the uniform. The next task was to wipe down all the surfaces he had touched. Then he went downstairs again to search the kitchen for food. As he had feared, there was not much to be had, but he stole what little he could locate.

Suddenly he remembered that his shaving kit and his supply of make-up were in the hands of the police. A chemist might remember if a woman bought a razor. Also, he'd heard that cosmetics were in short supply in wartime England. So he went back upstairs with the suitcase and helped himself to everything he needed from the bathroom and the bedroom.

Now he realized that he had no men's clothing at all. He returned to the first closet to see if he could find any items that he could wear in an emergency. He picked up a hat, and was delighted to find that the head of the tall thin man he had glimpsed leaving the house was only slightly larger than his, and he could easily remedy this by stuffing a strip of newspaper in the hatband. Next he tried on the shorter of the two overcoats. It was a few inches longer than he would have liked, but it would have to do. The brown leather shoes at the bottom of the closet were far too large, but he could stuff the toes with more newspaper. All the shirts and trousers would have looked ludicrous on him, so he went to the second closet and took a pair of slacks and a plain white blouse that might pass as men's clothing when worn under the overcoat. Yes, he would look like the victim of a German air raid, but that was not uncommon in 1941. He put the shaving equipment, cosmetics and the additional clothing in the suitcase; he would have to carry the hat in his other hand.

Next he had to get to the street. He left via the front door because it might be considered suspicious behavior if someone saw a woman walking past the side of the house carrying a suitcase and a man's hat. As he walked down the path to the front gate a postwoman rode past on a bicycle in the direction of Nelson Way. Kirchgässner turned his head to the side in the hope that she would not notice him, let alone be able to describe him accurately.

Now he needed somewhere to stay, preferably close to a public telephone, and with a garage that he could use to hide the car he was going to take. As he reached the sidewalk on Cavendish Street, he realized that acquiring a vehicle was not enough. Stealing a car was no problem; all he had to do was open the hood, hotwire the engine, close the hood, and drive off. The problem was that speed was of the essence when leaving the scene of an assassination. He had to have the ignition key of the car as well so that he could jump in, start the car, and drive off. An alternative was to leave the car running while he waited around the corner to kill Hess. But this was a time of fuel rationing, and someone would be sure to "do him a favor" and switch the car off.

The owners of "Rookery Nook," the house he had just burgled, had left their back door unlocked. Were they also careless enough to leave a car key lying around in full sight? He returned to the house, entered at the rear as before, placed the suitcase just inside the back door, tossed the hat onto the kitchen table and looked around the kitchen. No key. Searching through the drawers would be a waste of time; if the owners had left a key in the house, it would be in plain sight.

A methodical search of the rest of house, ending in the main bedroom, proved to be equally fruitless. Kirchgässner was about to try a different house when he had an idea. Peering out the window, he saw that Cavendish Street was deserted. He went downstairs and out the back door. Moving slowly to the front garden, he checked that there was still no one in sight. Satisfied, he walked to the garage. The wooden door had no padlock in the hasp. As rapidly as he could, he slipped into the garage and shut the door from the inside. The afternoon sunlight through the garage window revealed that the vehicle was a black, two-door, Morris Eight. And as he had hoped, the car was unlocked and the key was in the ignition.

He turned on the engine and looked at the fuel gauge. He was not surprised to see that the tank was nearly empty; fuel rationing in Britain was strict. Switching off the car, he returned to the house, took the suitcase and hat and stowed them in the trunk of the Morris Eight. He drove the car into Cavendish Street, turning left so that the car was pointing inland. He parked the car about fifty yards down the street. Then he went back to the house and closed the garage door, all the while checking to see that the street remained empty of pedestrians.

Kirchgässner returned to the car. As he opened the door and got in, a postwoman cycled past heading away from the coast. Was it the same one who had earlier cycled past in the other direction? When she passed him he had looked away, but he had caught a brief glimpse of her. This postwoman seemed to be the same person. But postal carriers are usually assigned a one-way route. So, who was this postwoman? Did she work for the Royal Mail, or was she an MI5 intelligence officer? Kirchgässner did not want her to know that he was headed toward the center of the village, so he made a U-turn and drove toward the sea, turning left at Nelson Way. As he passed the house on the corner and followed the road as it swung sharply to the left, he saw that the entire length of the beach to his right was lined with brightly painted wooden beach huts. In front of the huts were lines of the same defenses as on the beach that edged the nature reserve. He quickly realized that if he were to establish a new base in a holiday cottage on Nelson Way, there would always be the risk that someone living illegally in a beach hut might notice him. He had to look elsewhere for an empty house he could occupy.

The car needed gasoline and preferably plenty of it. Once more he made a U-turn and then drove north on Cavendish Street, toward where he thought the center of the village of East Clemford was located. A sign that read "Weedon's Garage" and a petrol pump with a frosted glass sphere on the top bearing the brand name BP in black letters told him that he had guessed correctly. Kirchgässner drew up on the forecourt. An elderly man wearing a blue boiler suit and a cloth cap came up to the driver's window.

"Can I help you, miss?"

"Three gallons of petrol, please," Kirchgässner said, handing over his fuel ration book. The right half of the front cover had been carefully removed; he assumed that, when a clerk issued a fuel ration book, that half was retained for official purposes. The fuel coupons inside the book were printed two to a page. The missing part of the front cover revealed a purple fuel coupon.

The attendant looked at the book and seemed worried. Taking the fuel ration book he replied, "And your National Registration Identity Card, please, miss?"

Kirchgässner relaxed. He immediately realized that he had forgotten Canaris's instruction, and assumed that that was why the attendant was perplexed. But the look of concern on the man's face intensified as he took the identity card.

"I'll just go inside to detach the coupon," he said, and started walking toward the office. His body language gave away that something was seriously wrong.

Kirchgässner got out of the car and followed the attendant into the building. The man was standing in front of a table strewn with papers of various kinds; a telephone stood on one side. Next to the telephone lay the identity card, placed on top of the fuel ration coupon book. He saw the man lift the handset and dial nine followed by another nine. The emergency number in Britain was 999—the attendant was phoning the police. Before he could dial the last nine, Kirchgässner slammed his hand on the switch hook to disconnect the call. As the startled man looked up at him, the German assassin smoothly took his ice pick out of his handbag and pressed it against the man's chest; the attendant could feel the razor-sharp tip about to pierce his skin.

"What's going on?" Kirchgässner barked. "Why are you phoning the police?"

The attendant was too frightened to speak. Helmut Kirchgässner glanced at the desk, saw two other fuel ration books lying there next to a small pile of detached petrol coupons, all printed in brick red, and quickly realized that he was a victim of MI5 deception. They had produced a fuel ration book with the petrol coupons printed in purple, taken the book to Cairo, and placed it in the battledress pocket of a soldier killed behind enemy lines on the Western Front. Then they had instructed everyone in Britain who handled petrol ration coupons to call the police immediately if someone tried to use a coupon printed in the wrong color.

The attendant had observed his face from close up, so Kirchgässner did not hesitate for an instant; he jerked the ice pick forward, stabbing the attendant in the heart. Taking great care not to get blood anywhere on his clothes, he withdrew the pick and wiped it on the man's boiler suit. Then he took the two brick red fuel ration books, his purple book and his identity card from the table and returned to his car. He was tempted to fill the Morris with petrol, but he knew that a woman doing that in smart clothes would attract attention. Also, another employee of Weedon's Garage might emerge, or perhaps even Weedon himself. The risk was too great; he reluctantly returned to the car and drove off to look for another petrol station.

He knew that West Clemford was crawling with police, so Kirchgässner continued north, driving across the bridge that spanned the causeway between Clemford Island and the mainland. He found himself in the outskirts of Colchester and soon saw another filling station. He drew up at the pump and handed one of the fuel ration books and his identity card to the attendant, a young woman also wearing a blue boiler suit. She handed the identity card back to him at once without glancing at it. Also, she did not check that the car registration number matched the number on the ration book.

She pumped three gallons into the tank. He paid her and then asked, "Can you suggest a place where

I can rent a room where the noise of my typewriter won't disturb anyone?"

"Your typewriter?"

"Yes. I'm a reporter. I'm working on a series of articles on how we women are not only doing the men's jobs while they're away at war, but we're doing them better than the men ever did."

The attendant sniffed. "I hope that you're going to explain why they pay us only half as much as the men we're replacing."

"Of course! That's the whole point of the articles: equal pay for equal work."

She smiled warmly. "Good for you!"

"Do you know somewhere I could stay while I write?"

"It'll be hard to get a room in the city—like most of Britain, we're packed to capacity with people from London whose homes were destroyed in the Blitz. Actually, the housing situation here in Colchester keeps changing. Last year, after the fall of France, invasion seemed inevitable. So they evacuated nearly half the inhabitants of some of the towns in East Anglia; Colchester seemed quite empty. Now that there doesn't seem to be any danger of the Germans coming here, most of the local people are back, plus numerous evacuees. We're glad to help them, of course, but as a result accommodation in Colchester is at a premium.

"Why don't you try a farm? It's inconvenient for most people because they don't have transportation from there to work or to the shops, but you have your car. And your typewriter won't be a problem if you get a room in an outbuilding."

"That's a good idea. Do you know of a farm offering accommodation?"

"Sorry, no. I'm a city girl. But if you keep driving on this road you'll eventually end up on the A12. When you see the signpost for Dedham, turn right. That'll put you in Constable country. There are plenty of farms there. I don't know if any of them have a room to rent, but you could ask."

"How far is it from here to the turnoff?"

"Oh, about ten miles, I think. Not too far. You won't use up too much of the petrol you've just bought."

"Is the signpost still there?"

"I should think so. They removed all the signposts and milestones close to the coast, even the railway station signs. But Dedham must be twenty miles inland, so they probably left the signpost alone."

Kirchgässner thanked her and drove off, adding another three gallons to the tank when he passed another petrol station where he used the second fuel ration book he had taken from Weedon's Garage. He continued onto the A12 and turned off to Dedham. As he did so, he could not miss seeing ahead of him in the distance the tall steeple of Dedham Parish Church, the one that Constable depicted in the background of several of his landscape paintings.

He drove into the quaint village and parked next to the red phone box outside the village shop and post office, on the corner of High Street and Mill Lane; the church he had seen was directly across the road. SS-Major Kirchgässner entered the shop. A middle-aged couple, whom he assumed were the owners, greeted him warmly.

The assassin established that he was a customer by buying an *East Anglian Daily Times*. Then he went into his reporter-with-a-noisy-typewriter spiel that had worked well with the young petrol pump attendant in Colchester. "So," he wound up, "can you suggest a farm near here where I can rent a room for tonight—perhaps part of a barn?"

The couple looked at one another blankly for a few seconds. Then the husband spoke. "Well, what with the men folk going to war, there are many farm families in the vicinity that have a room to rent. For example, there's the Morrisons."

"How can you possibly suggest the Morrisons when Mrs. Morrison—" and the wife gave her husband a meaningful look.

"Quite right, my dear, quite right. Not the Morrisons."

"Nor the Taylors, for sure," she added.

"Certainly not. And I wouldn't suggest that you take the vacant room at the Howards, either."

"Indeed not. Nor the Orfords."

"Definitely not the Orfords. And the Rutledges, neither."

"And we wouldn't recommend the Pointers," she insisted.

"Certainly not, my dear, certainly not."

"And don't even mention the Hoppers. Nor the Morleys."

"Indubitably not the Morleys. Under no circumstances whatsoever the room at the Morleys."

The woman smiled at Kirchgässner. "I'm really sorry we can't help you, madam. Good day!"

His year at Cambridge had inured him to the eccentricities of the English. He just smiled back politely, left the shop and post office, and got back into the Morris Eight. He turned left from High Street into Mill Lane, drove for about half a mile and then picked the next farm he saw.

"Do you have a room to let?" he asked the pretty young woman who opened the door.

"Come in, I'll call Mrs. Morrison," she said. "I'm Beryl, one of the Land Girls."

Seeing the blank look on his face, she continued, "After war broke out, I volunteered for the Women's Land Army. It's really hard work for a born-and-bred Londoner like me, especially getting up so early every morning, but the government wants as many people as possible to get involved with food production."

The German realized that he had blundered. *Everyone in Britain must know about the Land Girls*, he said to himself, *and especially a reporter writing an article on women doing men's jobs. I have to leave before they put my accent and my mistake together and call the police.* Aloud, he asked, "This is the Orford farm, isn't it?"

"No, it's the Morrison farm," Beryl said.

"Oh, dear, I'm on the wrong farm! Can you please direct me to the Orfords?"

"Yes, drive about two hundred yards in the direction of Dedham, and you'll see it on the other side of the road. Let me show you."

The obliging young woman escorted him back to his car and pointed in the direction of the Orford farm. Once Beryl was back inside the Morrison farmhouse, the ever security-conscious Kirchgässner drove along Mill Lane in the direction opposite to the one she had indicated. He drove along the country road until he saw a car parked on the grassy verge. He stopped behind it, checked that no pedestrians or other cars were in the vicinity, then quickly unscrewed and switched the vehicle registration plates.

Twenty minutes later he was ensconced in a comfortable room in a converted barn on the Morley farm.

CHAPTER NINETEEN
MI5 Headquarters, London
Saturday, May 31, 1941

"First let's review the situation in East Anglia," the air commodore said. "Agent WÜRZBURG is singing like a canary. It's true that up to now everything he's told us we've already heard from other captured *Abwehr* agents, but he's been in our custody for only three days, so there's hope yet that we'll learn something new and valuable from him.

"The bad news is that the assassin is nowhere to be found. However, we've received a police report from East Clemford that someone burgled a house and stole a car, a suitcase, women's clothing, make-up, and a man's razor."

"Sounds like the two German assassins we're searching for," Chulmleigh responded.

"Yes and no. I've asked Dr. Curtin, the head of our forensic laboratory, to join our meeting. I think I hear him outside now. Come in, Dr. Curtin. Allow me to introduce the members of my team: Lieutenant Wallstead, Lieutenant Commander Chulmleigh, Squadron Leader Harkness, Major Tupman, and Captain Marks." Curtin, a tall bald man with a pronounced stoop, nodded to each man in turn.

"Gentlemen, be seated. Dr. Curtin has something important to share with us."

"Thank you, Air Commodore. From the outset I must stress that everything I tell you this morning is strictly preliminary. We received the items that the officers found at Number Six, Estuary Drive, West Clemford only yesterday afternoon at about five. My assistants and I have been working through the night analyzing them, and we'll definitely redo our work later today after we've had some sleep.

"Air Commodore Pankhurst, you told me that you and your team had decided that there were two German agents, a man and a woman. At least one of them, perhaps both, arrived a short time ago in East Anglia from Germany, but it was possible that one of the agents was British. You therefore asked me to fingerprint every single item in the hope that we could find a print that matched someone we have in our files.

"I have to tell you that we found only one set of prints everywhere, including the woman's cosmetics and the man's razor."

"But they can't be identical twins," Chulmleigh interrupted. "One's a man and the other is a woman."

"Precisely," Dr. Curtin answered. "And in any event, identical twins have similar fingerprints, but they're never exactly the same. It's like your own hand—there are always differences between the prints of each of the fingers. The conclusion is inescapable: There's only one German agent, who dresses as both a man and a woman."

"And that's why they call him or her agent BROCKEN," Harkness said admiringly. "A Brocken Specter is an optical illusion. You see a man, but it's actually a woman, or vice versa."

"Perhaps I should stick my neck out just a little," Dr. Curtin said. "In general, it's almost impossible to tell whether a hair came from a man or a woman. But we can distinguish facial hair because it's coarse in appearance and has a triangular cross section. The two small snippets of hair we found in the razor are facial in nature. It's therefore more likely that agent BROCKEN, as you call him, is a man who sometimes dresses as a woman than the other way round."

"So," Captain Marks said, "agent BROCKEN is a transvestite."

"I wouldn't necessarily use that term," Dr. Curtin cautioned. "A transvestite is someone who derives sexual pleasure by wearing the clothing of someone of the other sex, and we don't know if that's the case here. It's quite possible that he dresses as a woman only for the purpose of facilitating his killings. After all, most of us are a lot less suspicious and on our guard if a woman approaches us."

"Are you saying that he's like an actor who wears women's clothing as part of his role?" Harkness inquired.

"Something like that. But let me make myself unambiguously clear," Curtin added. "One possibility is that agent BROCKEN is a woman who needs to shave her facial hair from time to time.

Another is that he's a transvestite. And a third possibility is that he's a male who wears woman's clothing for the sole reason of making it easier to approach his victims to murder them."

"Dr. Curtin," Pankhurst asked, "which do you consider the most likely?"

"You're asking a scientist who hasn't slept for nearly thirty hours to come to a conclusion based on only preliminary data. That just isn't reasonable. Having said that, I doubt that she's a woman who has to shave her face all the time, and my intuition tells me that someone who gets erotic gratification from wearing women's clothing is not going to be able to concentrate on killing while dressed as a female. That leaves only the third possibility: agent BROCKEN is a man who dresses like a woman when he kills.

"How sure am I? I'm not sure at all. And now, Air Commodore, with your permission I'm going home to sleep for a few hours."

"Of course, Dr. Curtin. Thank you for coming here and helping us to understand the situation, and many thanks for spending the whole of last night analyzing the data from West Clemford."

The scientist left the room. The air commodore turned to his team and asked, "What do we do now?"

"We lay a trap for agent BROCKEN," Captain Marks said. "He's in Constable country, and Campbell-White is there, too. We get the word out that Hess is suffering from some sort of breakdown, and to help him regain his sanity we're using painting therapy."

"Marks, did you say 'painting therapy'?"

"Yes, sir, that's what I said."

"There's no such thing, but do carry on. I'm curious to see where this nonsense is going."

"Yes, sir. Well, we'll take Campbell-White to Flatford Mill, where John Constable created those six large pictures, each one an absolute masterpiece of landscape painting. We'll provide him with canvas, easel, palette, paints, and the like. Carlyle will let agent BROCKEN know that we're bringing 'Hess' to Flatford Mill for painting therapy. Our officers will cover all the routes to the mill, which is in the middle of the countryside, and when agent BROCKEN arrives, we'll have him."

And Captain Marks sat back with a satisfied smile on his face.

"I really had hoped that at least one member of my team was sane," Pankhurst responded. "But we'll try your suggestion—mainly because everything else we've attempted has failed. It's twenty past ten now, and our man is due to be transferred from Braintree police station to Ipswich at eleven. If we haven't captured agent BROCKEN by the time Campbell-White arrives there, I'll issue instructions for your 'painting therapy' to start tomorrow.

"Personally, I don't think it's going to work. When agent BROCKEN arrives at Flatford Mill, he'll surely realize that the area is swarming with police. He'll stay well out of sight until the end of the day, and then he'll take a shot at Campbell-White as you escort him back to the car. However, as I said, let's give your plan a try. It won't do any harm, and we don't have any better ideas.

"Now let's turn to the situation in Scotland. Yesterday we followed both of Harkness's suggestions. Having checked that Lady Alison was at home in her cottage, we sent a man up a pole to turn off her electricity supply. Not surprisingly, she telephoned the local Electricity Department almost at once. We had three men standing by and we dispatched them to her house. They spent about twenty-five minutes looking in every room trying to find the 'fault' but to no avail, of course. Finally, not having found anything in the least bit suspicious, their leader made a telephone call to the Electricity Department, suggesting a way of solving the non-existent problem. Five minutes later the lights came back on. Lady Alison was profuse in her thanks."

"Sir, do you think she guessed that this was a ruse to search the cottage from stem to stern?" Tubman asked.

"I doubt it. The leader of the team is a qualified electrician, and he kept talking to her while the other two searched the premises. Noticing that she appears to know nothing about electricity, he bombarded her with appropriate technical phrases and jargon. And if she was feigning her ignorance of such matters, she would quickly have realized that the leader is extremely knowledgeable. So, no, I don't think she suspects anything. Other questions?"

No one raised a hand.

"I turn now to Harkness's second suggestion. We've checked that Lady Alison was telling the truth when she told Johnson that she paid for the conversion of Castle Robson into a convalescent home. Undertaking all those alterations at her own expense was hardly the actions of an *Abwehr* agent. Marks, I know what you're going to say: She did it to cover up the fact that she's an *Abwehr* agent. Am I right?"

"Quite right, sir."

"Anyhow, what she didn't mention to Johnson is that the vast grounds of Castle Robson contain numerous outbuildings, some of which have electricity supplies. And what's the significance of that?"

Lieutenant Wallstead put up his hand. "The transmitter responsible for the mysterious transmission on May 14th from the approximate vicinity of Oban was probably connected to an electricity supply, not batteries."

"Ten out of ten, Wallstead. With the permission of the convalescent home, we searched every outbuilding, with or without electricity. Of course, we told them we were inspecting the castle grounds with a view to expanding the facilities—we certainly didn't want anyone to know the real reason. And we found absolutely nothing there, either. Keep in mind that Mallaig is about forty miles from Oban as the crow flies, so it was possible but not too likely that the transmission two weeks ago came from Mallaig. Nevertheless, Harkness, those were two reasonable suggestions. Please keep at it.

"Now let's start again from the very beginning. We have only one suspect in the vicinity of Oban: Lady Alison, Countess of Mallaig. We've searched her castle—or more correctly, the grounds of her castle. And we've searched the cottage where she now lives. Before we cross her off the list, are they any other places where she might have hidden a transceiver?"

There was a long silence, and then Captain Marks spoke up. "Sir, I seem to remember that you said that the Countess comes to The Thistle almost every night. She even keeps her own bottle of whisky there.

"Here's what I've learned about her at our morning meetings: She's the Countess of Mallaig and the Chief of Clan MacRobson. She's wealthy—she paid for the conversion of her castle out of her own funds. She was educated at one of the best girls' schools in the land and is intelligent enough to get accepted to Oxford. And she's an accomplished equestrienne; her headmistress said that she was in the running for the British Olympics team.

"Sir, I don't claim to be an expert on the Scottish aristocracy or clan chiefs or champion horsewomen. And we all know that Lady Alison has suffered at least two serious nervous breakdowns. But it just doesn't make sense to me that she spends her evenings in The Thistle.

"And there's something else that's bothering me, too. Why does she have her own Lochervan whisky in that bottle? If she's of an egalitarian bent, then she'll consume whatever everyone else in The Thistle drinks. But if she's the kind of person who insists on drinking her own whisky and won't let anyone else enjoy her private tipple, why does she go to The Thistle and mix with the common folk at all? It just doesn't add up."

"What are you getting at, Marks?" Pankhurst asked.

"I'm saying that, if she's agent OBAN then the transceiver may be hidden somewhere in The Thistle, probably in the beer cellar."

This remark was met with total silence. Then the Air Commodore rushed off in the direction of his office, knocking over his chair in his haste.

"Well, Marks," Wallstead said, "I've never seen old Archie do that before. Either you're going to get a medal for this, or else there's going to be a vacant seat around this table tomorrow morning!"

***

After a country breakfast cooked by Mrs. Morley and served by her equally delightful husband, Kirchgässner drove into Dedham, arriving just before the church clock struck nine. He parked the black Morris Eight on High Street across the road from the village store and post office and entered the telephone booth.

"He's at Braintree police station. And the last two times they've moved him at eleven o'clock," Carlyle told him.

He returned to the car and looked at his map. The distance from Dedham to Braintree seemed to be about twenty-five miles, over good roads. He looked forward to a leisurely drive through the spectacularly beautiful Essex countryside.

***

The best-loved person in Braintree was undoubtedly Miss Delauncy, a teacher at a primary school for boys. In May 1939 she reached the official retirement age of sixty-five. Her former students hired the main room at the Literary and Mechanical Institute for her farewell reception, but even that large space was too small for the endless crowd of people who flocked there to wish her well. She shook hands with each person in the receiving line, greeting by name those men whom she had taught, which included almost all the civic dignitaries of Braintree.

She was respected as much as she was adored. Only a few people knew that her first name was Laetitia, but not for one moment would any of them dream of calling her anything but "Miss Delauncy." The townspeople agreed that, when in the fullness of time Miss Delauncy arrived at the Pearly Gates, she would look the keeper of the keys to the kingdom of heaven straight in the eye and greet him with a warm "Hello, Peter!" in the same encouraging tone of voice she always used in the classroom to her eight-year old charges. And St. Peter would no doubt reply, as respectfully as he could, "Good afternoon, Miss Delauncy!"

With the outbreak of war, younger teachers were conscripted and older teachers were pulled out of retirement. Miss Delauncy naturally did not wait to be asked, but reappeared in her classroom as if there had been no interruption in her selfless service to the shaping of the minds of boys. Children were evacuated from London as the German air raids intensified, and her classes grew in size. Miss Delauncy took it all in her stride.

That Saturday morning, Miss Delauncy was doing her shopping. As she walked around the corner from Coggeshall Road and reached the police station, she noticed two young men in tweed jackets and ties standing on the sidewalk, scrutinizing the passersby. Two uniformed constables walked out of the police station, followed by someone whom she immediately recognized as Rudolf Hess, handcuffed to a third constable. Her first thought was of the thousands of innocent children killed by Nazi bombs during the Blitz and Battle of Britain. Something snapped in her brain. Miss Delauncy moved as fast as she could toward the prisoner; the two constables in front politely allowed the elderly woman to pass them. As she reached Hess, with a sideways motion she flung her heavy shopping bag at his head.

Campbell-White ducked and the bag flew harmlessly through the air. As it passed over Campbell-White, Lionel Mortimer, one of the Essex watchers, came through the door of the police station behind the look-alike; he was carrying the radio and extension cord that MI5 had provided Campbell-White. Mortimer caught a glimpse of a woman apparently trying to murder 'Hess.' Having been warned that the German killer would probably be dressed as a female, he immediately dropped the radio equipment and bravely inserted himself between the Hess impersonator and the supposed assassin. Mortimer and Miss Delauncy collided, and the elderly woman fell backward onto the ground. Immediately the three watchers and a constable rushed to her assistance, leaving Hess largely unguarded.

SS-Major Helmut Kirchgässner stepped out of the clothing shop opposite, where he had been examining the goods on display while keeping an eye on the police station. As he took in the scene he drew his silenced CZ 27 from his handbag. The area in front of him was a mêlée. Four men were on the ground next to Miss Delauncy trying to revive her, and the other two policemen had their eyes on the schoolteacher instead of looking out for agent BROCKEN. Kirchgässner quickly fired two shots at Campbell-White. Both hit him in the chest, directly opposite his heart. Campbell-White slumped to the ground. Two policemen dragged him back into the police station, one still handcuffed by his left wrist to Campbell-White.

Agent BROCKEN slipped away in the confusion.

***

"Sir, it's Johnson. I'm speaking to you from the police station in Mallaig."

"Yes, Johnson. What have you found out?"

"The Earldom of Mallaig owns much of the village of Mallaig, including both sides of Highland Street. And that means that Lady Alison owns the building that houses The Thistle. The license is in the name of a Scottish private company, Mallaig Public Houses Limited. On Monday I can contact the Registrar of Companies and try and find out who the shareholders are. But my guess is that we'll find that Lady Alison owns the license, too. Fergus MacRobson is the licensee."

"Have you asked the local magistrate for a search warrant?"

"Yes, sir. He issued it, but with the greatest reluctance. I had to threaten him, extremely politely of course. He finally gave it to me with bad grace."

"He wouldn't be a member of Clan MacRobson now, would he?"

"You've got it, sir. It seems that it's just not done for a Scottish magistrate—or 'justice of the peace' as we call them here—to permit anyone to search the domain of their clan chief, and national security be damned. But I managed to change his mind."

"Well done, Johnson. Are you ready to move in?"

"Almost, sir. Yesterday we borrowed eight policemen from Fort William and other nearby towns; they include a detective sergeant. You'll be pleased to learn that none of them appear to be members of the local clan. Also, there's a training center for amphibious landing techniques at Inveraray on Loch Fyne, not that far from here. I took the liberty of phoning them as soon as I received your first message. They told me that a squad of Royal Marines are currently involved in an exercise on signaling procedures at Glasnacardoch, just outside Mallaig, and I requested that they be sent here at once."

"Excellent work, Johnson!"

"Sir, as soon as the marines arrive we'll get moving."

"Fine. I want you to execute that search warrant without delay."

"Hold on, sir, I hear a lorry outside. I think they're here."

"Good luck! Phone me as soon as you have some information."

"Yes, sir. Goodbye."

Johnson replaced the receiver and rushed outside. Twelve Royal Marines in full battle dress were forming up outside the police station. Johnson went up to their officer.

"Lieutenant, thank you for coming so promptly. We're about to execute a search warrant on The Thistle, a pub around the corner. I need your men to surround the building and make sure that no one gets in or out while the police go through every room. The pub is only about two hundred yards from here. The police are ready. Can you and your men follow us?"

"Certainly, sir. We're ready to move out."

Local inhabitants doing their shopping were astounded to see ten armed policemen running towards The Thistle, closely followed by a squad of Royal Marines. The marines formed a cordon around the building. Johnson looked carefully at the windows of the upper story, looking for any sign of Fergus MacRobson; it seemed reasonable to assume that he lived in the upstairs rooms.

Under the wartime regulations for that district of Scotland, the licensee of a pub could serve alcohol only between twelve noon and two o'clock, and again between six and ten in the evening, with an additional twenty minutes at the end of each period for patrons to finish their last drinks. It was now just before eleven o'clock. Accordingly, Johnson assumed that the bar would be locked, but that Fergus would be somewhere on the premises, cleaning the glasses from the previous night and preparing for the lunchtime session. So Johnson banged loudly on the door and shouted, "Police! Open up!"

There was no response from inside the building. He moved back and yelled loudly in the direction of the windows of the upstairs rooms, in case the elderly barman was taking a nap. But again there was no reaction. He nodded to a brawny sergeant who took a few paces away from the building, turned, and then charged at the door at full speed, shoulder first. As the wooden door cracked open, the sergeant nearly fell, but he managed to keep his balance. No one came to investigate the noise.

"Carry on as instructed," Johnson shouted. He had acquired the plans of the building earlier in the day and assigned search areas to each of the policemen. Because Captain Marks had predicted that the transmitter would be found in the beer cellar, Johnson had chosen that part of the building for himself, aided by Logan and Menzies, two of the constables seconded from Fort William.

Behind the bar, Johnson found a flight of stairs leading downward. He noticed a light switch and turned it on. The three men cautiously approached the cellar. They found themselves in a large underground room. Barrels of draft beer stood on their ends next to one wall; tubing connected them to the beer taps in the bar above. Three other barrels stood on their ends near the center of the room. The whole area was spotlessly clean.

"There's nothing here, sir, just those barrels. And there's nowhere to hide a radio. Shall we go upstairs, sir, and help the others?" Menzies asked.

"No," Johnson said. "This place is just too neat. Something is concealed here. Let's tap the walls. I'll start in this corner. You two go there and there."

The three men methodically rapped on the whitewashed stone walls. After a few minutes their knuckles were sore. As Menzies had predicted, their search was fruitless. Then Johnson had another idea.

"Maybe the radio is hidden under the floorboards."

"Doesn't look like it, sir," Menzies replied. "The floorboards are six feet long. None of them seems to have been cut."

"What about under a beer barrel?" Logan asked.

Menzies shook his head. "A full barrel contains thirty-six gallons of beer. It takes a strong man to shift nearly four hundred pounds by himself. It's bluidy hard work even for two. And they tell me that the landlord is old."

"What about under an empty barrel?" Johnson asked.

"Moving a barrel would leave a mark in the dust on the floor," Menzies replied.

"But look how clean this place is," Johnson said. "It's almost as if they keep it like this to ensure that shifting a barrel won't leave any trace."

"Yes, sir," Logan answered. "I think you're right. Menzies, help me move each of the barrels."

"No, wait," Johnson interrupted. "First let's check if there are any empty barrels. If there's a hiding place, it's surely under a barrel that's easy to move."

Logan and Menzies walked over to the three barrels in the middle of the cellar and closely examined them. All of them proved to be empty. They shifted each one sideways and examined the floor where the barrel had stood. Once more they came up empty handed.

"What about inside those barrels?" Logan suggested.

"Good idea. Let's check."

Logan and his colleague turned the three barrels on their sides and rolled them around.

"Sir, they seem to be empty. Do you want us to get some tools from the station and break them open?"

"No. If there were something inside, they wouldn't roll that smoothly. In any case, unless there's a way of opening one of them easily, there's no way anyone could store a radio there. It would be a pity to destroy those barrels unnecessarily, especially with wartime shortages."

Then Logan had another idea. "Those barrels over there have tubing connecting them to the beer taps. But what if one of them is an empty barrel connected to a dummy tube?"

Menzies scoffed. "That's ridiculous!"

"Menzies," said Johnson, "run upstairs and count the beer taps in the bar."

Menzies walked obediently toward the stairs, but it was obvious from his body language that he was convinced that he was on a fool's errand. Johnson could clearly hear the constable's footsteps overhead as he walked behind the bar. The MI5 intelligence officer realized that the wooden ceiling of the cellar was the underside of the floor of the pub. He looked up and shouted, "Menzies, how many beer taps?"

There was a pause and then the two men in the cellar heard a muffled voice saying "Eight, sir."

"Is one of them McEwan's Export?"

"Yes, sir."

"Deuchar's India Pale Ale?"

"Let me see. Yes, sir, I've found it." This time the constable's voice was from further way.

"What about William Younger's No. 3 Scotch Ale?"

"That one doesn't seem to be here. Let me check all the taps. No, sir, it's not here."

"Come back down, Menzies."

When the constable arrived, Johnson pointed to the beer barrels against the wall. "There are nine barrels there, and only eight taps upstairs. I think that Logan is right. Let's move the Younger's No. 3 barrel and see what's underneath."

Menzies rushed forward and felt the barrel. It seemed to be empty. He pushed it to one side. The three men immediately saw the trapdoor cut into the floor and the flush ring pull made of polished brass for opening the hatch cover. Menzies lunged toward it.

"Stop!" Johnson ordered. "There may be fingerprints. I've got gloves in my pocket." He slipped on a pair of gray cotton gloves and opened the hinged trapdoor. In the cavity below lay a suitcase. He reached in, undid the two catches and opened the lid. He shone his flashlight inside, revealing the transmitter and receiver modules of a German SE 85/14 radio. Johnson closed the suitcase and the trapdoor and moved the beer barrel back to where it had been.

"Thank you both for your help. But now it's a job for MI5. I want the two of you to stay here on guard until you're relieved. You've been issued with revolvers, probably for the first time since you finished your training. Don't hesitate to use them if you have to."

Johnson went back upstairs into the bar. Through the doorway he noticed that the rest of the police were standing outside. "Anyone find anything?"

They shook their heads.

"No papers? Nothing of interest?"

The response was the same.

"Thank you very much. Return to the station now. I may need some of you in a few minutes."

Johnson now approached the Royal Marines officer.

"Lieutenant, MI5 intelligence officers will soon be here to conduct a thorough search. In the meantime, instruct your men to not to let anyone enter or leave the premises, as before."

***

"Sir," Carlyle said over the phone to Air Commodore Pankhurst, "what happened at Braintree today was nothing less than a total fiasco."

"Tell me the worst."

Carlyle proceeded to describe the sequence of events. "The good news, sir," he concluded, "is that Campbell-White is alive. The body armor stopped the bullets, but he has a large bruise near the center of his chest from the two impacts. He's lying in his cell in Braintree police station. The doctor said that he's seen similar injuries from savage body blows to boxers or a vicious bouncer at cricket. He's prescribed aspirin and says that Campbell-White should be fine in a day or two."

"And Miss Delauncy?" the air commodore asked.

"She's in the William Julien Courtauld Hospital. Physically she's fine, I'm delighted to report, but there's a psychological problem. She keeps saying, 'I behaved far worse than any eight-year old boy. How can I possibly face the children?' We've sent her vicar over to talk to her, but I don't think that he or anyone else will be able to do too much. They tell me that she's an extremely strong-willed person."

"I think that someone from MI5 should go and see her. You'd be the best person."

"Me, sir?"

"Yes, you. You know precisely what you can tell her and what you can't. I'd appreciate it if you went to see her this afternoon. Now, do you think that agent BROCKEN believes that he killed Hess?"

"Of course! Why do you even ask that, sir?"

"Because he shot Campbell-White twice and there was no blood. Think about it, Carlyle—he must have seen his bullets strike his target in the chest. Also, surely he heard the metallic sound that the bullets made as the steel body armor stopped them? We need to know: Does BROCKEN think that Hess is still alive?"

***

"Sir, we discovered an SE 85/14 transceiver in the beer cellar of The Thistle, exactly as Marks predicted."

Johnson proceeded to explain to the air commodore what he had found.

"Excellent work, Johnson. Just hold on a minute."

Johnson could hear Air Commodore Pankhurst giving instructions to Captain Nicholas.

"Are you still there, Johnson?"

"Yes, sir."

"Your colleagues are helping to guard 'Hess' at Kilmallie police station, just outside Fort William. As many of them as can be spared will be with you in Mallaig in roughly an hour's time; Nicholas is taking care of it. In addition, an MI5 forensic team is on its way from Edinburgh. You can expect them in about four hours.

"Now," he continued, "what about the publican—Fergus MacRobson? Is that his name?"

"Yes, sir."

"Obviously he and Lady Alison are in this together. There's no way that he could run the pub, replacing the barrels of draft beer when they're finished, without knowing about the empty barrel of William Younger's No. 3 Scotch Ale connected to the dummy tubing. Also, that transmission from agent OBAN on the night of May 14th at a quarter past eleven—he must have known that she was in the cellar sending the message to Germany."

"Yes, sir, I agree."

"Does anyone else work in The Thistle?"

"Not that I know of. My guess is that, when a barrel of draft is empty, the brewery deliverymen set up the new barrel and take away the empty one, and they do it under MacRobson's close supervision. He'd never allow anyone other than Lady Alison to be alone in his cellar—they might cotton onto the trick with the tubing. Remind me to send a letter of commendation to the policeman from Fort William who tumbled to MacRobson's stratagem."

"Yes, sir."

"Now, where's the barman?"

"There was no sign of him inside The Thistle, sir."

"It's not quite opening time," Pankhurst said, "so it's not unreasonable for him to have gone shopping and not come back yet. Or perhaps he took a morning stroll around the village."

"But if he returned, he'd have seen the cordon of Royal Marines and probably realized that we'd found the radio."

"Yes, of course. Get every man you can to search the village. Make sure that he doesn't get on any of the ferries—once he escapes to the Inner Hebrides we'll have a devil of time trying to get our hands on him. Send some of your marines to the ferry wharf. I'll hold the line while you issue the order."

Johnson returned a few minutes later.

"While you were gone, Johnson, a few thoughts came to me. First, regarding that magistrate or justice of the peace who issued the warrant with such reluctance. You said that Lady Alison is the chief of his clan, so he's a MacRobson."

"Yes, sir. Oliver MacRobson."

"And the publican, Fergus MacRobson, is clearly also a member of the tribe."

"Yes, sir."

"Is there any chance that Oliver tipped Fergus off?"

"I don't think he did, sir. As far as I could determine, the reason that Oliver was hesitant to issue the search warrant is that Lady Alison is his chief, rather than a fellow member of his clan. In other words, it wasn't as much an issue of loyalty to the clan as obeisance to its head."

"Understood. Now, do you think he tipped off Lady Alison who then told Fergus?"

"Hmm. That I don't know. I can go and talk to him."

"Do that. But there's no hurry—the immediate urgency is to arrest Fergus MacRobson and Lady Alison. Which leads to my next point."

"Yes, sir?"

"The way I understand the situation, Fergus runs the pub singlehandedly, so Lady Alison couldn't possibly have stored the clandestine radio in his beer cellar without his knowledge. But there's another possibility, one that regrettably I've overlooked until now."

Pankhurst paused, and Johnson interjected, "You mean that Fergus MacRobson is agent OBAN, and Lady Alison is totally innocent?"

"Yes, that's exactly what I mean. So, the next step is clearly to interview Lady Alison. Be extremely careful—I don't want you to push her over the edge. She can't help us sort this out if she has another nervous breakdown and is unable to speak for months, whether or not she's an *Abwehr* agent. Find the local doctor, take him along together with a detective sergeant, and go and talk to her."

***

"Harbormaster?"

"Aye, Chief Inspector."

"I'm handing the phone to Mr. Johnson, from the government. He has some important questions to ask you."

"Good afternoon, Harbormaster," Johnson said.

"And guid day to ye, Mr. Johnson. What are ye after?"

"What ferries have left since nine o'clock today, and what's on the schedule for later?"

"Weel, at eleven a ferry left for two of the small isles, first Eigg and then Muck."

"Do you know Fergus MacRobson, the licensee at The Thistle?"

"Aye, of course. Why?"

"Was he aboard?"

"A dinnae ken, but I could ask around."

"Has that ferry arrived yet?"

"It's supposed to dock at Eigg at about noon, that's about ten minutes from now."

"Could you radio the captain and ask him about Fergus?"

"Certainly. Hold on, please."

A few minutes later the harbormaster returned. "Nae, Fergus wasn't on the ferry."

"And what about ferries leaving after eleven o'clock today?"

"There's a ferry leaving for Armadale on the Isle of Skye at the back o' noon."

"The back o' noon?"

"Aye, just after noon."

"Have they started boarding yet?"

"Nae. She's only just come in from Skye. The passengers are still getting off."

"Don't let anyone on board. I've sent two marines to the harbor. Tell them that I told you to instruct them to make sure that no one gets onto that ship. No one at all. I'm on my way to the Armadale ferry right now. Meet me there."

***

The Nazi assassin knew that his two shots were right on target. But the sounds of both impacts were definitely wrong. And there were no spurts of blood. As the killer tried to work out what had happened, he saw that Hess had collapsed and that the body of the burly policeman handcuffed to Hess by the left wrist blocked him from further bullets. A second policeman helped his colleague to drag Hess back inside the police station.

Kirchgässner quickly slipped his gun into his handbag. No one challenged him as he walked calmly toward his car, which he had parked around the corner in Coggeshall Road. The killer started the Morris Eight. As he slowly drove back to Dedham, he played over the events of the morning in his mind. It took him a while to realize that Hess was wearing some sort of body armor. During the Second World War, trials of body armor to protect against bullets were undertaken in Britain for the first time in February 1941; Nazi Germany had no similar program. It was therefore not surprising that, after firing the first shot, Kirchgässner did not immediately tumble to the fact that he should have aimed his second bullet at Hess's head.

At no time did the thought cross the *Abwehr* assassin's mind that the man he had tried to kill might be an imposter. He was also unaware that no one had seen him fire the shots. The three plainclothes officers had been solicitously tending to the elderly lady on the other side of the street, watched by the nearby uniformed police. The men would undoubtedly have heard the noise of the silenced weapon had it fired twice inside a quiet room. But with their concern fully focused on the recumbent woman, it was the thuds coming from the direction of where Hess was standing followed by the clatter of his fall that drew their attention; they did not hear the two soft popping noises from across the road. By the time they worked out what had happened, the street was empty.

Reaching Dedham, Kirchgässner drove around until he saw a farm sporting a "Room for Rent" sign.

"Mrs. Howard," he said, "I see that you have a room to let. I was wondering if I could stay here tonight?"

***

The harbormaster was a tall, harried looking, middle-aged man. The uniform of a Lieutenant Commander in the Royal Navy that he wore seemed to be two sizes too big for him. Johnson wondered whether the harbormaster had lost that much weight because of food rationing, the stress of his job, or whether he was seriously ill.

"Mr. Johnson?"

"Yes. Any sign of our man?"

"Not yet. Nae, I'm wrong. Look, here he comes."

Johnson looked back along the quay that led from the village to the ferry berth and saw Fergus walking toward him. He was carrying a small suitcase in his left hand. As he neared the ferry berth, he saw the two marines. He assumed that they were fellow passengers for Skye and kept on walking. Then he saw Johnson standing next to the harbormaster. He turned, dropped the suitcase and started to return to the village. It seemed that he was trying to run, but his age and physical condition precluded that.

"Stop that man!" Johnson shouted, hoping that someone on the pier would grab hold of Fergus MacRobson and prevent him from leaving the quay. But to the MI5 officer's horror, the nearest marine raised his Colt M1911A1 pistol and fired a single shot. MacRobson fell and did not move. Johnson rushed to him, closely followed by the marine who had taken Johnson's order too literally; the other marine remained on guard. The harbormaster was in a state of shock, unable to move. When Johnson reached Fergus, he could see that the publican was dead.

***

"Well, gentlemen, what are we going to do about agent BROCKEN?" Pankhurst asked. "Does he or doesn't he think that he killed 'Hess' this morning? If he believes that he assassinated him, then he's on his way back to Germany."

"But we have his radio, sir," Major Tupman said. "He's going to have to steal a radio to tell them when and where to pick him up. Hopefully, MI8 will locate him when he transmits."

"But where will he find a transceiver?" Harkness asked. "Civilians aren't allowed to have transmitting equipment."

"He knows that his assistant has one. We need to warn Carlyle at once," Chulmleigh said.

"Don't worry," the air commodore reassured him, "Carlyle is well aware of the situation. But there's also the other possibility: BROCKEN may think that Campbell-White is still alive. In that case, he's going to keep trying until he kills him. What do we do now?"

"Why don't we play a waiting game?" Lieutenant Wallstead suggested. "Let's see if he phones Carlyle tomorrow. He's phoned him every morning at nine o'clock without fail. That means that if he doesn't phone tomorrow morning we'll know he thinks that Hess is dead. And if he phones, it'll be to find out Campbell-White's new location."

"Or to set up a rendezvous with Carlyle to kill him and then use his transceiver," Chulmleigh added gloomily. "BROCKEN is undoubtedly going to murder anyone who can identify him.

***

"Good afternoon, Mr. Johnson. I see you've brought Dr. Finlayson with you."

"Yes, Lady Alison, and this is Detective Sergeant Moore. May we come in?"

"Of course. Please sit down."

They crowded into the small front room of the cottage. Lady Alison sat at her desk, with the chair turned round to face the room. As before, Johnson sat on the two-seater couch, the doctor was next to him, and the large policeman was perched on a small stool.

"Lady Alison," Johnson said, "I'm afraid I have some bad news."

"Is that why Dr. Finlayson is here?" she asked. "I'm not that fragile."

"I'm sorry to have to tell you that Fergus MacRobson is dead. He was shot at the ferry terminal."

"Shot? Who shot him?"

"He was trying to escape from Mallaig. A soldier misunderstood my—"

"Escape? What do you mean 'escape'? What was he escaping from?"

"Lady Alison, earlier today I found a German radio transceiver hidden in the beer cellar of The Thistle. Experts are examining it now, but we believe that it was used on the 14th of May to send a message to Germany in a book code."

"Is all this part of your circus clown act? If it is, I don't find it the least bit amusing."

"Lady Alison, I'm not sure you understand the gravity of the situation. Possession of a German radio transmitter is *prima facie* evidence of being a Nazi spy."

"Fergus MacRobson a Nazi spy? Don't be ridiculous."

"Lady Alison, the transmitter was found, as I said, hidden in the cellar of The Thistle. And you own the building."

"I inherited much of the village from my father. I may or may not own the building in Highland Street. I'd have to check on Monday morning with my factor—an estate manager knows these things. But what has all that got to do with the death of poor Fergus?"

"Here's what happened this afternoon. I obtained a search warrant for The Thistle. I knocked on the door, but Fergus was out for a walk. We broke in and started searching the premises. While we were doing that, twelve Royal Marines surrounded the building. I believe that Fergus returned from his stroll, saw the soldiers, and realized that the game was up."

"What game was that?"

Johnson ignored the interruption. "Fergus came here to get help from you."

"Balderdash! He hasn't been here for months."

"At the ferry port he was carrying a suitcase. Where did he get it?"

"I have no idea. Why are you asking me?"

"A number of people saw him walking through the village at about eleven o'clock. At that time he didn't have a suitcase with him. He couldn't go back into The Thistle to pack a bag because it was cordoned off by the marines."

"He could have bought it in the village."

"A suitcase bearing your coat of arms?"

The Countess of Mallaig smiled sadly. "Mr. Johnson, as you so quaintly put it, the game is indeed up. Yes, Fergus came here late this morning. He told me that he'd done something wrong and had to leave for the islands at once—the police were at The Thistle waiting to arrest him. He asked for my help as his chief. I have a small suitcase that I keep packed in case I have to travel at short notice. My cousin, the Duke of Bute, comes to stay here every so often; he leaves some of his clothes in the second bedroom. I took my items out of the suitcase and gave Fergus some of my cousin's clothes."

"Did Fergus tell you what he'd done?"

"No. When I asked him, he said it would be better if I didn't know. That way I couldn't be charged with aiding and abetting a criminal or, worse, being an accessory after the fact. Of course, I now realize that the real reason he didn't want to enlighten me is that, if he'd told me that he was a Nazi spy, I'd have obviously summoned the police at once. I wouldn't have lifted a finger to help him.

"Yes, Mr. Johnson, I did help one of my clan members to escape. But I certainly had no idea what he'd done and, I must tell you, I have the greatest difficulty believing that he was a Nazi spy. In fact, the reason I helped him is that I assumed that what he'd done was really minor. As far as I'm concerned, Fergus MacRobson, may his soul rest in peace, was no criminal."

"Lady Alison, yesterday we turned off your electricity."

"You did what?"

"And when you phoned the Electricity Department, we sent three of our men here. Their leader kept you engaged in conversation while the other two searched the cottage."

"This is an outrage! I shall complain to the Home Secretary. He's my uncle."

Once again Johnson ignored her interjection and continued calmly. "When they left, they took one object from the cottage."

"And what was that?"

"A glass."

"A glass?"

"Yes, they took a glass from the draining board in the kitchen."

"And why would they do that?"

"Because when you washed it you left your fingerprints on the glass, fingerprints that exactly match the fingerprints we found on the SE 85/14 transceiver we found in the beer cellar of The Thistle."

There was dead silence. No one moved. It was as if the world had stopped rotating on its axis. Then the Countess of Mallaig spun round and reached into the drawer of her desk. Johnson, who had been watching her closely, jumped up and smashed the revolver out of her right hand before she could raise it to her head.

"You bastard! You've broken my wrist!"

"Sergeant, take her away."

Dr. Finlayson was about to protest, but said nothing.

***

The smile of Air Commodore Pankhurst's face was radiant. His eyes shone with delight.

"Gentlemen," he began, "we've been receiving good news from Scotland all afternoon. There are still some questions that need answering, but overall the situation is excellent. Marks, you were quite right. Well done!

"Let me summarize what happened, what we know, and what we still don't know. Most importantly, we've found a suitcase containing an SE 85/14 transceiver. As Marks correctly deduced, it was in the beer cellar of The Thistle. Our people are still examining it, but they're all but certain that that was the device that agent OBAN used on May 14th to send a radio message to Berlin. For one thing, the wavelength on the dial of the transmitter corresponds exactly to what the two mobile units reported—agent OBAN forgot to change it when he or she put it back in its hiding place.

"I said 'he or she' because we're still not sure who agent OBAN is. The barman and licensee of The Thistle, Fergus MacRobson, is dead. We're trying to find out as much as we can about him. Was he agent OBAN or just a Nazi sympathizer who worked with agent OBAN? We simply don't know yet.

"Now I turn to Lady Alison, the Countess of Mallaig. She's highly intelligent, cunning, and calculating, but Johnson managed to bluff her twice when he went to interview her. She denied all knowledge of anything, admitting only that she'd given MacRobson a suitcase containing some of her cousin's clothes to help him 'in her capacity as the chief of the clan,' and insisted that it simply wasn't possible that he'd done anything serious. Then Johnson told her that the men who came to her cottage to fix the electricity took away with them a glass with her fingerprints on it. Of course, they did no such thing—they had their instructions and they stuck to them. Next he told her that we'd found her fingerprints on the transmitter. In fact, the forensic team arrived in Mallaig more than two hours later from Edinburgh. But she believed both his assertions; Johnson can be very convincing. She drew a loaded pistol from her desk drawer—and we need to find out how the searchers missed it yesterday—but Johnson was able to knock it away before she could shoot herself. He broke her wrist in the process, but that's neither here nor there in the overall situation.

"Is Lady Alison agent OBAN? Again, we just don't know. We arrested her, and once again she's had a nervous breakdown. She's sitting in her cell in the police station in Mallaig, not moving, not eating. It's almost as if she's in a trance."

Captain Marks put up his hand. "Yes, Marks?"

"Sir, I don't believe it."

"You don't believe what?"

"That she's had another nervous breakdown. I have no doubt that the first two breakdowns were genuine. But this time she's just pretending in order to avoid being questioned."

"Marks, you've been right about her all along. You seem to have some sort of special insight into Lady Alison. Could you expand on what you said?"

"I'm sorry, sir, but I can't. I'm not a psychiatrist and I don't pretend to know how her mind works. I just intuitively seem to understand her on some level. I'm afraid I can't explain it any more than that."

"Well, I'll pass your remarks on to Edinburgh—that's where they'll take her tomorrow morning. If you're right, we should be able to learn from her who agent OBAN is."

"That may not be necessary," Harkness said.

"Oh?"

"We gave the name 'agent OBAN' to the person who sent the message nearly three weeks ago. If agent OBAN didn't change the wavelength on the transmitter, then I suspect that he or she didn't wipe the suitcase and its contents, either. By now, the forensic team should have a preliminary report."

"Quite right, Harkness. I'll have a quick word with Captain Nicholas and come right back here."

The five officers sat back and relaxed until the air commodore returned less than half a minute later.

"I bumped into Captain Nicholas on his way here with the preliminary report. It says here that the fingerprints of Lady Alison are on the suitcase and the radio. They've found no other fingerprints so far.

"Well, gentlemen, now we know. Agent OBAN is Lady Alison, the Countess of Mallaig. For now, we'll lock her up under Regulation 18B of the Defence (General) Regulations 1939. It allows us to detain anyone suspected of being a Nazi sympathizer for the duration of the war. I know what you're going to say, Marks, that she's a good deal more than just a sympathizer. But under the circumstances, including her two genuine nervous breakdowns, it might just be easier to lock her up safely until all this is over and deal with her then, depending on her mental health at that time."

"Sir," Wallstead spoke up. "Is it possible that Fergus MacRobson was merely a dupe of Lady Alison? Maybe she told him, correctly, that all transmitters had to be handed in, but gave him some convincing reason why she needed to keep hers?"

"Yes, that's possible," Pankhurst said. "But MacRobson is dead, and the countess isn't saying anything, at least for the time being. In fact, we may never know the truth.

"In the meantime, we can congratulate ourselves. We've located both German transceivers, so the Double-Cross System is safe—for now. Agent NORFOLK is in custody here in London and agent OBAN is locked up in the police station in Mallaig. But we have one vital unsolved problem: Agent

BROCKEN is still on the loose. We have to capture him, and soon, before he kills anyone else.

"And there's another problem. Canaris sent agent BROCKEN to kill Campbell-White in East Anglia. Has he sent someone else to kill Worthington in Scotland? If so, we need to take precautions. But if he hasn't done so yet, we need to transmit a message to Canaris that will prevent him sending another assassin. How do we do that?"

"Can't we utilize subagent URIAH HEEP who's been following Worthington?" Major Tupman suggested. "We know that Canaris believes virtually everything that PICKFORD sends him."

"But does he? PICKFORD told him that there are two Hesses at large in Britain. Clearly one of them has to be an imposter, possibly both. But before Canaris could find out which was the real Hess, he sent agent BROCKEN here to kill Campbell-White. Now, why would he do that?"

"Sir," Chulmleigh suggested, "is it possible that he came to the conclusion that Campbell-White is the real Hess?"

"And why would he do that?" Pankhurst responded. "On the contrary, he received a radio transmission from agent WÜRZBURG, alias Hermann Leichtal, telling him that the man in Chelmsford is an imposter. And thirty-six hours later agent BROCKEN phoned Carlyle."

There was silence.

"Maybe it's the other way round," Chulmleigh offered. "Maybe he deduced that both men are imposters and he wants them both killed."

"But why?" Pankhurst repeated.

"Because," Harkness said, "Hitler ordered all his agents in Britain to find Hess and kill them. But Canaris needs them to get back to work gathering information for the *Abwehr*. Only when both Hesses are dead will his agents be able to return to their normal intelligence-gathering tasks. Or, more accurately, to our disinformation dissemination work!"

"That makes sense. Do you all agree that, if we want to ensure that Canaris doesn't send another assassin or calls off the man he's already sent to Scotland, we need to kill Worthington?"

Seeing the shocked looks on their faces, he quickly added, "What I meant is that we need to send a message to Canaris from PICKFORD stating that Worthington is dead."

Now there were nods all around the table.

"Fine. Where's a good place to hide Worthington away until we find BROCKEN? It has to be somewhere where no one will let on that he's there. Any ideas? In a military base?"

"Yes, sir," Tupman said. "But we need to change his appearance first."

"Good suggestion. I'm sure he won't mind, if we explain the reason. And we'll send a message via PICKFORD to the effect that URIAH HEEP reported that the Hess in Scotland is dead."

"Perhaps shot trying to escape?" Tupman suggested.

"In view of what happened in the harbor in Mallaig earlier today, that sounds credible. Anything else?"

"Sir," Harkness said, "I'm not sure that I like the idea of sending that message via PICKFORD. I know that we're pretty sure that the *Abwehr* believes everything PICKFORD tells them. But if Canaris were totally happy with what PICKFORD is telling him, he'd have waited until either subagent URIAH HEEP or subagent EBENEZER SCROOGE reported that the Hess he was following is an imposter. At that point he'd send in an assassin to kill the real Hess. Instead, he just sent BROCKEN to kill Campbell-White."

"What do you suggest we do instead?"

"Let's search the pub and Lady Alison's cottage for the book."

"The book?"

"For the book code. Then we can send a message in that code to Canaris."

"But everyone's Morse code 'fist' is different, just like handwriting," Pankhurst objected.

"Yes, sir. But as far as I know, our receivers record every message they detect. After hearing her transmission, a Morse code expert here at MI5 should be able to copy her fist with reasonable accuracy. The Germans must know that Lady Alison has had two major nervous breakdowns. She's highly unstable, and I believe that any significant differences between her fist and the fist of whoever transmits our message will be put down to that."

"That makes sense. Now, should we use both routes to inform Canaris that the Scottish Hess is dead?"

"I don't think that would be a particular good move, sir. If Canaris starts to suspect the authenticity of our message to him in the book code, it'll jeopardize future messages from PICKFORD. Agent URIAH HEEP should just say that he last saw Hess in Kilmallie and he's looking for him."

"You're quite right," Pankhurst said. "Also, I think that the Double Cross team should compose the two messages. They've been playing with Canaris's mind for such a long time that they'll know exactly what to say and how to say it. But there's still one big problem: How will we know which book to use? There are probably hundreds in the cottage."

"Well, sir, if we were to attempt to decode the message of May 17th using each book in turn, all but one book will yield nonsense. That's the brute force approach. The other way is for Johnson to go through the books in the cottage and see if he can select a few likely candidates. That should speed up the process."

CHAPTER TWENTY
Duntress Castle, Renfrewshire, Scotland
Thursday, September 9, 1993

"Did you ever discover anything more about Fergus MacRobson?" Benedict asked. "Was he a dupe of the countess, a German sympathizer, or an *Abwehr* agent in his own right?"

"We never found out," Sebastian said. "He was a lifelong bachelor and he had no siblings as far as we knew, so when the war ended there was no reason to investigate further to potentially clear his name."

"And Lady Alison?" Benedict enquired.

Hamish flashed Sebastian a warning look. Benedict noticed nothing. Sebastian said as casually as he could, "She died in prison."

"How did she die?" Benedict wanted to know. Sebastian thought quickly. He knew that his son was extremely squeamish about all things medical, so a gory explanation would quickly lead to Benedict changing the subject or even leaving the room. "She died of an aortic aneurysm, early in 1944, I think. From the postmortem they learned that she was born with a weakness in the wall of her aorta, the main artery in the body. The aorta ruptured and the massive internal hemorrhaging killed her very quickly. There was no warning. An aortic aneurysm is usually symptomless. Rupture is sudden—and fatal."

As Sebastian had anticipated, Benedict said, "I'm just going outside for a quick breath of fresh air," and ran from the room.

Sebastian closed the door behind him and turned to Hamish. "Is she still in the Glasgow Hospital for the Criminally Insane or whatever they call it these days?"

"Yes. She's been there for more than fifty years. It must be unendurable to be a sane person living in a place like that."

"Well," Hamish replied, "we both know that it was her decision to fool the psychiatrists and pretend to have that third nervous breakdown. She thought they would detain her 'at His Majesty's pleasure' until the war was over. Then she would make a miraculous recovery and be released. After all, the authorities review the files of prisoners who've been found guilty but insane at regular intervals. If it's clear that they're no longer a danger to themselves or others, they can be set free. But what she didn't know is that the Home Secretary almost always imposes a minimum term of imprisonment. And in her case, it was life."

"I'm getting old and forgetful," Sebastian said. "Remind me how that happened. Wasn't the psychiatrist a relative of hers, or something like that?"

"Not quite, but you're close. The judge was certain that this time she was pretending to be insane and had hoodwinked the psychiatrists. Because she'd been found guilty of treason during time of war, he wanted to sentence her to death, but he couldn't go against the psychiatric evidence. However, he found a clever way around the problem. He had no choice other than to find her guilty but insane, and he correctly sentenced her to be detained at His Majesty's pleasure. But he asked the Home Secretary to impose a minimum period of life. The Home Secretary at the time was her uncle by marriage, and he was only too delighted to comply with the judge's wishes. After all, Lady Alison was the proverbial blot on the family escutcheon, and having her out of the way on a permanent basis made a lot of powerful people feel considerably more comfortable."

"And releasing her would do nothing but open the equally proverbial Pandora's box," Sebastian added.

"Precisely. And the fewer people who know about the situation, the better. If someone like your do-gooder son Benedict were to learn about it, we'd never hear the end of the matter."

CHAPTER TWENTY-ONE
MI5 Headquarters, London
Sunday, June 1, 1941

"Good morning, gentlemen. I've instructed Captain Nicholas to come here the moment that Carlyle phones in his report. Oh, here he is. Come in, Nicholas."

His aide handed a sheet of paper to the Air Commodore. "Thank you, Nicholas. Please come back the instant you hear anything else.

"Now, gentlemen, it seems that agent BROCKEN phoned Carlyle punctually at nine this morning as usual. He wanted to know where Hess was. As we agreed, Carlyle told him that PICKFORD's radio message this morning stated that Hess is injured and is recovering in a military base somewhere. That was a good move, I think, because it's common knowledge that soon after we captured the real Hess, we treated his injured foot at Maryhill Barracks in Glasgow. I therefore believe that, when Canaris reads the message, it'll seem reasonable to him."

Air Commodore Archibald Pankhurst paused to gather his thoughts. "Well, now we're sure that BROCKEN realizes that he didn't kill 'Hess.' And we know that in a day or two he'll learn that Campbell-White has recovered. And when Carlyle tells him Campbell-White's new location, BROCKEN will surely be waiting outside the next jail or police station. With Miss Delauncy safely out of the way, we'll get him this time!"

"Sir," Tupman asked, "are you sure he'll be there the next time?"

"What are you saying, Tupman?"

"Well, sir, yesterday agent BROCKEN was able to fire two shots at the look-alike without being arrested because our men were more concerned about Miss Delauncy than catching the assassin. That's not going to happen the next time, and BROCKEN knows it. Also, the members of the MI5 team were somewhat slipshod. Instead of the seven watchers fanning out in the street before the police brought 'Hess' out, there were only three of them. I don't know what the other four were doing; Mortimer arrived late on the scene and knocked Miss Delauncy over. And there were supposed to be four policemen accompanying Campbell-White, but only three were there. I have no doubt, sir, that you've had a word to two in certain people's ears, and that from now on every move will be carried out by the book. But I'm equally sure that BROCKEN knows that, too. So I would be somewhat surprised if he turns up at the next police station, unless he's there as a pure observer."

"I agree with Tupman that BROCKEN won't try to kill Campbell-White there," Wallstead said, "but I think he'll be there to follow him and kill him at his next destination."

"Which will be Flatford Mill," the air commodore announced. "Marks, your painting therapy starts as soon as the look-alike has recovered. By the way, you need to know that there's been one change to your plan. We agreed yesterday that Carlyle would tell BROCKEN about the 'painting therapy' when he phoned. But there's no way that Carlyle, playing the role of a PICKFORD subagent, could possibly have found out about Flatford Mill.

Next he turned to Wallstead. "Yes, Lieutenant, you may be right. Realizing that security will be unbelievably tight at the next police station, BROCKEN may certainly follow the police car or van in the hope that everyone in the security detail will be more relaxed at the end of the trip and therefore more careless.

"Now let's return to the situation in Scotland. All is well there, but there's one issue we still need to settle: What do we tell Worthington? This morning Johnson informed him that tomorrow we're moving him to a military camp. Actually, we're sending him to No. 1 Combined Operations Invasion Training Centre at Inveraray on Loch Fyne—that was where those Royal Marines who surrounded The Thistle were based."

"Including the marine who shot and killed Fergus MacRobson," Tupman added gloomily. "As a marine myself, I'm not too happy about the way that we're turning out trigger-happy soldiers."

312

"Yes, what happened is truly regrettable," the air commodore said. "But let's try to put that behind us. Johnson told Worthington that, for his own protection, we're changing his appearance before we transfer him. More precisely, we're going to trim his eyebrows, then color his hair and eyebrows brown. And then we're locking him up, for his own safety, in a military base. What's Ernest Worthington thinking at this moment? He's incredibly intelligent, but even a halfwit would realize that changing his appearance so that he doesn't resemble Hess must mean that we no longer intend using him as bait to attract agent OBAN. And that can only mean that we've captured her. Very soon he's going to start to wonder why we're still keeping him under lock and key. What, if anything, do we tell him when he asks the obvious questions?"

"Sir," Harkness said, "I think we need to tell him the truth—he'll work it all out anyway. If we give him the facts, he'll continue to cooperate."

"But will he?" Chulmleigh asked. "Once Worthington realizes that he's going to stay locked up until we can resolve the situation in East Anglia, I think that he's going to try to escape. If he does get away, he could start talking. And one word about Hess doubles may lead to agent BROCKEN realizing that the *Abwehr* has sent him to kill an imposter, escaping our net, and returning to Germany."

"I respectfully disagree," Wallstead said. "Worthington is far too intelligent to even think about escaping. I'm sure he realizes that all he has to do is sit tight for at most a week or two, and he'll get his unconditional pardon. But just to be safe, Johnson needs to unambiguously remind Worthington of the terms of the agreement and caution him to hold on a bit longer."

***

"Logan, do you know what a book code is?" Johnson asked.

The constable on loan from Fort William shook his head.

"Well, you start with a book—we call it the 'key text.' And you use the book to encrypt and decrypt your message. This is the message that our suspect sent to Germany on the night of May 14th, using the radio that you found in the beer cellar of The Thistle. The message begins '19 6 5 4'. The first number is the page number in the key text; the second number is the line number on that page; the third number is the word number in that line; and the fourth number is the letter in that word. That means that, if you turn to page nineteen in the key text, go down to line six, find the fifth word in that line, and take the fourth letter in the word, you'll have the first letter of the message."

"What book is the key text, sir?" Logan asked.

"That's what we're here to find. We need to look around Lady Alison's cottage and determine which book she used for her code. For example, here's a book next to her bed called *The History of Argyll* by Angus C. MacInnes. Take out your notebook and pencil. I'm turning to page nineteen. Here's the sixth line. Word five is 'mountain,' so the first letter in the message would be 'n.' Write down 'n' in your notebook. Now, if this were the key text, the second letter would be 'w.' And the third letter of the message would be 'g.' Do you know many words beginning 'nwg'?"

Logan shook his head emphatically.

"Well, I think we can safely discard this book. The problem, Logan, is that there are hundreds of books here in Lady Alison's bedroom on those shelves over there, and I really don't look forward to going through each one to check if it's the key text that she employed. Instead, we need to use our heads. In order to decode this message, the Germans need to have an exact copy of the key text in Berlin. Not too many Germans are interested in the history of Argyll, so it's unlikely that they could've acquired a copy of the MacInnes book there. It's got to be a book that they could find in a Berlin bookshop. The Nazis would need two copies: one to give to Lady Alison when she came to Germany for her to take back with her to Mallaig, and one for them to keep."

"They burn books in Germany, sir. It's got to be a book that the Nazis didn't ban."

"Good point, Logan. And here's another clue: Lady Alison studied economics at Oxford. Do you see any books on economics?"

They went over to the wall of books. Logan started from the top shelf on the left; Johnson worked his way from the right. Suddenly Logan called out, "Sir, here's a book called *The Economic*

Consequences of the Peace, by someone called John Maynard Keynes."

"Actually, his name is pronounced 'Canes.' Wait a minute, I think you've got it. It's a work that opposes the terms of the Treaty of Versailles, so the Nazis would have liked that one—there surely were copies in some Berlin bookshop or other. And I'll bet that most Germans would have no idea how to pronounce his name correctly. We're looking for a *key* text, and here's a book by *Key*nes."

"I didn't know that the Germans go in for puns, sir."

"They don't, and they certainly wouldn't make an English pun. Lady Alison must have chosen the book. Let's see if you're right. On page nineteen, the sixth line reads, 'When President Wilson left Washington he enjoyed a prestige and a.' So, the fifth word is 'Washington' and the fourth letter of that word is 'h.' Logan, write down that letter. The next one is an 'e.' Write that down while I look for the next one. Yes, after that we have an 's.' And then there's another 's.' Well done, Logan, you've found the key text!"

CHAPTER TWENTY-TWO
MI5 Headquarters, London
Monday, June 2, 1941

"Gentleman," Pankhurst announced, "there's good news from Scotland. Last night we sent a message to Canaris purporting to come from Lady Alison. Of course, we encoded it using *The Economic Consequences of the Peace,* a somewhat ironic title now that I come to think of it. We sent it at a quarter past eleven, her usual time, though not her usual day, and we transmitted it from the beer cellar of The Thistle. Fortunately we were able to find someone at the Royal Navy signal station near Ganavan to copy her fist; they tell me that he did an excellent job."

"Isn't there a risk that he'll talk about it to his fellow sailors, or his friends and family?" Wallstead asked.

"Well, as you all know, there's always a risk of a security breach, but we've done our best to persuade him to keep his mouth shut. He's an older sailor, a married man with four daughters. I think he's mature enough to realize that it's really important for him to say nothing to anyone. We've given him a reasonable cover story, too—he's to tell anyone who asks where he was yesterday that we needed him to try out some new signaling equipment. His commanding officer has assured me that we needn't worry about it.

"Next on the agenda is our newly out-of-work impersonator in Mallaig. Yesterday afternoon Johnson told Worthington essentially everything regarding our activities in Scotland—as we previously agreed, he'd probably have worked it all out by himself anyway. Then Johnson informed him that Campbell-White's part in Operation OTTAWA was not yet complete and, for his fellow look-alike's safety, Worthington has to stay at a military camp for probably another week, two at the very most. He then warned the jewel thief that we've informed the servicemen at the Combined Operations camp that we'll be holding a civilian in the prison there, and the level of security has been heightened. One of the items that Johnson took particular care to tell Worthington when he spoke to him was a detailed description of the shooting of Fergus MacRobson. Consequently, locking Worthington up inside a camp of trigger-happy soldiers, sailors and especially marines should ensure that he won't try anything.

"Finally, Campbell-White's bruised chest is healing nicely—he can move about with almost no discomfort. So we're taking him to Dedham Vale today for painting therapy.

"Here's our plan: Flatford Mill is situated on the Stour River, in a rural setting, surrounded by farms, meadows and woods. There's a public footpath that takes you from a gravel parking area to the mill—it's a walk of about a mile and a half. The route goes through a meadow, over a style into a sheep pasture, then it skirts the edge of a wood, passes through a cow pasture, and so on. At one place there's even a sort of dark tunnel formed by high hedges on both sides of a narrow path closing in over the top.

"Constable's masterpieces show that the area was quite heavily wooded in the early 1800s, but fortunately there are almost as many trees in the area today, so it's an ideal location for an ambush. Before Campbell-White arrives, we'll place snipers wearing ghillie suits in trees along the public footpath."

"What's a ghillie suit, sir?" Harkness asked.

"It's clothing designed to resemble heavy foliage, ideal for hiding unobserved in a leafy tree. To make a ghillie suit they start with a camouflaged battledress in shades of green and attach loose strips of burlap and jute made to look like leaves. Then the sniper breaks off sprays of leaves from the tree he's hiding in and fastens them to the ghillie suit. If he does it the right way, then when the wind blows, the leaves on the suit move the same way as the leaves of the tree."

"What a great new invention!" Harkness exclaimed.

"Not quite," Air Commodore Pankhurst said drily. "Scottish hunting guides, ghillies that is, have been wearing them for decades. And our snipers used them forty years ago in the Boer War.

"Returning to our plan," he continued, "instead of the usual three-car convoy there'll be only the one unmarked car with four of our men in police uniforms escorting Hess. The whole object of the exercise is to lure the assassin to the mill, so we've instructed the car driver to just continue at the same speed if he observes agent BROCKEN following him on the road from Braintree. When they arrive at the parking area, their orders are to leave the vehicle without the slightest delay and immediately take the footpath to Flatford Mill. That will minimize the risk of BROCKEN shooting Campbell-White, or our MI5 officers for that matter, as they leave the car. We want the assassin to follow the route of the police party, giving our marksmen an opportunity to shoot the German assassin as he tails his target. Of course, everyone in the police car will be wearing body armor, just in case. Especially Campbell-White."

"What about the painting equipment?" Tubman asked.

"They'll leave all the stuff in the boot of the car, ready for Plan B. Plan A is what I've just outlined: BROCKEN follows the police car to the mill parking area and then pursues our Hess impersonator on foot and our snipers get him. But if that fails for any reason then, once Campbell-White has reached Flatford Mill, one of the policemen will return to the car for the equipment for the painting therapy. The snipers will now form a protective cordon around the location that we've selected for our budding artist to assiduously apply pigment to canvas. There are a number of large trees as well as a few old buildings in the area, giving excellent concealed positions for the sharpshooters."

"Sir, I have a question about Plan B," Chulmleigh said. "If agent BROCKEN fails to follow our car, how will he know to go to Flatford Mill to find Hess?"

"Carlyle had orders to tell the assassin about the painting equipment, but not Flatford Mill, when he phoned this morning at nine o'clock, as he has done every day so far. Agent BROCKEN is in Constable country, so he'll obviously put two and two together."

***

Helmut Kirchgässner left the Rutledge farm where he had spent the night and drove back to the village of Dedham. He had stayed for three days in a row on farms in the area, so there had been no opportunity for him to change out of his persona as a woman.

Just before nine o'clock, he parked his car next to the telephone booth in High Street, across the road from Dedham Parish Church with the steeple that he had seen in the background of a number of Constable paintings.

"Is your mother still suffering from pneumonia?"

"Only in her lower left lung today."

"Where is he?"

"Yesterday they took him back to Braintree police station. But something odd is going on. After they took him inside, I saw them loading art equipment into the boot of the black unmarked car that they use to transport him from place to place."

The materials that the police had piled into the trunk of their car intensely aroused Kirchgässner's curiosity. But almost enough time had gone by for MI5 to trace the call, so he quickly said, "I'll call you back."

Three minutes later, agent BROCKEN was again on the line.

"What art equipment?"

"The usual sort of thing: an easel, at least two canvases, and several brushes of different sizes. There was a large wooden box that I assume held tubes of oil paint. I couldn't see everything—their bodies blocked my view."

Kirchgässner hung up immediately. He instinctively realized that the British would foil any attempt he might make to kill Hess as he left Braintree police station—this time they would be ready for the assassin. He needed to find a different way of murdering Hess. As he exited from the telephone booth he glanced up at the parish church directly across the road. The steeple and Carlyle's list of painting supplies gave him an idea. He returned to his car to think it through.

He knew that, when John Constable started to record the beauty of Dedham Vale on canvas, he painted the steeple, towering over a green canopy of trees in the background of his landscapes, in its actual location. But as his skill grew, in his later works he frequently placed the square steeple on the canvas where he thought it would most improve the overall composition of his painting. Also, if he felt that the picture needed it, he would increase the height of the steeple in order to achieve a more harmonious effect.

When Kirchgässner fired those two shots at Hess in Braintree, he was dressed as a woman. Unaware that the guards had been so preoccupied with the elderly lady who had fallen that they had not observed him, he assumed that the police expected to see a woman assassin once again standing in front of Braintree police station with a gun in her hand, this time ready to fire at Hess's head. And when they spotted her they would surely kill her before she could shoot Hess again. Instead, like Constable, he needed to paint a somewhat different picture. When he reached Braintree he would park the Morris Eight in Coggeshall Road as close as possible to the police station and remain behind the wheel, waiting for the unmarked police car to turn into the major road out of the town. Furthermore, he would wear a man's hat and coat over his woman's outfit. If the police even noticed him in his car, they would see a far less threatening image: a different person, in a different place, sitting and not standing. In all probability they would ignore him. Then he could follow the black car to its destination and murder Hess as he exited from the vehicle.

But what about those art supplies? Why had the police loaded the trunk of their car with items needed for painting in oils? The only explanation that came into his mind was that they were taking Hess to an art gallery where he would sit in front of a masterpiece and copy it, the way art students gain insight into the creative process. But why would the

British organize such an activity? It made no sense at all.

He had almost two hours before Hess was scheduled to leave the prison and Braintree was less than twenty-five miles away. So he decided to sit and think the problem through for another minute or two. However, he could not think of any other reason for the painting supplies. Then he realized if he were to follow Hess into an art gallery without looking out of place, he would need to be considerably more smartly dressed, and that would mean changing into the second set of women's clothing that he had taken from the house in East Clemford.

But where could he change into the other outfit? He recalled that, when he stopped at the village shop and post office three days earlier, he had seen a wooden sign reading "Public W.C. 200 Yards" that pointed toward the lane on the east side of the church. High Street was deserted, so no one saw a woman in a floral rayon day dress, hand-knitted cardigan, and flat shoes take a suitcase out of the back of the Morris Eight and cross the road in the direction indicated by the sign. A few minutes later a woman wearing high heels, stockings, a tea dress, and a well-cut swagger coat with a fur trim walked back to the car. SS-Major Helmut Kirchgässner replaced the suitcase in the trunk, got back into the car, and drove off in the direction of Braintree.

After a few miles he looked around. There were no other cars in sight, no pedestrians, and no farm workers in the fields on either side. He pulled off the road onto the verge where a clump of mature trees would screen the car and got out. Kirchgässner unlatched the trunk once more, opened the suitcase, and quickly took out the overcoat he had left on the top when he repacked his clothes before leaving the public restroom. Taking off the swagger coat, he put on the man's overcoat. Then he reached into the trunk, took out the man's hat that he had left there for the last three days, jammed it firmly on his head, and continued on his way.

***

"Donndorf," Admiral Canaris said, "we've received two messages. Last night agent VALKYRIE sent a brief signal from Scotland. All she said was, 'Hess killed trying to escape.' Why would an impostor want to escape? And why would the British shoot a look-alike?"

"I have no idea, Admiral. It makes no sense to me."

"And in his message this morning, PICKFORD stated that subagent URIAH HEEP reported that he saw Hess entering the police station in Kilmallie on Saturday morning. He didn't emerge on Sunday morning at ten o'clock as expected. Also, the plainclothes and uniformed policemen who escorted Hess into Kilmallie police station on Saturday left on Sunday morning in groups of two or three. That tends to confirm what agent VALKYRIE told us.

"Could it possibly be," Canaris continued, "that we've got this all wrong? We know that the man in

East Anglia is an imposter—agent WÜRZBURG told us that. It's inconceivable that he made up the report about the boy, the sharp stone, and the aristocratic accent—that definitely happened. But perhaps the man killed in Scotland was the real Rudolf Hess."

"It must have been Hess. The British could have no conceivable reason for killing a double," Donndorf insisted. "Admiral, we have three independent reports: Agent WÜRZBURG assured us that the man in East Anglia is an imposter; agent VALKYRIE told us that the man in Scotland was killed; and subagent URIAH HEEP informed us that the man in Scotland has disappeared and there's no sign of his guards, either. The only conclusion that I can come to is that Deputy *Führer* Rudolf Hess is dead."

"I agree. I'm going to see *Herr* Hitler this afternoon to tell him that his execution order has been carried out, albeit by the British. What irony!

"One other thing, Donndorf. I want you to send a message to all our agents in Britain informing them that Hess is dead and instructing them to immediately return to their assigned duties. You were quite right—the enemy has been using Hess and the look-alikes to provoke our agents into transmitting a radio message to us so that the British can locate and arrest them. Let's hope that as many of our people as possible receive that order you're about to send out instructing them to stop looking for Hess. After all, Rudolf Hess is dead, so any *Abwehr* agent who reveals himself to the British by sending a radio message to us will be giving up his freedom, and probably his life, in return for telling us about the location of an imposter. What a waste!"

***

"Gentlemen," Air Commodore Pankhurst said, "about two hours ago, Ernest Worthington escaped."

The five officers exchanged looks.

"What happened, sir?" Tupman asked.

"We taught Worthington the subtle art of pretending to be someone else, and he was able to successfully impersonate Rudolf Hess. But Worthington also used the skills that he'd acquired to teach himself how to masquerade as Canavan. It seems that, while playing endless games of chess, Worthington observed Canavan as closely as he'd watched Hess. When he was alone, the jewel thief probably practiced in front of a mirror until he was sure that he could successfully pretend to be his chess opponent.

"Worthington somehow managed to get his hands on a disguise that we'd provided our intelligence officers, specifically a large handlebar moustache. He also must have purloined one of our small bottles of spirit gum to fasten the moustache to his upper lip. How did he steal the two items? The man was a highly skilled thief—taking the moustache and the gum must have been child's play for him.

"When he arrived at the base this morning, we think that he noticed that Canavan was nowhere

327

around. So Worthington decided that this would be an excellent time to escape by impersonating his chess opponent. Four of our men in police uniforms were escorting Worthington to the military prison. As they entered a building near where the car was parked, Worthington observed a door marked "Officers' Latrine" and asked if he could use it. Up to now he's always been extremely cooperative and well behaved, so they didn't suspect a thing. He went inside, quietly bolted the door behind him, affixed the moustache with the spirit gum as quickly as he could, and jumped out the window.

"Both Canavan and Worthington are tall and thin. Both were wearing a tweed jacket, an open-necked shirt and flannel trousers. As of yesterday afternoon, both had brown hair. And as of this morning, they both sported a large brown handlebar moustache.

"Worthington copied Canavan's loping gait as he walked toward the car that we'd used to drive him from Kilmallie police station to the camp outside Inveraray. Our four men were still inside the building and they had no idea that their prisoner had made a dash for freedom. Two Royal Marines who'd seen Canavan earlier this morning now saw Worthington and were convinced that the man about to open the car door and drive away was Canavan. So they waved to him. Worthington waved back, apparently exactly copying Canavan's wave to the two marines earlier that day, and drove off."

"How did he start the car, sir?" Wallstead asked.

"Our men can't find the ignition key anywhere. It seems likely that he picked the driver's pocket. Again, that would be easy for a man with his skills.

"Of course, we've set up road blocks," Pankhurst continued. "But Worthington has outsmarted us so far. He drove into Inveraray, parked the car in front of the historic jail, tore off the give-away handlebar moustache, and disappeared."

"Disappeared, sir?" Marks asked.

"We can't find him. As far as we know, he hasn't left Inveraray, but a search of the village has so far yielded nothing. Of course, we're going to keep looking until we find him. I fully appreciate that Worthington wants nothing more than to stay hidden. But there's always the risk that he may talk, and the success of Operation OTTAWA therefore depends on Worthington keeping his mouth shut. And if we have to shoot him to ensure his silence, so be it."

"But sir," Marks insisted, "surely the risk that Worthington might say something to someone is infinitesimally small? As you just said, his sole objective is to remain at liberty. The last thing he'd tell anyone is that he's a fugitive Hess impersonator."

"I take your point, Marks, but there's a Nazi assassin on the loose and we cannot take the slightest chance. Worthington took the decision to escape, and now he must face the consequences.

***

Seated behind the wheel of the parked stolen car, Kirchgässner saw the unmarked black car turn into Coggeshall Road. There were four uniformed policemen in the vehicle, with a fifth man, in civvies, seated in the middle of the back seat. The SS-major started the Morris Eight, pulled out into the road, and followed the police car. Regular glances in his rear-view mirror reassured him that no one was shadowing him. As he drove behind the police at a safe distance, he realized that he was retracing the exact route he had taken to Braintree earlier that morning, but in the reverse direction. He saw the car in front slow down, turn off the A12, and drive toward the village of Dedham. Kirchgässner feared he might lose Hess if the police suddenly swerved into a side road, so he started to close the gap between the cars. When the police reached Dedham Parish Church, the driver turned left into Mill Lane, then passed first the Morrison farm, and then the Morley farm. Kirchgässner could not work it out: Why were they driving Hess through Dedham Vale? Then it suddenly dawned on him: They were taking Hess to paint at Flatford Mill.

He knew he was correct when the car in front of him slowed and then turned left into a wooded lane at a sign that read "Flatford Mill Parking." He saw the vehicle turn right about a hundred yards down the lane. He did not want the police to see him, so instead of following he continued a few yards past the turning and parked on the side of Mill Lane. Removing his man's hat and jacket, he put on the swagger coat again. The loaded CZ 27 went into the right side-pocket of the coat, and the ice pick, spare magazine, and silencer for the CZ 27 in the left side-pocket. Ready for action, he got out of the car and started to walk around the corner toward the mill. As he did so, he wondered if he should change back into his other clothes, which would be far more appropriate for a stroll in the country, but there was no time to do that—he might lose Hess. Also, when he tried to kill Hess in Braintree, he was wearing the floral day dress. Kirchgässner was unaware of the fact that the police had not noticed him there because they were all tending to the elderly lady who had fallen, so he decided that it was definitely to his advantage to be seen wearing a completely different set of clothing.

When he reached the spot where the police car had turned off he noticed that a thick screen of trees and bushes surrounded the unpaved parking area. The empty police car was standing in the center under a large oak. There was no sign of Hess or his escort. Kirchgässner assumed that, for the sake of security, the policemen had rushed their prisoner toward the mill, and one of them would return later for the oil painting equipment. He tried the trunk of the car; it was unlocked. Inside he saw the items that Carlyle had enumerated. He quickly closed the trunk before anyone could see what he was doing.

Looking round, Kirchgässner saw three different paths starting at the parking area. At the entrance to each path was a wooden post with a sign fastened on the top that stated "Public Footpath" but imparted no additional information. He listened carefully in the hope that the police were talking sufficiently loudly for him to determine in what direction they had taken Hess, but he heard nothing.

Kirchgässner was well aware that, with tourism at a standstill and motor fuel rationing stringently enforced, the chance of another car arriving at the parking area for the mill was slim. On the other hand, he knew that the British love to walk in the countryside, so he stood near the police car, hoping that a Dedhamite on a morning stroll might come by and direct him to Flatford Mill. Minutes passed. Just when it seemed that he would have to throw in the towel for the day, he saw two middle-aged women walking briskly toward him along one of the footpaths. They were thin and of above-average height. Both wore hand-knitted woolen sweaters, tweed skirts, thick woolen socks, and hiking boots.

The woman on the left shouted across to Kirchgässner, "You look lost."

"Yes, I certainly am," he said with a broad smile and walked toward them. He greeted both women, and then addressed the one who had spoken to him.

"I'm trying to get to Flatford Mill. Which path do I take?"

The woman replied, "My dear, there are stones everywhere on the route to the mill—your high heels will break off before you know it and you won't be able to walk any further. And you're wearing nylon stockings. The wild grasses in the meadows will tear them to shreds, and there's no way you'll be able to replace them these days. Why, some of the lasses are going so far as to put make-up on their legs to make men think that they're wearing stockings, and then drawing a black line on the backs of their legs to represent the seam. We live just around the corner. Come with us, I'll lend you a pair of thick socks and an old pair of boots that I was going to give away— your feet look roughly the same size as mine. When you get back from the mill, you can return my things and put your stockings and your own shoes on again. By the way, I'm Miss Mason, and this is Miss Fortescue."

"That's most kind of you, Miss Mason, thank you so much. I'm Miss Green."

"Are you from these parts, Miss Green?" Miss Fortescue asked as they walked out of the parking area.

Kirchgässner thought quickly. What possible reason could he give for visiting Flatford Mill in wartime, when tourism was all but forbidden? He managed to come up with a good answer.

"Actually, Miss Fortescue, it would be correct to say that as of yesterday I'm from these parts. The Nazis bombed my flat in London. They reduced the entire building to a pile of rubble while I was at the National Gallery listening to a lunchtime piano concert given by Myra Hess. That's why I'm wearing these most unsuitable clothes for a country ramble; they're all I own. I have a brother who has a farm near here, and I've just been evacuated to Dedham Vale to live with him. I love Constable's glorious landscapes, they're so very English, if you know what I mean. So, even though I arrived here only last night, I had to walk to Flatford Mill to see where he painted those memorable masterpieces, city clothes and all."

"We're so sorry that you've lost everything, Miss Green, but welcome to Dedham Vale."

"Thank you, Miss Mason. I'm most grateful to my brother for letting me live on his farm."

"Dorothy, do we know a farmer named Green?" Miss Fortescue asked her companion.

What do I say now? Kirchgässner asked himself. Then he remembered the congenial Mr. Morley whose farmhouse, he knew, was within easy walking distance.

"Actually, Miss Fortescue, my father was killed in World War One, and my mother remarried a man named Morley."

"Oh, so the delightful James Morley is your stepbrother!" Dorothy Mason said with a girlish giggle. "How lucky you are! We think he's the nicest man in these parts. What a pity he's married!"

But Helmut Kirchgässner was not out of the woods yet.

"Miss Green," Miss Fortescue asked, "please excuse my forthrightness, but do I detect the slightest touch of a German accent?"

Fortunately for the assassin, he had prepared an answer to that question. "Yes, indeed. After the end of the last war, my stepfather was seconded to Germany for several years. He was with the Foreign Office, and they transferred him to Berlin."

"But James doesn't have any sort of German accent," Miss Fortescue said accusingly.

Damn the woman, he said to himself, *why doesn't she leave me alone?* Aloud he answered, "As you know, my stepbrother James is somewhat older than I am. In 1919 he had nearly finished school, so he stayed in England and joined us in Berlin during the holidays."

Before Miss Fortescue could torment him with further penetrating questions, they arrived at a large and rather ugly two-story house with a red tiled roof.

"Come in, Miss Green," Miss Mason said, pushing open the unlocked front door.

Helmut Kirchgässner found himself in a paneled entrance hall. To his right was a large mahogany hallstand with umbrellas, walking sticks, coats, and a variety of headgear all neatly arranged in their proper places. A Georgian rosewood drop-leaf table stood on the left. Dorothy Mason saw him looking with interest at the only two items on the table, photographs of tall young second lieutenants wearing immaculate British Army uniforms of the First World War. The silver frames were as highly polished as the surface of the table.

"Our fiancés," she said in a matter-of-fact voice. "They were both killed at the Battle of Passchendaele. The death rate for junior officers on the Western Front was over 70 percent. I will never forgive the Germans for what they did to a whole generation of young men. Now please come into the front room. I think you'll be comfortable in the floral patterned easy chair, the one over there with its back to the French window. Agatha, will you please put the kettle on—let's have a cup of tea and some scones."

"Please don't go to any trouble on my behalf, Miss Mason."

"Nonsense, my dear, we always have tea and homemade scones when we return from our morning walk. As you'll soon find out, Miss Green, Agatha really knows how to make a good cup of tea. We were both in Queen Alexandra's Imperial Military Nursing Service during the First World War. We served on the Western Front, near Ypres. We quickly discovered that nothing has the power to make a wounded soldier feel better than a nice strong cup of tea. So Agatha made it her business to learn how to make tea the way the men wanted it, and she still makes it that way. I'm sure you'll enjoy it."

"I know I shall."

"And while Agatha makes the tea and bakes the scones, I'm going to find those boots for you. I can't remember if I put them in the cupboard in the scullery to give to the church jumble sale or in the attic for the Boy Scouts' bring-and-buy sale. Let me see now." And she left the front room, closing the door to the hallway behind her.

Kirchgässner wanted to get on with his mission right away, but he realized that he had to stay. Yes, he could return to his car, take off his high-heeled shoes and stockings, and put on the other pair of shoes he had stolen from the house in East Clemford. Being flat soled, they would probably be fine on the path to Flatford Mill. Even better, he still had Flying Officer Emily Duxton's black lace-up shoes in the suitcase in the trunk—they would be ideal for the terrain. But the problem was that the two women had not indicated which of the three public footpaths he should take. Also, he knew from his weekends as a student in East Anglia that British footpaths rarely go directly from Point A to Point B. He needed detailed guidance as to which stile to cross, which gate at the end of the next field to take, and so on. Impatient as he was to kill Hess, he knew that he had no choice but to sit back in the easy chair and wait up to half an hour for Agatha Fortescue to mix and bake the scones, while Miss Mason looked everywhere for a old pair of boots that she'd probably given away months before. Then he would have to indulge in meaningless small talk over tea with the two former nurses, all the while coming up with reasonable answers to Miss Fortescue's probing questions. But eventually he would learn the precise details of the route that would take him to where Hess was engaged in painting Dedham Vale so that he could walk there and murder him.

Suddenly the door opened and Dorothy Mason stuck her head in. "The boots weren't in the scullery cupboard. I must have put them in the attic for the Boy Scouts." The head disappeared and the door closed again.

A minute later it was Miss Fortescue's turn. She came in and announced, "I've mixed the scones, but the dough has to sit for a short while. Then I'll cut it and put the scones on a baking sheet."

Before the assassin could reply, Miss Fortescue withdrew and shut the door.

Next, Miss Mason was back with another brief news bulletin. "Not in the attic. Maybe the garden shed?" Once more, SS-Major Helmut Kirchgässner had no opportunity to even acknowledge receipt of the latest report.

One announcement followed another in dizzying succession. The unending series of communiqués began to disorient him. In Kirchgässner's mind, the door to the hallway was starting to resemble the wooden door of a cuckoo clock: The door opened, a cuckoo emerged, the bird squawked and then immediately disappeared again. He sat in the floral chair, tensely waiting for the next dispatch from the front.

But then Kirchgässner began to think. Scones, he recalled, are made from flour, butter, and milk. All three ingredients were strictly rationed. He had no doubt that in the vicinity of Dedham, as in every other agricultural district, there were a handful of corrupt farmers who would illegally sell items subject to rationing at outrageous prices, and that some shopkeepers were equally venal. But he could not see either Miss Mason or Miss Fortescue participating in any sort of black marketeering. Consequently, how could they possibly "always" have scones with their tea after their morning walk? In fact, it now seemed unlikely that Miss Fortescue was actually making scones at all. Perhaps the two women were keeping the door between the front room and the entrance hall closed so that he would not notice the absence of the smell of freshly baked scones. When the tea finally arrived, sans scones, they would probably cover themselves by claiming that the scones burned in the oven.

But why were they pretending to make scones? And what should he do about it? His number one priority was to find out how to get to Flatford Mill. Returning immediately to the parking area would surely be counterproductive; there was no point in his standing and waiting there in the highly unlikely event that someone else who knew the route to the mill might pass by. No, his best chance—probably his only chance—of finding Hess was to stay with the two middle-aged spinsters, even though it was now clear to him that they were both completely demented. Perhaps the loss of their fiancés more than twenty years ago had unhinged them.

Twenty-five minutes from the time that he first sat down in the front room, the door opened yet again, and Miss Fortescue came in. "The scones are almost ready," she announced. "I'll just open the French door to the garden. We need a little fresh air in here, don't you think?"

The German assassin was all too familiar with the English fetish for "fresh air," so he just smiled at Agatha Fortescue as she opened the glass-paneled door to the outside, using a conveniently placed garden gnome with a red hat as a door stopper to keep it fully open. "But we certainly don't want a through draft now, do we?" she asked rhetorically. "I'd better close the door to the hallway on my way back to the kitchen." She left the room, closing the door behind her.

Suddenly a deep voice from behind him bellowed, "Police! Don't move, or we'll shoot," and men rushed in via the French door that Miss Fortescue had propped open on their instruction. He felt the barrel of a gun pressing firmly into the back of his head.

Hearing the order shouted out by their commander was the signal for three armed men standing in the hallway to fling open the door to the front room and burst in, weapons at the ready. Kirchgässner was surprised to see that all three men wore ghillie suits. "I want you to put your hands straight up in the air," the deep voice behind him declared. "Keep them far away from your pockets."

Several more men piled into the front room via both doors, some in police uniforms, the others wearing ghillie suits. A bulky policeman grabbed each of Kirchgässner's arms. The men pulled him out of the easy chair, searched him thoroughly, removed his weapons from his coat pockets, and cuffed his hands tightly behind his back. As they marched him out of the house, he heard Miss Fortescue asking insistently, "Inspector, as former military nurses we could instantly tell that what we were seeing was a man dressed as a woman, so we telephoned you as soon as we got home and we kept him here for you because we're fully aware that it's illegal for a man to masquerade as a woman in public. But don't you think it's verging on overkill to come to our house with a dozen or more heavily armed policemen just to arrest a harmless queer? And usually it's impossible to find a constable in

Dedham when you need one, so how did you manage to get so many of your men here so quickly? And another thing, why are almost all of them wearing ghillie suits? Aren't policemen supposed to wear uniforms so that we can tell that they're policemen? And this is a house, not a forest, so why are they in ghillie suits in the first place? And why are they dropping leaves all over our carpets?"

SS-Major Helmut Kirchgässner had no illusions as to the dismal future he was now facing. The British would inevitably hang him for the murder of the two Royal Air Force officers and the garage attendant. There was no way out. But at least the formidable Miss Fortescue was haranguing someone else for a change.

CHAPTER TWENTY-THREE
Duntress Castle, Renfrewshire, Scotland
Thursday, September 9, 1993

The coal fire in the grate had long since gone out. An autumnal night chill gripped the great hall of Duntress Castle. But neither Sebastian nor Hamish noticed the cold as they remembered the spirit of jubilation that they experienced that afternoon when they heard that agent BROCKEN was safely in custody.

"What happened to Worthington?" Benedict enquired.

Hamish smiled indulgently. "The rogue got away. He died about twenty-five years ago at his home on a beautiful island in the Bahamas. His much younger wife took his papers to the British consulate in Nassau, the capital. From what Worthington had told her and the documents that he left behind, we were able to piece together what happened.

"While we were escorting him around Western Scotland, in addition to taking the handlebar moustache he had apparently stolen two or three other small disguises and kept them in his pockets. We never thought that it was necessary to search him, of course. The items enabled him to make his way from Inveraray to Colchester, of all places."

"Why Colchester?"

"Well," Hamish said, draining the last of the whisky in his glass, "it seems that for years he'd been cheating Joost van den Beeck, his partner in crime. Worthington had stored the cream of the proceeds of his jewel robberies under the floorboards of his bedroom and then taken them across the Channel to Belgium. But items that were not unique and could therefore be easily sold to a fence he kept somewhere in a house that he owned in Colchester, together with emergency funds. During his years as a thief, he'd established a second identity—that wasn't as hard to achieve before the war as it is nowadays. The Colchester house was in his other name, as was the set of new personal documents that he'd obtained. He stayed in Colchester for the rest of the war, once or twice taking the train to London to sell stolen jewelry when he ran low on money. Soon after the war was over he acquired a passport in his new name and used it to leave England and go to Switzerland. At the bank he used his old identity papers to prove that the money in the account was indeed his. After a lengthy stay at a luxurious hotel in the Alps, he traveled to the Bahamas. He settled down there and married a beautiful Bahamian."

"And Campbell-White?" Benedict asked.

"As we'd promised him," Hamish answered, "he received an unconditional pardon. He re-entered the army, now as a private, and he trained somewhere in Australia—in Townsville, if I remember correctly—

to become a coastwatcher. He set up base in Guadalcanal at the end of 1941 and radioed reports of Japanese air force and naval movements to Port Moresby in New Guinea. In May 1942, the Japanese invaded Guadalcanal. We evacuated the island, but Campbell-White refused to leave, as did a number of missionaries who were providing medical and educational services to the islanders. Campbell-White went to the copra plantation he'd managed and recruited the workers there as core members of a sizeable guerrilla band that he assembled to harass the Japanese ground troops and report their movements to us. Then the United States Marines landed in the north of Guadalcanal in August 1942. Campbell-White's team of jungle fighters joined the American forces in fighting off the unrelenting Japanese onslaught; the intense combat went on for months.

"Toward the end of November 1942, the situation of the missionaries became untenable. Campbell-White organized an operation to bring them through Japanese-held territory to the area controlled by the Americans. As the small party, including about half a dozen guerrillas, came within hailing distance of the American lines, some forty Japanese soldiers hiding in the lush tropical undergrowth ambushed the convoy. Campbell-White stayed behind to fight them off singlehandedly, allowing everyone else to reach safety unscathed. Sadly, the American troops who rushed out to help him arrived after he ran out of ammunition. His loyal band of guerrillas buried him where he fell."

"And what's the name on his headstone?" Benedict asked.

"I know what you're getting at," Sebastian said. "Yes, he did change his name when he received his pardon. But after he died, his family agreed that his unending heroism during his year on Guadalcanal had totally wiped out the shame of the past. The American commander on the island wrote a detailed report to our Minister of Defence strongly recommending the award of the Victoria Cross to Campbell-White for his valor in the face of the enemy in saving the missionaries. And the Duke of Exeter's Own Cavalry reinstated him posthumously; they even promoted him. So the headstone reads something like this:

"Major the Honourable Frederick Campbell-White, V.C. 10th Lancers. Killed in action 3 December 1942 heroically protecting the lives of unarmed civilians. Age 26.

"Rest in Peace."

AFTERWORD

The characters in this book are all figments of our imagination; none of them are based on real people. Where we have given characters the names of historical figures, such as Admiral Wilhelm Canaris and Rudolf Hess, statements attributed to them are all fictional. Also, all the commercial establishments in this story, including The Thistle, The Mitre, and Weedon's Garage, are equally fictitious.

On the other hand, almost all the towns and villages mentioned in this book are real, including Thorpe-le-Soken and Tolleshunt D'Arcy, and we have described them as accurately as we could. Clemford Island does not exist, but it is based on Mersea Island. We have used real street names wherever possible, except where this might mislead the reader into believing that he or she has identified an imaginary establishment. For example, we have located The Thistle on Highland Street, Mallaig; there is no such road.

One of the readers of an early version of the manuscript loves single malt Scotch whisky. He asked us how he could acquire a bottle of Lochervan, preferably the eighteen-year old, "the crowning glory of the whisky maker's art." Sadly, we had to tell him that the only place where he could find Lochervan is between the covers of this book.

ACKNOWLEDGEMENTS

We warmly thank Howard Aksen, Belinda Barbizon, Aaron Binkley, Rosalind Fischl OAM, Joe Kensell, Johan Koeslag and David Thorpe for taking the time to read the manuscript and for their many constructive suggestions. We greatly appreciate their help.

Again we are most grateful to our developmental editor, Michael Mann, for his meticulous reading of the manuscript and his helpful comments and suggestions. For the sixth time, it has been a delight to work with our publisher, Jennifer Chesak, of Wandering in the Words Press. And for the sixth time, we also thank her for designing a striking cover.

STEVE SCHACH

Steve Schach, a native of Cape Town, South Africa, moved to Sydney, Australia, in 2009, after twenty-six years as a professor at Vanderbilt University in Nashville, Tennessee. Before he began writing thrillers, Steve wrote thirteen best-selling software engineering textbooks, which are used in universities all over the world. Down Under, Steve intended to become a full-time grandfather, and limit his intellectual activities to solving cryptic crossword puzzles and avidly watching *Sesame Street* with his grandchildren. However, the urge to write proved to be far too strong to overcome. Wandering in the Words Press has previously published five of his thrillers, most recently *Bakerloo Line* in April 2015, co-authored by Sharon Stein.

SHARON STEIN

Sharon Stein is a pediatric radiologist. Born in Cape Town, South Africa, Sharon was a professor of radiology at Vanderbilt Children's Hospital in Nashville, Tennessee and an examiner for the American Board of Radiology. She is a former president of the Southern Pediatric Radiology Society. In 2009 Sharon moved to Sydney, Australia with her husband, Steve Schach, to be with their grandchildren. She is an accomplished cook and baker who loves to share her recipes and techniques. This is her third thriller co-written with Steve Schach; Wandering in the Words Press published the first, *Coopers Island*, in October 2013.

www.ingramcontent.com/pod-product-compliance
Lightning Source LLC
Chambersburg PA
CBHW061317170626
46817CB00001B/210